DESIRES *of* innocence

Mary Tibble

Pen Press Publishers Ltd
London

First published in Great Britain by
Pen Press Publishers Ltd
39-41 North Road
London
N7 9DP

ISBN 1 900796 46 5

A catalogue record of this book is available
from the British Library

Cover design by Catrina Sherlock
from an original idea by Mary Tibble

Dedication

To *Ray* for his support and encouragement

CHAPTER 1

Jane Downing had been discovered dead in her apartment, on the outskirts of Morpeth in the north. Her body had been laid across the bed and shrouded in a white silk nightgown, as if trying to create that final dramatic scene on a film set. Her hair had been brushed, each strand perfect, and between her hands was placed a red rose. The finale was a small note at the foot of the flower bearing the words, *FORGIVE ME, MY BEAUTIFUL CLEOPATRA*.

She bore no other signs of bruising except the purplish markings about her neck. She'd not been raped or abused in any other way, though there was evidence that sex had taken place shortly before death. Whoever had killed this innocent creature, had felt some love towards her, there was too much care taken to ensure her dignity was preserved even in death. This theory was strengthened with the discovery that she was about four months pregnant...

Her parents had never been introduced to the boyfriend, whom she'd met whilst working at a local florist, but every time she visited her mother she was full of excited chatter about the new man in her life. Jane had only ever referred to him as Antony, she'd jokingly told her mum that he always called her his '*Cleopatra*'. Armed with this information, the police were fairly certain that the murderer was her latest lover.

They had dated when his job brought him to the area, but her mother insisted that during this time Jane had never been happier.

Her murder had affected them badly, especially when they discovered she was carrying a child, their grandchild. The shock caused her father to suffer a heart attack, and her mother had become drawn and grey, unable to eat or sleep properly.

Chief Inspector Jennifer Lawson had been asked to take charge of the case, normally she was based at the 'Yard' but was staying with her brother Frank at his home on the Scottish border for the New Year. Being fairly close to where the murder took place, she had received a phone call from her superior requesting her to visit the scene. From all accounts, this was a strange case and the local police had asked for some assistance.

Jennifer had battled her way up through the ranks of the establishment having to prove herself to the fullest to climb each and every rung of the ladder.

Jennifer, although on holiday herself, had left details of her whereabouts just in case. Being single, she'd volunteered to work. This was to be her first murder case. Good fortune had ensured Jennifer was in the right place at the right time.

Jennifer was my mother's best friend, they'd been inseparable as children and though their lives had travelled along different paths, their early bonding had ensured contact had been maintained no matter what. Jennifer had often baby sat when I was young and had become a second 'mum', so when my decision to rejoin the learning tree had placed me at an establishment close to her home, it was only natural that I would try and see her whenever possible.

Sabrina, my pal from the university, and I made regular visits to her home at Greenwich during term time and although I found our evenings most intriguing, Sabrina did not always appreciate them. I must admit I always wanted to talk about the world of crime so I can't really blame her for the way she felt.

I had invited Sabrina to stay with us at home for Christmas but she was off to Italy to spend the holiday with her family while Jennifer and I spent Christmas with my parents. Mum and dad had been invited along with Jennifer and I to Scotland for the New Year but they'd already made arrangements with my sister to celebrate with her. It was probably the wiser choice, they wouldn't have appreciated the persistent snowfall we'd had to endure during the drive.

Jennifer needed a break. To ensure she didn't drive, I hired a car and we arrived safely despite many roads being shut. The dedicated creature she was, Jennifer only lasted a day before making some excuse to check in at the local station, just incase. Being without wheels she persuaded me to take her, I agreed on one condition - it was a quick visit. I'd sat parked for some thirty minutes before the urge to track down Jennifer and extract her from the premises overwhelmed. For a small station it was busy, I stood politely trying to attract some attention. When none was forthcoming I grabbed the next uniform that passed. Eventually Jennifer appeared, in an excited state.

A call had come in, the body of a woman had been found in Morpeth. The only problem was, no transportation, all station cars were out. I couldn't believe how fast my brain reacted with an offer to take her. At first she dismissed the thought but astonishingly and to my amazement, I persuaded her.

A young constable had been assigned to give directions. He hastily opened the car door for Jennifer. He never enquired who I was, his fresh faced appearance gave rise to the notion that his time with the force could be counted in months rather than years, so he probably thought it best not to question such a senior ranking officer.

We pulled up to a pretty house, its thickly thatched roof easily bore the heavy blanket of snow that clung and disguised its natural beauty.

Jennifer was met by the local sergeant who guided her up the path towards the house whilst trying to part with as much information as possible on the short journey. I got out of the car and stood by the gate making polite conversation with our young escort.

I manipulated the conversation remarking on the many snow tracks leading to and from the house, evidence of much exerted activity. I was hoping he would give away some little snippets of information but it soon became evident that he knew very little himself so I would have to wait and see what I could milk from Jennifer later. It was cold, the frozen air was penetrating the heavy overcoat I was wearing and my feet were becoming numb even with my vain attempts to stamp some feeling back into them. I was more than glad when Jennifer emerged from the house knowing that we would soon leave and return to a rather large log fire that Frank had kept burning during the entire duration of our stay.

On the drive home I was full of questions but stayed silent, Jennifer was deep in thought and wouldn't appreciate any kind of interruption. I tried getting warm in the bulky but necessary fur coat I wore, pulling round the welcoming folds. Jennifer seemed oblivious to the sub zero temperature, she'd got the first scent of the chase and was relishing the hunt.

Frank must have known we'd be cold upon our return, the fire was burning fiercely and two hot steaming bowls of home made soup were magically produced. It was not until we were relaxing full bellied, enjoying the warmth from the flames that crackled in the hearth, that I felt it a safe time to broach the morning's events.

I noticed Jennifer's glazed eyes now showed tiredness, perhaps with the realisation of the mammoth task before her, heading a murder investigation. She had very little practical experience or the knowledge needed to successfully complete such a feat. In the few moments that we sat quietly, her face emitted many unspoken thoughts. I realised that Jennifer's need to suppress the many conflicting emotions coursing through her weary mind killed any sensible conversation, all that remained was her incessant chatter.

She'd assisted with many similar investigations and whether they had been in God forsaken hovels or palatial residences, they had displayed the scars of their grizzly past. Not so in this instance. Jennifer had found it uncanny to walk into a room where a murder had been committed with no obvious signs that it had taken place. The room hadn't been touched since the removal of the body and apart from the dust to trace fingerprints the place was clean, everything neatly in place.

The only fingerprints found were those of the victim's but surely there had to have been more evidence to pursue? My question was quickly answered, all the door handles and most of the surface areas had been wiped of any possible tell-tale marks, either Jane had been an obsessive cleaner or her murderer had rigorously cleared up after himself.

If he had been a fairly regular visitor as Jane's mother suggested there should have been other signs of his presence, aftershave on the bathroom shelf, a razor, something. The only things that adorned the shelves of Jane's bathroom were those associated purely with a woman, cute shaped bottles full of perfumed liquids all oozing pure femininity.

There had been nothing to even suggest the presence of anybody except Jane. The police had systematically searched through every item of clothing, read all papers and letters, checked each room and cupboard thoroughly, nothing, the only things in the flat were those belonging to the deceased. They'd hoped to be lucky with the little tatty-edged once red address book that a keen eyed bobby had rescued from behind the bedside cabinet, but upon checking found all the names and addresses related to family or girlfriends. The contents of her handbag hadn't helped either, full of nondescript incidentals that roll about adding unnecessary weight to an already bulging container.

They were really quite flummoxed, the killer had been very clever indeed to keep his identity secret, he must always have contacted her, not she him. In a last vain attempt they examined the florist customer listing; if he regularly made purchases it was likely that his details had been registered. For such a small company they kept detailed notes, how often a purchase was made and the type of flowers bought, but after many hours spent visiting each address recorded they eliminated all but one name. Was this the person they sought? The answer to that question was no, eventually that lead also ceased with the discovery that the missing link had emigrated some months previously.

The only logical conclusion to be drawn was that the irregularity of his visits suggested he was possibly some kind of sales rep, but a fussy one, bringing with him and using only his own things. He must also be very successful at his chosen occupation, having sufficient funds to squander on taking Jane out. Her mother was delighted at her daughter's catch, there was no run of the mill restaurant in his phone book, he had expensive tastes and only frequented the very elite of eating establishments, often after a trip to the theatre. This abundance of free cash would indicate that he was single, a wife and kids can quickly consume large chunks of any man's income.

That was as much readily available information as Jennifer had on this mysterious character and the case had given it all freely. With very little else to tell, she decided it was time to shower and make some calls to her office. I was somewhat surprised at her comment as she headed towards the door that she'd only revealed a fraction of the facts in this case, nothing that wasn't already common knowledge. I, on the other hand, rather felt we'd covered them all, but I was content to leave it be. Mind you, I had to turn my back to conceal the grin on my face as Jennifer finished our conversation saying that she needed to call her office and as she felt it only right to keep such calls private, she would use the phone in her bedroom.

I noticed she'd forgotten to take the note pad on which she been scribbling, she couldn't afford to forget anything. I knew she'd be back upon realising her mistake. If I'd asked, she would probably have shown them to me but I didn't like to push the point.

I scanned the pages, it read like a fairytale; white dress, satin sheets. Who could kill such a sweet soul? There was a brief description of the actual body, a fair-skinned girl with heavy dark bruising on her slim throat. His hands must have easily wrapped around such a fragile form, slowly allowing his fingers to meet as they ended her life.

I made out I was reading the paper when Jennifer reappeared looking for the pad. Oh, naturally I gave the pretence of not noticing as I attempted to fill in the ten minute crossword on the back page, only glancing up when I thought it safe to do so, but she seemed in a hurry grabbing her notes.

I lay back on the sofa as the heat from the fire was beginning to make me drowsy. I closed my eyes and changed my thoughts to the next day, New Year's Eve. Frank was hosting a party for his neighbours and knowing how they celebrated such occasions up here, it promised to be a long affair. I needed all the rest I could get to stay the course, so I decided to relax until then.

The following morning I awoke to the smell of cooking, our host was preparing nourishment for the intended guests and I felt it only proper that I should play my part by offering to sample the said delights before they were served. Frank must have been awake early as the first goodies were already cooling on the kitchen table, home-made oatcakes and wholemeal rolls and as I entered the room, a large lump of beef was returning to the oven after basting. Just as I finished my task as official taster, Jennifer appeared looking for some breakfast.

She was going back to the station at Morpeth for further discussions so I was happy to stay to assist Frank and judging by the pile of dishes in the sink, he needed it. When we'd completed our duties Frank poured us a large whisky each, supposedly to get us in practice for the evening.

Jennifer returned mid afternoon, after having achieved little further progress than on the previous day, there had been no breakthrough with the specimens the police had removed from Jane's room, a selection of fibres and hairs that had been slipped into little plastic bags then whisked away for rigorous scrutiny under laboratory microscopes. There was only one further small but significant point, forensics had managed to finish testing a hair that had been found within the bedding, one which could possibly have been overlooked but for a keen eye.

It belonged to a man between twenty-five and thirty-five in fine health, the lab report also stated the hair was in good condition, obviously from a well kept head. It was the wrong colour to be the victim's nor could it be matched to any member of her family or friends.

The tests carried out on the body found traces of skin under her fingernails. Her lover was of European origin but had a naturally tanned skin, probably from one of the warmer countries and vaginal swabs confirmed the presence of semen. DNA could match either but without a suspect this was an impossible task. It was fascinating what could be discovered from such an innocent piece of evidence such as an eyelash or nail clipping and I secretly hoped that it might be me who would, one day, be conducting the tests and helping with a police enquiry.

This news although important was not of much use, most of the suggestions as to whom it might be were based on pure theories and ideas, they desperately needed more pieces of the puzzle which as yet had not been laid on the table. Jennifer spent a long while going over and over the case notes searching for that clue that might have been missed. Eventually I intervened, she was looking tired and in need of a rest and as it was going to be a late night, I suggested she lay down for an hour. I didn't think she would take my advice but, for once, she agreed with me and disappeared to her room for a well earned nap.

The evening was a great success, the guests arrived at short intervals just after 8pm and were soon in full party mood. Later Frank removed the dust from the ivory keys on the old piano in the corner and everyone joined in the singing. The hour was late and after a little too much to drink and eat, I played safe by just listening. As the magic hour approached, somebody produced a set of bagpipes and started to wind them up, and the

New Year was piped in to the sounds of *Auld Lang Syne*. It must have been after three o'clock before I gave up, wishing everyone a Happy New Year before negotiating the stairs on hands and knees. I don't remember much after that but when I eventually opened my eyes the following day, I lay on top of the bed still wearing my underclothes. I must have sat down to remove my tights and passed out because I still had one leg in them.

I tried to focus on the face of my watch. When it became visible, I noticed that the thumps in my head were at two second intervals, the time 2.55pm. I had slept for twelve hours. I felt terrible, I plunged myself into the bath trying to muster up some life but it wasn't working. Frank and Jennifer took one look at me when I joined them, confirming I looked as bad as I felt. I struggled through what remained of the day before Jennifer ordered me to bed, we had a long journey home next day and I had to be fit. When I awoke the following morning I did feel a little better but having to travel didn't improve things. I was glad I'd had the forethought to name us both on the car leasing forms, I was in no fit state to drive. I ended up lying across the back seat where I slept until a gentle hand shook me from slumber.

Jennifer dropped me at the lodgings which I shared with Sabrina, luckily she wasn't due back for a couple of days. Just what I needed to recoup, peace and quiet.

Her arrival was announced by the slamming of the front door followed by hurried footsteps before she finally burst in and dropped her luggage on the floor. I was sure there was a lot more than what she went with.

Of course she wanted to fill me in about her holiday,

chattering away hardly pausing for breath. Her family had been a little disappointed because her brother Jonathan had been unable to make the festive family gathering, he'd had to remain here due to pressure of work but her mother was insistent that he make the next time which would probably be Easter. Sabrina had been shopping with the aid of her father's flexible plastic friend and by the amount of the clothes she'd bought, it had to be very flexible indeed. She had purchased a rather nice little item for me, a silk blouse which had small embroidered flowers on the collar, it was of excellent quality and not the type I could afford.

I let her glide to earth slowly from her brief but well funded break back to reality. We would be starting a new term at university and needed to switch our brains back into the learning mode ready for our return.

Life took a slow pace for a while, dark nights made us unwilling to leave the warmth of our cosy rooms in the evening, it was a case of nourishment, homework and bed. We did continue our once-a-week visit to Jennifer but Sabrina soon made excuses to opt out. I couldn't blame her, although I tried hard I was unable to crush my obsession concerning the death of Jane Downing, I think even Jennifer found my constant hounding a little monotonous at times.

On one of my later visits, I found out that a witness might have seen the murderer's car. One of the villagers riding home from the pub that night on his bicycle, apparently saw a large dark car at about 10.30 that night. He remembered mumbling to himself about the owner having too much money. The police were curious as to why he had taken so long to come forward but it transpired that the old chap's son had collected him that following morning and taken him, as he did every year, to the caravan park he managed. It was only on his return after his customary month away that he learnt of the investigations and thought to inform the local bobby about the vehicle he'd encountered that night.

With this additional information, the police again interviewed most of the locals and only one, who they discovered was the local busybody, had noticed the presence of a strange car. All she could reveal was that it was definitely large, black and had some kind of bright yellow sticker in the window but she hadn't taken note of the make or number plate. The yellow sticker may have been that of the supplier and the police were exploring this possibility.

As the weeks rolled by little if any progress was made. All the garages and hire companies within a twenty mile radius had been checked out and although many did advertise themselves by placing stickers in their cars, none used the bright yellow type they were searching for. Jennifer was rapidly coming to the conclusion that they would never solve the case and I believed she was probably right.

There were fevered attempts to solve the case quickly but due to the lack of suspects less and less time was given to her murder. Jennifer who'd made frequent visits to the north, finally returned back south and the file on Jane Downing was left open.

My visits were returning to normality, our conversations were of family, friends, university and forthcoming holidays, even Sabrina had started joining us again. The half-term was fast approaching and

Sabrina was once again preparing to jet off to the parental home. This meant that I'd be on my own for a week.

Jennifer had promised to attend three functions that a friend of hers was holding, most of the guests were extremely rich and important people in government and city business. The first was to be on Saturday evening at his modest abode situated in Mayfair and I was invited.

I was glad it was on a Saturday, it gave me chance to visit the hairdresser to have my hair professionally styled, normally I would pin it up myself but this was a special evening calling for that expert touch and I wanted to look my best for Jennifer's sake. I was going to splash out on a long evening dress, but Jennifer insisted she had several and one of them must be suitable for me.

I had never had cause to don a long dress before and it felt quite strange, luckily Jennifer and I were about the same size. After shuffling through her wardrobe pulling out one dress after another, I eventually chose a powder blue dress that was figure hugging to the knee then straight with a slit at one side that opened to half way up my upper leg and it had little shoulder straps which I removed. To be quite honest, it was the only one I found suitable, all the others were a little old fashioned in style. With my hair pinned up in a French plait, my neck was left a little bare but after selecting some drop pearl earrings and necklace from Jennifer's well stocked jewel box, a pair of slip on strapless shoes and the stroke of a make up brush, the transformation was complete.

"You look lovely Carol," said Jennifer. "That dress fits you perfectly, it never looked that good on me."

"Well, I am a little taller maybe that's why it looks different," I replied.

"Yes, you're a little slimmer too!" she said. "Are you nearly ready?"

"Yes, when you are."

"Right, I'll just get my jacket and we'll go," said Jennifer.

As she reappeared, I could see she was wearing a rather dainty bolero type jacket decorated with sequins and tiny satin bows.

"What a beautiful jacket," I said admiringly.

"Yes isn't it, I got it in Paris, I fell in love with it as soon as I saw it in the shop window, cost a fortune though," she replied. "But I didn't pay for it, it was a gift."

"Oh yes!" I said giving her a sly look.

"Hm, he's a lovely man, runs his own company but pressures of work kept us apart never allowing our relationship to develop past the boundary of good friends," she had a sparkle in her eye as she spoke.

"Do you still see him?"

"Oh, a couple of times a year."

"Well next time it might be a good idea to rekindle the fire," I suggested.

"Maybe...well shall we go?"

Jennifer's friend, Judge Wilkins, had invited her as he had done on many occasions to his functions, her presence fulfilled two purposes; firstly as a guest and secondly in her professional capacity, he felt happier having someone with a keen eye present. His guests were all wealthy and most were wearing expensive jewels, a temptation for any thief but up until now, Jennifer had only ever needed to participate as a guest.

As we arrived I noticed the procession of luxury cars ferrying people up the drive to the front door, Jennifer's small hatchback was very out of place so we sneaked in unnoticed and parked before anybody spotted which car we'd got out of.

"There's an awful lot of money people here Jennifer," I muttered to her quietly, "I hope I don't show you up."

"Don't be silly, just mingle, make polite conversation and enjoy yourself."

As we entered the house, we were greeted by the host Judge Wilkins and his wife.

"Hello Jennifer, it's good to see you again, I hope you've been keeping well," he enthused genuinely.

"I'm fine thank you, I have brought a friend with me this time," she told him. "You have always said I could."

"Of course, I wish you would bring a guest with you more often," he said reassuringly.

"This is Carol Johnston, her mother and I have been good friends for a very long time, she spends a fair bit of time with me while at university."

"Welcome Carol, you look delightful, I'm sure you will draw more than your fair share of the young men's attention tonight," he replied. "Most of my guests are of a more mature age and the younger ones find it a little boring at times."

We were escorted to the main reception area where several people stood in small clumps chatting and drinking champagne. The judge was right in his observations. There were only two men nearer to my age and they were surrounded by several older ladies, all plying for their attention.

Jennifer introduced me to some of the guests she knew but our conversation was a bit limited once they found out my business was handling the birth of babies and not money. One chap said, "Oh that must be interesting." He might have been convincing but for his pained expression. From then on I took to just listening rather than talking, making the customary nod of the head when and where appropriate. Eventually Jennifer left me to complete the second reason for her invite, she felt guilty at abandoning me but I wanted to try some of the delicious food on show, that task would keep me occupied for some time.

I was so involved choosing from the array of designer dishes that I never heard the approach of a young man, in fact he made me jump when he spoke.

"Excuse me madam, may I be so bold as to introduce myself?"

I quickly turned around to be confronted by a tall slim man with dark skin.

"What?" he must have noticed the shock on my face.

"I frightened you, I'm sorry," he said gently. "Only I was eager to make your acquaintance, excuse me, I will leave."

"No, no it's alright," I reassured him.

"My name is Prince Ahmed," he said, taking my hand raising it to his lips.

"Well I'm pleased to meet you Prince Ahmed, my name's Carol Johnston, why don't you have some food?"

"No thank you, I only eat what my personal chef prepares."

"OK but I think you're doing yourself an injustice," I laughed.

He was a very nice person and comfortable to talk with not like the others.

"If you don't mind, it's awfully stuffy in here. Shall we get some drinks and sit out in the garden?" I asked

"Yes, I'd like that."

The waiter fetched us some liquid refreshments before we descended into the garden. As we did so, I noticed a rather large man who looked most uncomfortable with the restraints imposed by the suit he wore. He had stood anonymously at the edge of the room and followed us around at a respectable distance. As we crossed the lawn, the prince raised his hand and immediately the chap stopped and stood discreetly to one side.

We sat in the refreshing evening air while the prince told me all about himself. He was born in Saudi Arabia the first son of seven, his father whose wealth was originally built by the sale of oil was a hard man not wanting his sons to live off his success but to make their own way in the world. He insisted that his sons were educated in England at the very best schools, most of them had finished their education but two were still at Eton.

He went on to explain that he was in England to expand his shipping business by opening a UK office to deal with all the documentation that was currently being handle by an agent on their behalf. He had originally borrowed a sum of money from his father to buy an ailing shipping company and within five years had not only turned it into a profitable asset but paid back his debt as well.

As for his personal life, he was married, only having one wife so far but keen to advise he could have more. His wife was pregnant with their first child which of course he hoped would be a son. It was natural in his country to have large families but western life had had some effects on him, one was to limit the amount of children he fathered. I found that a contradiction to his eagerness for more wives but said nothing.

As I listened to his dreams and aspirations, I took an overall review of his appearance. His skin was not deep in colour but dusky as though sprinkled with coal dust, his eyes were the traditional dark brown as was his hair, common of his origins. His suit I'm sure was an Armani, most distinctive and of expert tailoring. On one hand was a gold ring, a heavy chunk of metal that hung from his slim hand, I kept staring trying to make out the pattern. He must have noticed my interest, extending his hand towards me so I could inspect the heavy band. It was a work of art, wide and hand carved and mounted on top in a heavy clawed setting sat a large tear shaped ruby

I expressed my admiration of the fine jewel, apparently his father had had them especially made. He'd given one to each of his sons as a gift, referring to it as a tear of life's blood and he believed while they wore them they would always be blessed by wealth and happiness. It was only the view of an old man but until now was working. The prince owned a successful business, while two of his brothers were high executives in the banking world and a third had just graduated at medical school as a doctor. The rings were held as a sacred family heirloom, the only people to possess one other than his brothers were his wife and two of his father's closest friends. New rings had to be made when needed under the strict instructions that they were only to be given in very special circumstances.

My life compared to his was mundane, boring even but he listened to my rendition with much enthusiasm as though trying to feel the pleasure and pain of my past existence.

My upbringing was very simple, part of a family of four, my dad worked hard and he always managed to find sufficient money each year to provide us with the customary two week holiday at a seaside resort. My sister was married at twenty to an accountant and seemed happy, while I chose to help the world out by delivering babies, a booming profession. The news of my new venture to become a forensic scientist was greeted by a bemused look.

In answer to his question why, I explained that I'd reached the limits of the birthing game and had no desire to become a doctor but at the same time, wanted to pursue something still of medical grounding. I did mention my passion for amateur crime detection and the vast role forensic investigation played in the conviction of an offender, and if I wanted to pursue this career, it necessitated going back to school to gain further qualifications.

The prince politely stated that becoming a midwife was a worthy choice for a woman, I chose to ignore his sexist remark as I was sure it wasn't meant in the manner it was said. He wanted me to describe what was involved with the delivery of a baby, as a father-to-be he didn't have the first clue of what happened. He sat silently taking in every word as I started with the first pang of a labour pain through to the cutting of the cord. He posed a couple of questions before asking me would I do him the honour of delivering his first child. Surely he wasn't serious, he'd only just met me. I smiled nervously as I suggested that with all his money, he could have the top gynaecologists and paediatricians in the world perform that function, they were more qualified if something should go wrong.

"You underestimate your capabilities, Carol and besides you have already brought several lives into this world most successfully."

"I know but what you're suggesting is different," I replied.

"What, just because I have money, does that make my baby different, such as needing a doctor with a title to hand?"

"No, I didn't mean it like that, I just meant your wife could have the best that's all."

"I have listened to you for over an hour and all the time you spoke it was with pride and love of what you do, money can't buy that. I know my child will be safe in your hands and if something should go wrong then so be it, Allah will decide."

I was still issuing my refusals when Jennifer appeared, looking for me.

"Found you at last," she said. "Hiding out here with a handsome man?"

"May I introduce Prince Ahmed, a very nice but somewhat stubborn man."

"Pleased to meet you, I hope Carol has not dominated you for too long."

"Not at all, Carol has proved to be a most charming companion with whom to pass the evening," he replied in his quiet voice. His compliment was unexpected and if the night had been lighter, I'm sure they would have noticed the blush that now warmed my face.

"We're the only guests left so I think we'd better leave, the judge looks exhausted," said Jennifer.

"Yes, we must go, can I offer you ladies a lift home?" asked the prince.

"No thankyou, we have our own car," I said.

"Then at least permit me to escort you to your vehicle."

As we bid our hosts good night and left, I noticed the large man once again following at a discreet distance. The prince opened the car door for me to step in, again he raised my hand to his lips before saying goodnight.

"I will make the necessary arrangements for your visit and send you details," he said. "I meant what I said before and I won't take no for an answer, you hear?"

With that, he slammed the door and walked in the direction of a limousine parked by the front door.

Jennifer was inquisitive. "What was all that about?"

I relayed what had happened that evening and although I found the idea daunting, she insisted it would be a great opportunity encouraging me to grasp it with both hands. When I told her of my fears she said I was being silly, pointing out the amount of people that miss out on things in life through worrying about what might happen and as usual she was right.

When I got indoors I noticed how late it was, tiredness now overpowered me and I headed for bed.

The subsequent parties at the judge's des rez were very tedious, I got chatted up a couple of times by some over zealous young men but their conversation was staid, they were more interested in spouting their supposed importance in companies that were unsurprisingly owned by their fathers or some childless aged uncle. As the drivel poured from their mouths about their supposed achievements it only emphasised their failures, I wondered how they'd fare if they had to do battle on the real ladder of working life, fighting for every promotion instead of the lift taking you effortlessly to the top floor.

These people were the future top management of successful companies but how could they appreciate what they had without proving through hard work and skill that they were the best for that position?

I have always been of the opinion that a good leader should know what it's like to toil as one of the menial cogs in the vast company machine. Showing the men and women they employ that they can and will stand by their side on the production line, gaining education no school can teach, that of people, each one different, displaying the ability to govern them whilst taking into account their individual identity and needs. These men, people who wouldn't know what a sweeping brush was let alone which end to grasp, they thought they knew it all but really they knew nothing.

When I found myself bored with conversation I took to the beautiful garden, more than content to sit peacefully alone admiring the colourful and somewhat exotic blooms that surrounded the regimental, manicured lawn, grateful when Jennifer was ready to leave.

I should have appreciated the efforts of Jennifer to keep me occupied during the break from study, she involved me as much as possible in her affairs. I think she'd hoped if I was confronted with enough of the harsh realities of life it might thwart my ambition of becoming a forensic scientist. She never understood why, after studying nursing and specialising as a midwife, I had stopped and changed my course so drastically, veering into an area that saw mostly death and very little life.

My father had taken voluntary retirement from the company he had worked at since he was 27 years old, they had to reduce the workforce and when the opportunity arose my father grasped it, he had always been shrewd with money, making sure he had banked enough into his pension to ensure both he and mum were comfortable during their golden years. The package offered by his firm had been exceptional, leaving him with several thousands of pounds surplus. After buying a new car and taking one or two dreamt of holidays, his final gesture was to donate a chunk of the remainder to me, this would provide sufficient funds for me to cease work and return to university, to go back and study full time for a degree in science. I would never have been able to save enough out of my salary to take three years out of work, even so I had to operate a very tight budget and my father's teachings from a young age helped.

I could manage this year, I had been lucky meeting Sabrina, her parents paid the rent on the little flatlet she had and her offer to share was eagerly accepted. I tried to pay my share but she wanted company which I provided and so my only overhead was to share the fuel and telephone bills and of course, food for the table. Next year I knew that I would have to find a part time job to boost my depleted bank balance, it would be unfair to ask my father for any more money.

I presumed that Sabrina would go to Italy for the summer but no, she had decided to stay at the family house here and I was delighted when she invited me. At first I made the customary refusals but she only had to insist once to convince me.

I had been faced with returning to my parents whom I loved very much but they lived life on the slow track now, boredom would set in quickly if I spent the time with them. They were more than understanding at my decision and hoped I enjoyed the break. Dad offered to pay for my stay but I couldn't and wouldn't take a single penny more from him, he had worked hard and had already helped me more than I could ever thank him for, besides Sabrina had told me Jonathan, her brother, paid all the bills as he lived there most of the year. The two remaining weeks were quick in passing and we soon found ourselves packing the bulging cases into the boot of her little hatch back car.

The journey wasn't too unpleasant, the sun had made the interior of the car hot but we'd been lucky not meeting too much traffic, the breeze rushing in through the open windows was sufficient to keep us relatively cool. I knew that her family had money but I was still amazed when Sabrina pulled up the private drive of what I could only describe as a mansion.

Once unpacked, Sabrina and I sipped iced coffee and relaxed on the patio, it was the first day of our holiday and I couldn't believe my luck at being invited to such a fantastic house. I met Sabrina at university, she was taking a business course preparing herself for the eventual return to Italy and the family business. We had taken to one another instantly and we socialised as much as possible during our free time.

Sabrina's parents were Italian, although she along with her two brothers was born in England. When her parents returned to Italy about four years ago to take charge of the family wine business, the three children decided to stay, and their parents provided a house that they could all share. Mind you, what a house! From a distance you could see what seemed to be a house built into the side of the hill. The front was protected by a high wall that was camouflaged by great swathes of climbing flowers that clung tightly to trellis work but had been carefully trimmed away from the arch containing two mighty wrought iron gates.

Once through the gates there were several stone steps that lead to the front where you entered a walled patio area well stocked with several sun loungers, a barbecue and trailing green plants which covered the overhead trellis creating natural shade. At the far end of the patio there was a further set of steps which lead up to what I could only describe as a naturally made dam. There was a stream which flowed at the back of the house down the hill. The ground of the stream had been redeveloped so that the water flowed down a waterfall into a plateaued lake about ten feet wide and fifteen feet long with the banks on either side being built up with beautiful coloured stones. The water, upon reaching a certain height, then flowed out at the other end to continue its natural course. Due to the constant flow, the water stayed quite clear and clean, this enabled the pool to be used as a natural swimming pool during the summer months, it also received natural shade from the evergreen trees on the far side.

The rest of the house was also as impressive as the outside. The kitchen was full of all the modern gadgets, the bedrooms large with ensuite facilities, tastefully decorated in subtle pastel shades and the lounge-come-dining area was spacious and had a large panoramic window overlooking the green fields of the valley. I had assumed that her parents were fairly wealthy but this place must have cost a fortune and although it was on the edge of a cosy Oxfordshire village, it still seemed isolated. The only thing to spoil its perfection was the modern building of some two storeys further up the hillside which housed the local constabulary, however the evergreens had been strategically planted almost obscuring it from view. The only advantage of having the strong arm of the law so close would be to deter burglars from making uninvited visitations.

"My brothers come and go I'm afraid," said Sabrina, "but I know that Jonathan will be here by the end of the week as he has two meetings in London and prefers to stay here when he can. Andrew will come in the next couple of days, that's if he can tear himself away from his following of young ladies."

I didn't really mind if they joined the party or not. I could certainly manage to enjoy myself without them. However, I had seen some photos of her two brothers, both looked as though they should have gone into male modelling so I did want the opportunity of meeting them, especially Jonathan as he was nearer my age than Andrew. Sabrina herself was quite stunning, she had retained the dark smouldering features of her parents, she was small but perfectly formed with long flowing dark brown hair, she was going to be a catch for some lucky man. I on the other hand, had blond hair and green eyes, with skin that would burn and blotch at the very sight of the sun, so I appreciated that the patio had a large shady area.

"This house is fantastic Sabrina, it's better than a villa in the south of France, how did your parents ever find it?"

"As all three of us had chosen to stay in England, they spent many months trying to find a suitable house, but couldn't find anything that lived up to their expectations. With three young people sharing the same house it had to be large enough to give us sufficient room."

"What about the place you already lived in?"

"That was too big, besides it would be mainly Jonathan who would live there, both Andrew and me had made our own accommodation arrangements while studying, pointless footing the cost to upkeep such a place."

"Then why not three separate places?" I asked.

"Mum and dad didn't like the idea of us all being separated, especially me, they're a bit old fashioned and wanted big brothers to watch over me. Not that we really see much of one another with Andrew and myself at university and Jonathan trying to set up his own practice."

"But in theory you all live apart," I replied.

"Oh, strangely that was acceptable as it was regarded as only a temporary situation."

"Well at least you're all happy," I said as I reached for the sun tan lotion. "What shall we do about dinner?" I asked, changing the subject.

"I'll tell you what," said Sabrina, "if you don't mind waiting till later to eat, we can take a nice stroll down the lane to the local inn and have a meal there."

"Great, I didn't really fancy cooking anyway." It was such a glorious day and a walk when the sun was ebbing would suit me just fine.

I proceeded to lay back on my lounger, close my eyes and dream of sun-kissed beaches and clear blue seas, not that I would ever have the money to experience either. About six o'clock the pangs of hunger were beginning to be felt and we both decided that nourishment was needed. We forced ourselves to move from our comfortable beds and return to our rooms to change.

My bedroom was nearly the size of my parents' house in total. There was a king size bed which was set on a raised floor, there were stacks of pillows to laze across and a duvet of the size I had never seen, all were covered in a rich pink floral linen that seemed to emit the scent of fresh roses. The rest of the room was adorned with wardrobes, cupboards and a trinket laden dressing table, finally there was the addition of the modern world in the form of a television and video. The bathroom was spacious and cream in colour, the taps were gold and all towels were of the same pink shades as the bed clothes, there was even a matching bath robe. A person could quite comfortably have lived in this room, let alone just sleep.

As the weather was warm and we were to walk to the inn, I slipped on something loose and comfortable, shorts, T-shirt and flat sandals, and joined Sabrina in the living room as she was finishing a phone call.

"That was Andrew. He is going to try and get here tomorrow if he can scrounge a lift."

"Good, I'm looking forward to meeting him."

"The feeling would appear to be mutual," said Sabrina with a cheeky smile on her face. "Anyway, are you ready?"

"Yes let's go eat, I'm starving, I hope there's something nice on the menu."

The inn wasn't too far away, and upon entering it seemed dark but with the windows and doors open it made it a nice cool place for us to sit and eat.

As the evening progressed, the inn became quite full and stuffy so we decided to retire to the sanctuary of the garden. Most of the clientele were middle-aged but at about eight o'clock three chaps and two young girls turned up.

"Hello, Sabrina," said one of the men. "It's nice to see you again, are you here for the duration of the holidays?"

"Yes, how are you all, any new gossip?"

"None, you know nothing much ever happens around here."

"Why don't you join us?" said Sabrina. "Meet my friend Carol Johnston, she'll be staying with us up at the house".

"Pleased to meet you Carol, I'm John, this here is Pete, Steve and Jill and Angela."

We spent the next hour chatting, me finding out about these new acquaintances while Sabrina caught up on all the village news of the last six months. We were so deep in conversation that we didn't notice we'd been joined by another person. Steve introduced him as David Long, he was tall, fair haired and casually dressed. As their eyes met, an instant magnetism formed between him and Sabrina and a secluded conversation ensued for quite a while until a gentle nudge reminded her I was still there. At about nine, we decided to return to the house, it was becoming dark and Sabrina didn't think it too safe to wander down the unlit lanes late at night. As we stood so did David.

"Carol, David is leaving now so he's kindly offered to walk us home, isn't that nice of him?" said Sabrina.

"Yes," I answered, feeling somewhat superfluous.

We said our goodnights and promised to see them all the following evening.

As we left one of the girls, Angela, caught up with us, "Is Andrew coming soon?"

"Yes he is, tomorrow or the day after," said Sabrina.

"Oh good, I'll see him then, goodnight."

When we had walked a safe distance and were out of ear shot, Sabrina explained that Angela had a crush on Andrew and usually pestered the life out of him but he'd never taken a serious interest however, he managed to tolerate the attention. He hoped her infatuation for him would eventually fizzle out as she became older and found someone more suited.

"Mind you," I said laughingly, "I can understand why she chases him, after seeing the photos of him, he is a very good looking chap. She had better watch out, I might take a fancy to him myself!"

"Oh no, I think once you've seen Jonathan you'll quickly change your mind."

"What do you mean?"

"Well although Andrew is a very good looking boy and I would never admit to either of them I found one better than the other, I personally think Jonathan has something more."

"In what way?"

"I don't know, its difficult to explain, wait till you meet them both and make up your own mind."

We were only a couple of hundred yards from the last house in the village when we approached what I would regard as the nearest thing to a lay-by you could get on such a narrow lane. A young man sat in a parked metallic grey Ford escort, wearing a white T-shirt and sun glasses. He had the window open and had obviously heard us coming. As we got nearer, he suddenly grabbed a map book and started to study it in great detail.

I glanced in as we passed and started to chuckle to myself.

"What's so funny?" quizzed Sabrina.

"No wonder he's lost," I said. "Didn't you notice, he's got that book upside down, he'll be turning left when he should be turning right!"

As we strolled home, David explained that he'd recently been posted to the new police station, the one across from the house and that he'd luckily found lodgings with an old lady who owned a cottage about a mile further on. His new landlady apparently felt much safer with him there, up until now she'd been on her own and the cottage was in a rather remote place. His move was due to his recent promotion to sergeant, the little station he had been at previously already had a sergeant and was too small to warrant another, so he'd requested a transfer and had been fortunate to get a placement at this new branch.

When we arrived back at the house, Sabrina asked David in for coffee. He accepted her offer but with the understanding it would have to be quick as he was on early shift the following morning. I stayed for what I considered a polite length of time and then made myself scarce by going to bed, David was obviously smitten by Sabrina and I thought he would appreciate some time alone with her.

I had been in bed reading for about an hour when I heard the front door shut, David had obviously departed, within seconds Sabrina was bounding through the door, courteously asking if I was asleep but even if I was wanted me to waken. She was in an excitable mood saying she wasn't sleepy and it soon became apparent that she liked David. It was ages before she stopped talking about him. David had expressed a wish to take her out one evening but she thought it selfish to leave me on my own. I told her not to be so silly and go enjoy herself, that I would be alright with her two big brothers to watch over me. My decision brought a beaming smile to her face. She decided to telephone David the next day to let him know. Eventually she left to take a bath, I could now do what I wanted to do earlier, sleep.

British weather being what it is, when we awoke the following morning it was raining, so we decided to have a lazy morning and go the pictures in the afternoon.

We had a rather large breakfast, which I cooked. Sabrina wasn't the domesticated type and didn't portray the typical Italian mama who spends most of her time in the kitchen. This filling repast would keep us going until early evening when we were going to indulge ourselves with a selection of scrumptious delights from the local Chinese take-away.

"I expect by the time we get back Andrew will have arrived," said Sabrina.

"Good, we'd better get enough food for three then," I said.

The film finished about six o'clock and when we came out it was raining heavily. We hoisted the coats over our heads and made a quick dash up the street to the take-away.

We hadn't a long wait and soon left fully laddened with a variety of dishes, the rain had eased slightly but we didn't want to tempt fate and made a hasty dash for the car.

The smell of food as we drove home was making our mouths water and we hoped that Andrew had eaten already and was not hungry, thereby leaving more for us.

As we drove up to the house, there were no visible lights.

"It doesn't look like Andrew has made it yet, maybe he couldn't find a willing victim to give him a lift," said Sabrina.

"Oh well, we shall just have to eat his share of the food, we can't let it go to waste."

As we entered the house, we could see there was some subdued lighting from the front room.

"Andrew must be here after all," said Sabrina. "Hi Andrew, where are you?"

As we entered, we heard a scuffling from the front room. A tall young man sprung up from the sofa and gave a broad grin, while a young lady also emerged hastily adjusting her clothing.

"Sorry to disturb you, you were obviously busy," said Sabrina lightheartedly.

"No that's alright, Julie very kindly gave me a lift and I invited her in for a coffee."

Julie was obviously embarrassed by the whole situation and Andrew gently but quickly ushered her out the door showering her with apologies as she left. I have always found it quite amazing how some men are born with the ability to talk their way out of this kind of situation without offending, and even leaving their prey eagerly awaiting their next encounter.

Sabrina and I meanwhile retreated to the kitchen, we were both very eager to eat. We set a third place and had already tucked in by the time Andrew reappeared still grinning.

"Andrew, meet Carol," said Sabrina as another mouthful of food disappeared.

"At last, it's good to meet you, Sabrina has told us so much about you, nothing bad of course, but she has been quite excited about you spending the holidays with us."

"I'm glad about that, I wouldn't want to make the wrong impression."

"Have you eaten, Andrew?" asked Sabrina.

"Yes, we stopped off for a meal on the way down, I thought it best as I wasn't sure what you had planned for this evening. Mind you, that smells good so I might just try a little!"

"You seem to know a lot about me," I said as we finished our meal, "but I don't know much about you."

That comment was like opening the flood gates, over the next hour he never stopped talking, only momentarily to take a breath. Andrew had made the bold decision to study interior design, much to the disappointment of his parents who hoped he also would eventually join the family business, but he had other ideas. He wanted something different and had a flair for art which he wanted to exploit to the full. It was also an occupation that he could continue, whichever country he decided to settle in.

Although he still had a year to go before finishing his course, he had already redesigned the homes of many of his parent's affluent friends and even though money had been no object, they were highly delighted by his work, more than eager to show off their new abode to all friends and colleagues alike most of whom were also very wealthy. Within no time, Andrew had managed to set himself up with a nice little business, travelling to all parts of the country redesigning everything from town houses to country retreats and making lots of money.

Andrew displayed a somewhat smug self admiration for one property he had particularly enjoyed restoring, a small castle in the lowlands of Scotland near the boarder, and produced pictures he'd taken before and after, photographic evidence of his vast talents. I had to admit his work was good, to boost his ego I suggested that if time allowed we'd view its true glory during the holiday.

This ability also showed in his appearance. Although his clothes were of a casual design, they were lavish and well made. His trousers were correct in length not using his shoes as support, his shirt was pristine white and crisply ironed to ensure those perfect creases, even his shoes were of hand-made leather and polished to a high shine. I was aware that he was a very nice looking chap; he had inherited the dusky Italian features like Sabrina, his hair was dark brown and parted in the centre, it had a natural wave, but not too curly and had a beautiful sheen any girl would be proud of. His eyes sparkled and his nails were properly manicured, he obviously took great pride in the image he portrayed, it was not difficult to see why he had a large following of admirers but above all his finery, he was very natural and relaxed, able to mix at all levels of the social scale. I felt he was the kind of person who'd impress all, in different ways, regardless of age or gender.

"Oh, by the way," said Sabrina, "young Angela was asking after you yesterday, wanted to know if you were coming to the house during the holidays."

"I suppose you said yes. You know she'll spend most of her time attempting to get as close as possible to me and constantly stare all the while."

"Don't be so horrid, you should be pleased that she shows an interest in you, no matter what you think, she will make a good wife for the right man," Sabrina said defensively.

"Yes! But not me thank you, so no matchmaking please!"

"Anyway, I think you'll notice a change in her this time, those baby looks have faded and she has a very nice figure," said Sabrina. "What do you think Carol?"

"Well although I've never met her before I would have to agree that Sabrina's right, she is certainly very attractive."

"Hm...it may be worth another look then... can't miss an opportunity now can I?" said Andrew with a glint in his eye.

"Oh by the way, I telephoned David and he will meet us at the inn tomorrow." said Sabrina.

"Who's David?" quizzed Andrew.

"He's a young man that has taken quite a shine to your baby sister but I rather think the feeling is mutual," I replied.

"I better meet this person then," said Andrew with mock gravity although I think he was quite serious.

"You will," said Sabrina. "And I expect your best behaviour, not like the last time I introduced you to a boyfriend, you spent the whole evening scowling at him and making sure we were never alone!"

"No I didn't."

"You did so don't deny it. I don't interfere with your girlfriends," said Sabrina.

"That's different," argued Andrew.

"No it's not, I am entitled just like you to see who I want, and don't want to have to gain the approval of my brothers every time."

"End of round one," I said, butting in. "Shall I make some coffee?"

"Sorry Carol, yes some coffee would be fine," said Sabrina apologetically.

The atmosphere quickly returned to normal and the rest of the evening was just spent lazing and chatting, we decided that the following day we needed to stock up with food. Jonathan was due the day after that and he apparently was very fussy, preferring to cook and eat at home.

As I lazily slouched in a comfy armchair Sabrina and Andrew gave me a potted biography of their older and successful bother. As I knew very little about him, I let Sabrina do all the talking. I learnt he was a solicitor who now had a very successful practice based in Mayfair, and like Andrew had also been lucky when starting out, mummy and daddy had introduced him to all the right clientele. Sabrina told me he worked long hours, but recently he'd been deluged not only from local clients but from all over the country forcing the need for more space and man power. I learned that he'd spent time visiting different areas of the country looking for suitable premises. I was puzzled as to who would manage this second office but Sabrina was quick to provide me with the answer; simple, he'd met another solicitor, a James Williamson and they were to form a partnership. However, I got the impression that James didn't like the south much preferring the new outlet to be more northerly.

I found Andrew's frankness that Jonathan could not appreciate the plain and abrupt northern way somewhat amusing, he was probably by now experiencing withdrawal symptoms from the finery he had become accustomed to. If he was finding northern life so distasteful, I wondered how Jonathan and James relationship could be amicable. Maybe the secret was because they were so totally different, Jonathan liked his fancy food and fine wines and James was more than happy with a pie and a pint of bitter.

I realised that life had been more than favourable to this family in all aspects, that automatic success waiting as if passed down the generations like a family heirloom. My immediate thought was of how lucky they'd been but the more I listened the more my opinion altered, these children of rich background hadn't taken a free ride on the backs of their elders but studied and worked to achieve their goals in life, they rightly deserved the rewards now in abundance even if money had smoothed their rocky path.

As I retired to bed, I wondered if I'd ever manage to reach the goal I'd set myself especially changing directions at a later stage, but many had done so before and achieved more than ever dreamed of, so there was every possibility of my doing the same. Everybody needs to strive towards something and my ideals gently carried me into the twilight zone of slumber.

CHAPTER 2

I was late waking the following morning, mind you we had stayed up late. Sabrina and Andrew were already dressed and ready to leave when I poked my dishevelled head round the bedroom door. I made a speedy retreat to the bathroom emerging in record time only stopping briefly to grab a slice of cold soggy toast as we left.

I could not believe the amount of food that was being piled into the two trolleys as we systematically toured the isles of the vast superstore the following day. Andrew and Sabrina were like a plague of ants grabbing at various fresh and packaged goodies. Only the best fresh produce was picked, the highest quality meats and complete cheeses, some of which I had never seen before. I was shocked when the cashier finally totalled up the bill which didn't include any wine or spirits... these, I was informed, were to be purchased from an off-licence who specialised in red Italian wines, Jonathan's preferred tipple.

We struggled to the car and packed the large stack

of bags as best we could, slotting each one together like a jigsaw, filling the boot to capacity.

We drove to a small village, the sort that if you blinked you'd miss, we turned into a small side street and parked outside a shop which didn't look very special.

It turned out to be a very deceptive place. Upon entering, it was like stepping back in time, say a hundred years or so. We had to duck our heads as we stepped through the door. Inside there was no gaudy modern shelving, just solid highly polished dark wood and a heavy brass edged counter that stood at the far end where an antiquated till sat. The shelves were stocked with an unbelievable selection of wines, certainly labels that you wouldn't find on your local supermarket shelf.

The owner appeared from a back room, his manner and dress complementing the surroundings. He referred to us as 'sir or 'madam', terms which no shopkeeper had used for many years but nevertheless, it made a most refreshing change. There was a long discussion on the assortment of wines available, this merchant obviously knew his customers well and made some suggestions and recommendations of which wines to choose. We eventually left with three cases full of different bottles which had to share the back seat with me due to the lack of boot space.

It took us nearly an hour to put everything away upon our return, we were totally exhausted! I made some coffee and we all slumped onto the kitchen stools for a well earned break. I had already got out my cheque book to pay my share but Andrew told me to put it away, all the food bills went straight onto a family credit card and would be paid for by Jonathan. This was normal procedure when they were at the house and it meant that no one felt guilty about inviting their friends as and when they wanted to. Jonathan felt this was only correct being the eldest, he also often used the house to entertain his clients, he therefore liked to keep the cupboards well stocked necessitating the purchase of fresh items only if he was having a dinner party.

It had been raining on and off most of the day but by evening time it had eased, the sun had finally emerged from behind the receding black clouds gently drying the earth and offering the promise of a delightful sunset. We decided to have any early 'half' at the inn and grab a pizza from the landlady to bring home, our last junk meal before indulging in the finer foods which we would undoubtedly be savouring after tonight. Andrew thought this was a great idea and although he kept reiterating his attitude towards Angela, we both felt he was showing a more than eager desire to go out, especially for someone trying to avoid an unwanted admirer.

When we arrived at the inn, the group we had met previously, were already well installed in a corner of the bar. Angela had carefully positioned herself at one end of bench leaving just enough room to squash one more person on the end, thus ensuring that person would have to sit very close. Andrew, of course, was in a teasing mood and at first declined the offer to sit proposing that either Sabrina or myself should take the place. With one look at each other, we visually agreed not to play his game and acquired a couple of stools from another table, this left only Andrew standing so eventually he conceded and sat down much to the delight of Angela. Sabrina and I made conversation with the lads whilst Andrew spent most of the evening talking at Angela, she in turn just gazed on starry eyed, treating every word like an utterance from the gods.

David did not make an appearance until much later, at the last minute he had to assist with the transporting of a prisoner to London. Sabrina introduced her new man to Andrew, who under her strict instructions, welcomed him and shook his hand before returning his attentions once more in Angela's direction.

At about eight o'clock both he and Angela suddenly stood up.

"It's such a lovely evening, we thought we'd go for a walk," stuttered Angela.

Andrew had taken an interest after all, we both just smiled at him, he was already sporting that cheeky grin he was wearing the first night I saw him at the house.

"Will you be back...or shall we go home by ourselves?" asked Sabrina.

"Oh I'll see you at home...I think that's best."

"What about the pizza, do you want us to save you some?"

"Eh...no I'll sort something out for myself later thanks."

David was invited to join us for supper and we left carrying a very hot pizza and a large bag of the landlady's freshly cooked chips, it all smelt wonderful. As we walked home, we again noticed the escort car parked in the lay-by as on the previous evening but this time the owner was nowhere to be seen. I remember remarking that it would be impossible to get lost in the same place twice but Sabrina said he might be visiting someone local. David had a look around but could see nothing wrong so we carried on walking.

Over supper David explained that he just found out

that a position had become vacant for a plain clothes officer at the branch and he was seriously considering applying for it, he had decided to discuss it with Inspector Connel who was the senior officer. While we were on the subject of the police Sabrina told David about Jennifer Lawson and how she would often tell us of the unusual and funny cases she had dealt with over the years. My interest in the police practice of solving crime was met by raised eyebrows.

I boasted that I'd been privileged to accompany Jennifer to a 'scene of the crime', but went on to say that much to my disappointment, I'd been left outside in the company of a poor unfortunate bobby whose only involvement in the incident was he happened to be on duty at the time, but he had been quite handsome so I didn't mind. Listening to Sabrina, I got the impression that I was a very large handful for Jennifer to cope with, it meant her often giving in and feeding my unending curiosity of her work.

We'd been home only an hour when Andrew reappeared looking bedraggled, apparently they had eventually gone back to Angela's place and not surprisingly, ended up in her bedroom. They had been relaxing on her bed when her parents returned home unexpectedly early from the cinema. Angela panicked and pushed him out of the window closely followed by items of clothing and his shoes. It was a good job that she lived in a bungalow otherwise it could have been quite a nasty experience. He had to carry his shoes as his clumsy retreat had landed him in the flower bed and due to all the rain we'd had recently, his feet were covered in mud. Sabrina made it very clear that it was his own fault, told him to stop treading mud into the carpet and go take a shower. He was obviously not too perturbed, still managing to raise a smile as he departed to the bathroom on tip toe. Both David and I managed to keep serious faced during his scolding by Sabrina but no sooner had his bedroom door shut than we burst into stifled laughter.

David, at this point, thought it best to leave and Sabrina showed him out, I could just hear them talking and with the snippets I overheard, it became obvious he was again asking her out. The talking finally stopped and it was a long while before she reappeared, they had undoubtedly found a better use for their lips than verbal communication.

When Sabrina returned she was in a buoyant mood, David had offered to take her to dinner one evening which she readily accepted, but wanted to wait until Jonathan had arrived so as not to leave me on my own. This fitted in with David's plans, he would be busy over the next week especially as he didn't know what he may have to do if he applied for the new job.

It was about ten thirty when the telephone rang and Sabrina answered.

"Hello Jonathan, how are you?"

By her responses, he was obviously explaining where he was and when he would be arriving.

"OK, we'll see you tomorrow evening about seven then. You take care driving there's been several accidents on the motorway due to the holiday rush. I'll get Carol to cook something nice for dinner. Bye, see you tomorrow."

Just then Andrew appeared dressed in a large white towelling dressing gown.

"Who was that on the phone?" he asked.

"It was Jonathan, he's in the north Yorkshire area looking at more offices," explained Sabrina.

"When's he coming home?" asked Andrew

"Tomorrow, about sevenish, I told him I would get Carol to cook him a nice meal."

"Thanks," I said. "Talk about drop me in at the deep end, with what you've been telling me I don't think my cooking's up to his standards and expectations."

"Whatever you prepare he will eat and I'm sure he'll enjoy it. I haven't found anything wrong with your cooking yet and I've had plenty," Sabrina said in a reassuring voice.

"I'll go make us some coffee," said Sabrina.

"I'll just watch the news if nobody minds, just in case."

Andrew looked at me a little strangely.

"It's alright, Carol's become a proper little detective since living in Greenwich," said Sabrina.

Once again I heard her rendition of my persecution of Jennifer.

"During our little get togethers, Carol can't help but change the subject, not satisfied until she has dissected every minute detail," said Sabrina with a scolding tone to her voice. "Although Jennifer is always pleased to see us, by the end of the evening the relief on her face shows she's glad we're leaving. I have even suggested we send Carol on one of those murder mystery holidays, let her solve a riddle of her own and I'm sure the people she'd be with wouldn't mind her constant chatter especially if they were as interested as her!"

Sabrina was right, even other friends at the university had often hinted that I should become a police woman but I didn't fancy walking the beat or typing up report after report on a stolen car or missing cat. The road I'd subsequently chosen would specialise in one area, not generalise.

There was no mention during the brief news update, which came as no surprise. I was about to launch into that all too familiar topic of conversation but was cut short by a momentary glance from Sabrina that said, in no uncertain terms, she didn't want to hear another word. I felt it best to comply with her wishes, even the best of us can be a real bore to others when we continually harp on the same subject. I know, I've been at the receiving end on several occasions, it has the effect of grating on one's nerves, a term of speech only but a suitable description nevertheless.

Unfortunately, my mind had again received a spark of stimulation, retrieving details and images of the victim. At this point, I thought it best to make a quick departure, Andrew seemed a little bewildered at my decision to retire early but Sabrina just gave an understanding smile as I left the room. I lay awake for about an hour recalling and mulling over the facts in my mind, trying to make some sense of the whole affair.

I must have drifted off to sleep because the next thing I remember was Sabrina knocking on the bedroom door at about ten past eight to see if I would like some coffee. I had slept well but was in no rush to leave the comfort of my large bed so took the opportunity to relax and read until nineish before getting up.

CHAPTER 3

The day was promising to be very warm with the sun already shining brightly. None of us really fancied much for breakfast, just toast. Jonathan was due later and a substantial evening meal would be expected.

"Have you decided what you are going to cook tonight, Carol?" asked Sabrina.

"Well yes, I thought maybe some home made chilli with rice, it'll keep if Jonathan doesn't arrive on time. Also some fresh bread and a light fruit salad to follow."

"That sounds great," shouted Andrew from the patio. "Are you going to come and have a swim, it's a beautiful day and not too hot yet so Carol should be alright."

We both did a speedy change and joined Andrew who already sported a pair of brightly coloured trunks. I had to admit that when Andrew was stripped of his clothing he really had a very nice body, deeply tanned but a little lacking in muscles. I do prefer a man to have a healthy sized chest.

The natural pool was fantastic. You entered by the steps at the far end of the patio and as I stared down into its depths, I could see that steps had also been set in the other side thus enabling you to have easy and safe footings into the water. God, it was cold as I hesitantly dipped one set of toes below the surface. The sun had not been up long enough to completely take off the chill. I stepped in very gently, unsure of the stony bottom. Although the base was made up of large rounded pebbles, they were smooth and felt natural to tread on. Once I had checked out the bottom I decided it just best to plunge in, trying to ease oneself in gradually was proving to be painful.

I swam out to the centre, the deepest part could be no more than about five feet, and being six two, I could stand up with my head above water. As I looked across, I could see where the water was entering from the stream, it was like a miniature waterfall and with the sun shining directly on it, it made it a wondrous focal point full of rainbow coloured bubbles floating outwards from its base. I swam over and positioned myself below the fall, it was exhilarating, taking my breath away as each iced droplet touched my warm flesh. I stayed for what seemed an eternity, not wanting to move, letting the water torment my skin. It was only when Sabrina spoke that the spell broke and I emerged. I swam across to join them, my body must have become accustomed to my watery surroundings, I was beginning to feel warmer and more relaxed.

"This is really lovely," I said.

"It is rather isn't it," exclaimed Sabrina. "You can just see over the edge where it leaves, I like to watch the water flow down the rocky base, always reminds me of a child skipping."

I swam over to the other end. To the right side the stones had been purposely built up to channel the water's flow, which dropped sharply and ran on down the hill between high slopping grass banks, it then veered off to the right and eventually out of sight.

We spent most of the day just lazing about, swimming now and then when overheated, or stretched out on the loungers reading and an abundance of chilled juices and fruit ensured we stayed refreshed inside.

Whoever had overseen the planting of the floral decor had chosen well, the overhead trellis heaved with a blanket of green leaves spasmodically interrupted by hanging blooms of yellow and red. Around the edges were strategically placed earthen pots that overflowed with smaller but highly perfumed flowers and herbs. I closed my eyes and tried to identify each one by smell but found it impossible.

"What are you doing?" asked Sabrina, obviously my deep breathing exercise had caught her attention.

"Trying to pick out the different flowers," I said, laughing. "But my nose isn't sensitive enough."

"I know what you mean, one second there's mint and the next roses," said Sabrina.

"Who chose the plants?" I asked.

"I did actually," trumped up Andrew with a proud look on his face.

"Should have known, the well planned colour scheme should have told me," I replied.

"Well, I have to be able to design the exterior of a building as well as the interior," he said.

"Never thought about it really, I suppose you must," I said. "You must be quite an expert on flowers and plants then."

"Not as good as I'd like to be but I manage with a little help and advice from a friend of mine who's a landscape gardener," said Andrew.

"That's handy," I said closing my eyes again, the warmth of the day was making me sleepy. It was a little before five when consciousness returned once more. I took a last dip to liven up my senses before leaving Sabrina and Andrew still bathing to make ready the evening meal. I had prepared and just started cooking when they both appeared looking quite refreshed.

"Oh no!" shouted Sabrina, "I've forgotten to go to the off-licence, Jonathan won't be happy, he always likes to finish a meal with a cognac or something."

"Don't worry," said Andrew. "We'll get changed and go now, he's not due for at least another hour, we should be back by then."

With a speedy transformation they were ready to leave.

"You don't mind, do you?" said Sabrina. "We'll be as quick as we can."

"No, that's alright, I have plenty to do. See you later."

I switched on the television once they'd gone, flicking through the channels to find something suitable to watch while I prepared the fruit salad. The news was starting on One, that would do.

I had been chopping away, careful to avoid my finger tips when the newscaster made a brief mention about the murdered woman. I ceased my furtive activity and turned up the sound to hear what was being said. The police had found another witness who'd seen the car, a BMW, that fateful night and were proceeding with their enquiries on the information given. However it was confirmed that the police were still without a suspect.

"I wish they could get a lead," I muttered to myself.

"A lead to what?" came a gentle, sultry reply.

I instantly turned around, knife still in my hand. "Jesus

you nearly frightened the life out of me!" I screeched.

"I'm sorry," he said. "Are you alright?"

"Well no thanks to you," I said, my voice still sounding a little shocked. "I didn't hear you come in."

"I didn't mean to scare you, let me introduce myself, I'm Jonathan and I presume you are Carol," he said. "You're just as I imagined, Sabrina did a good job of describing you. By the way where are my beautiful sister and fun loving brother?"

"They've just popped to the off-licence, they'll be back shortly," I explained. "I have been elected to make dinner, I hope you like chilli."

"Yes, especially when it's home made," he said in a very charming and reassuring voice.

"That's alright then, would you like some coffee, dinner will be about another hour?" I asked.

"That would be nice, I'll take my bags to my room, freshen up and join you shortly."

I managed to calm myself down, made some fresh coffee and waited. Jonathan returned after about ten minutes. The only lights on were two small round spotlights that shone down at angles and although the day was still bright, the design of the house kept it naturally dark. As he approached, I saw the outline of a tall, well built man with broad shoulders. The nearer he got, the more I could define his features. He sat himself on one of the stools by the breakfast bar directly opposite in exactly the direction of one of the beams of light. He truly was a magnificent creature.

He must have thought me very strange; I just stood for ages with my mouth open, staring at him, taking in his every detail. He wasn't just handsome, but breathtakingly gorgeous. His hair was dark blonde, not dark like the others. It was parted to the side and although well cut, fell casually across his forehead. He did however, have those eyes, very dark and very deep especially in such subdued light. The contours of his face were such that it was as though it had been chiselled and smoothed from fine stone, not a blemish to be seen, but darker of course, there was no shadow of a beard even this late in the day. They say beauty is in the eye of the beholder, and to me he typified beauty. He had changed into a black polo neck top which was hugging the contours of his body like a second skin. He was muscular but not overly, a pair of black cord trousers finished his ensemble, well fitting but not tight. I thought to myself, "I hope he loves swimming I'd like to see more of this body!"

I was suddenly brought back to reality when again he spoke.

"I think something's boiling over," he said in a raised voice as he jumped up from his seat.

I grabbed at the pan of boiling water, pulling it away from the heat, allowing it to cool.

I felt aware of his closeness. As I turned around, Jonathan was standing immediately behind, pinning me in a corner. His eyes were just gazing into mine and I could feel myself being drawn even nearer to him. Very briefly our lips met and I felt as if in a hypnotic trace, unable and unwilling to break free.

It was only the arrival of Sabrina and Andrew that halted our embrace. The shocking realisation that I could have possibly let a man I had known only moments make such undefended advances left me in confused silence.

"We saw your car in the drive, you got here earlier

than expected," noted Sabrina, giving me a smile. "I can see you and Carol have already met and are getting on very well together by the way you were...helping her cook."

"Yes I made good time," said Jonathan. "Anyway, it gave me a chance to meet Carol on my own. She is delightful and every bit as beautiful as you described, Sabrina."

He lifted his eyes once more towards me, I was experiencing a strong desire to turn back the clock but this time wished there to be no interruptions. This feeling unbalanced me and I made haste to change the subject.

"I hope this chilli is good. Sabrina told me you really only like the best and it's not exactly to any known recipe, just my own."

"When someone cooks from the heart, then normally what they produce is a delight, which I'm sure yours will be," said Jonathan in a voice that produced an instant calm.

"Have you settled down now?" Jonathan asked me.

"Yes I'm OK," I replied.

"What happened then?" asked Sabrina.

"When I arrived, Carol seemed so engrossed in the TV she never heard me, gave her quite a fright when I spoke," said Jonathan.

"Let me guess, she must have been watching the news," replied Sabrina in a somewhat sarcastic tone.

Jonathan gave that all too familiar puzzled look at which Sabrina told him she would explain later.

Time to make myself scarce, so I set the table and finished off dinner.

"OK come and eat," I shouted.

Over dinner they chatted about what they had been up to since last they met at the house. Sabrina and I were obviously at university, Andrew was about to sit his final exams and had just completed two houses, one near Penrith and the other at Banbury. Jonathan had been relentlessly driving up and down the country looking for suitable premises and thought he had found the ideal place situated in York but wanted to take James to view it. Andrew also wanted us to see the castle he had renovated, the prize of his ever increasing photo collection of achievements, so it was suggested that we all go.

The final topic of conversation was about me, Jennifer Lawson, and my undying interest in police affairs. I was beginning to have a complex about it all especially when I listened to Sabrina. She made me sound a nuisance and I probably was.

"I see," said Jonathan, glancing up momentarily, his eyes still dark but different, a cold icy stare. "You like to solve mysteries do you Carol?... Interesting."

His look had unnerved me slightly. "No, not always but there's something intriguing about this one and I just like to keep updated on what's going on," I said quietly, trying to play it down.

Eventually everybody had finished and Jonathan sat back in his chair; he had made no remarks during dinner about the food I had produced. It's not uncommon for people who don't like something to say nothing rather than offend.

"That was an excellent meal Carol, your culinary skills are very good, I hope you will treat me to further delights while you're here," said Jonathan now in a very complimentary tone. Was he just talking about food?

"I'm pleased you liked it," I said, unable to control the beaming smile I was now sporting.

"We told you not to worry, it would be fine," coaxed Sabrina.

After clearing up we retired to the front room with a pot of fresh coffee.

"Would you all like a cognac?" asked Jonathan. "You did buy some didn't you?"

"Of course," said Andrew disappearing to rummage through the bag of goodies they had bought. "Here you are."

"What have you done to your hand?" asked Sabrina noticing the inconspicuous plastic stuck to Jonathan's palm. I hadn't noticed before but once mentioned its presence was quite apparent.

"Oh it's nothing, I cut it on a door handle at one of the offices I went to view. The man from the estate agent panicked when he saw the blood and insisted he take me to the nearest hospital to have it seen to," he replied laughingly. "I think he was frightened I might sue them so he wanted medical assurance that no serious damage had been done and that my hand wasn't about to drop off!"

"Well, he was right to make you have it seen to properly, is it alright now?" she asked.

"Yes much better, the plaster is really only to keep it clean."

It didn't affect his grip on the large glass of brandy he was holding so it was obviously on the mend.

I made an excuse of being tired after the first drink and retired to bed much against their pleas to stay.

Although I had been made very welcome, I thought it would be nice for them to chat together without me present, also my mind was thinking about other things. I wanted to call Jennifer again to try and arrange for us to meet. However, my attempts proved fruitless, she must have gone out for the evening. I would have try again in the morning.

CHAPTER 4

The following day was another scorcher and my three hosts spent most of the day sun bathing. I stayed as long as the heat permitted before slipping away to try telephoning Jennifer again. This time I was more successful and we agreed to join up that evening about six thirty. I asked Sabrina if I could borrow her car and shortly after tea, I left for Greenwich.

For once the timing was perfect, I arrived at Jennifer's home about six forty-five just as she was getting out of her car.

She made some iced coffee and we sat relaxing on her small balcony. The sun was cooler now and most pleasant. She obviously knew why I had phoned and resigned herself to yet further grilling from me until this endless case was solved. Unfortunately, the investigations regarding the car had still drawn a blank on the mysterious car. It could have been anybody, the road on which Jane Downing had lived joined two busy roads and was often used as a convenient short cut by people who knew the area.

One unusual fact had recently come to light; Jane's

mother had been pruning the roses one afternoon when she'd remembered Jane telling her that 'Antony' loved flowers and knew them all by their proper names, an important fact but he could still be anything from a keen gardener to a botanist. Jane also mentioned his liking to wear a fresh button hole every day, usually a rose, so where did he purchase his supplies from before meeting Jane? Roses are not a cheap item even when readily available. Jennifer said the police would check just in case the local florist had such a client but it seemed, unless they were extremely lucky, they didn't hold out much hope of it leading anywhere.

I left Jennifer's and arrived back at the house just before eleven. Sabrina was still up but Andrew and Jonathan had gone to bed. Andrew had over indulged himself at the inn that night, fallen over on the way home and had been promptly ordered to bed by big brother immediately upon their return.

Jonathan's reason for slumber on the other hand was totally different. He had a meeting on a golf course near Cheltenham with a client early the next morning, this person could prove to be an important contact so he needed to be fresh and alert.

I was tired and ready for bed but Sabrina had waited for my return and was not about to be put off, it was the first chance since her brothers had arrived for us to indulge in a girlie chat. She followed me into the bedroom, I washed and changed into my night clothes while she proceeded to make herself comfortable across my bed. I could sense her mild irritation at not being able to command my full attention with idle conversation. When she was ready to tell of the genuine topic for this late rendezvous, then I would listen.

"Well?" quizzed Sabrina.

"Well what?" I asked, trying to sound indifferent although I instinctively knew what she was hinting at.

"Oh, don't give me that look, I saw you last night in the kitchen, you and Jonathan were really getting to know one another as I recall."

"No...he was just helping me with a pan of hot water," I answered not ready to give in so easily.

"OK, I won't push the point. So what do you think of my two charming, successful brothers?" said Sabrina. "Which do you prefer?"

"They're both very nice. Andrew is certainly good looking, a little flighty but great company."

"Yes, he does charm the ladies somewhat and he's lucky not to have landed himself in hot waters before now. He's come very close I can tell you, just look at last night with Angela," said Sabrina. "But he still goes back for more, he won't learn. However, I'm more interested in what you thought about Jonathan."

"What can I say? He's gorgeous, he must have thought me a bit of a dumb head when we first met," I told her. "All I did was stare."

"Yes, he does seem to have the power to overwhelm women and from what I saw he appeared to be having the same affect on you."

"I wouldn't have said that," I denied.

"Oh yes he was, you were kissing!" exclaimed Sabrina, raising the tone of her voice slightly.

"No we weren't, we were just very close, he was helping me and he can help me anytime he likes," I said, with a huge smirk on my face.

"Hm...be careful. As I said, he has a way with the ladies but none have managed to trap him yet, especially in a long term relationship. When they become too serious or involved he disappears straight out of their lives," stated Sabrina with a note of warning in her voice.

"OK, I'll remember."

I fancied some cocoa and as the milk heated, I filled Sabrina in on what information I had found out from Jennifer although it wasn't very much. I also said I hoped she didn't mind but I'd given their telephone number to Jennifer just in case. The hour was late, the cocoa drunk, bed was the only place I now wanted.

The following day I slept late and rose just after ten. Jonathan had already left and Andrew was eating breakfast on the patio unaffected by the previous evening's activities. The weather was warm but the sun was constantly ducking behind the passing puffy, white clouds.

"Where's Sabrina this morning, not up yet?" I asked.

"No, not yet," replied Andrew.

"I'll go and see if she wants some coffee, what about you?"

"No thanks I've just finished a cup," he said.

Sabrina was sitting up in bed with the curtains still closed, apparently she was feeling ill. It was that time and a migraine headache was developing causing her to feel nauseous. I furnished her with some water and aspirins insisting that she try and sleep it off.

Andrew was somewhat unconcerned that Sabrina felt unwell and after a brief moment of false sympathy for his sister, suggested that I spend the day out with him. He had to visit a house to estimate for the redecoration of the master bedroom, we would go there first, take a picnic and stop at a little place by the river that he knew of for our lunch. The idea sounded appealing but I wanted to check that Sabrina didn't mind being alone. A few pitiful mumbles said "go and enjoy yourself" and she was sure she'd be alright after a nap.

Andrew quickly packed a cooler box with wine, bread, cheese and fruit. We threw a couple of travel blankets in the boot with the cooler box and set off.

It didn't take too long to reach the house. Actually I would have called it a mansion. It had large, wrought iron gates which were electronically opened from the house. After muffled communication via an intercom system, we drove into the forecourt which was adorned with artistic stone statues of lions. I was more than willing to wait in the car whilst Andrew went about his business, but he insisted I go with him as his assistant for the day. The owner was not at home but the butler had been issued with instructions to show us the master bedroom and provide us with anything we may need.

I must admit it did appear dowdy upon entering. The furnishings, although once of an expensive nature, were now worn and faded, the old fashioned pink roses no longer enthused boldness but had receded, indistinguishable from their surroundings. It had been the bedroom of the new owner's mother and unlike the rest of the house, had not been redecorated for some years. Maybe the reluctance to wipe away familiarity and fond memories was reason enough for such neglect.

The old lady had recently met and married her third husband who was an extremely wealthy man. He owned a large cattle ranch in Texas where she now resided. She had no need of the house or any monies that could arise from its sale so she'd kindly donated this desirable residence to her daughter who had always lived with her.

The daughter's decision to change bedrooms was a chance for Andrew to once again put his special talent to use. The room was vast and fairly square, opposite the door there were two arched patio windows that allowed in ample light and opened out onto the garden.

The furniture was dated. Great heavy, deep wooden wardrobes and drawers lined the edges and against one wall stood a four poster bed which, in earlier days, must have been a fine piece but years of unnoticed abuse had marred its beauty.

Andrew drew outlines of the available space, strutting from one side to another as if trying to view every angle. Finally, after taking some measurements and information from the butler about the new resident of the room, what kind of lady she was and her preference of colour, we were finished. As we departed through the front door, he advised the butler that he would send through some sketched drawings and ideas within a week.

"There, that didn't take long did it?" he said. "We can take a leisurely drive to the river, I know of a very quiet spot, nobody has stumbled across it yet except me, I hope."

We approached the river down a track, the sort that you would find running through a wooded area. It opened out into a wide grassed bank that was sheltered each side by small trees and bushes, it then sloped gradually down to the water's edge. Very picturesque. Andrew parked the car to one side and we spread the rugs out on the bushy grass on the far side which offered the only available shade. It was very peaceful and he was right, unless you knew where it was, you could never find it. Andrew had apparently spied it one day while sailing down stream with a friend on her cruiser.

Lunch was good and afterwards we laid back to relax. With the heat of the day and several glasses of wine I felt a little lightheaded.

"I suppose Sabrina warned you away from me and Jonathan," he said, out of the blue. "She normally does to all her friends."

"No, actually she hasn't. I hope she considers me sensible enough to look after myself."

He turned towards me propping himself of his elbows. "Do you like me, Carol?" he sounded like a young child asking for reassurance.

"Of course I do. What a daft question!" I said almost laughing.

"No, I'm serious."

I opened my eyes and looked up. He was serious, he was asking with a look of sincerity in his eyes. I stopped giggling, this was a side that I hadn't seen or anticipated from a person who so far had portrayed a light-hearted carefree attitude to life.

"Honestly, I mean it, I do like you," I said, reassuringly.

"Good," he said, relaxing slightly.

Without any warning, he leant over and kissed me, passionately I may add, his hands caressing my body but never touching forbidden parts. I was stunned for a moment, my immediate response was to return his embrace but only momentarily before gently pushing him away, permitting me to sit up. His actions had taken me completely by surprise and it took me a few minutes to fully realise what had happened.

"I think you're wonderful Carol, very special," he said and with the way he looked, I was convinced he meant it.

My God, I'd only been at the house for a week and already had an encounter with not one but both brothers. This was all happening too fast.

He moved towards me again but I drew back defending what personal space I still had with raised hands.

"I'm sorry," he said, "I've offended you. I didn't mean to, please forgive me, but you did say you liked me."

"Yes, I do like you Andrew but I'm not sure yet if it's in the way you want. Anyway I thought you were after Angela," I said. "Look, let's just be friends for now and if anything further is destined to happen between us, then so be it, OK?" I said, looking at him for understanding.

"You're right, I'll back off," he said. "But don't wait too long, somebody else might snatch me away," he said jokingly and giving me that cheeky grin I had seen on our first meeting.

We finished the last of the fruit and wine before finally packing up and setting off home.

Whilst driving back, I reflected on what had happened. It puzzled me. Was Andrew really interested in me or was he trying it on as he did with his other girl friends? I felt I didn't know him enough to make that decision but if he really was serious, things could become very interesting. Mind you, I was already sure that if I had to choose between Andrew and Jonathan, there was no doubt in my mind. It would be Jonathan.

"So, my assistant for the day," he said snappily, "what

ideas do you have for re-vamping that tardy old bedroom?"

"Lilac," I replied.

"Lilac! Why lilac?" he sounded puzzled by my decision of colour.

"It's a very unexploited colour and I like it," I said.

"OK, continue," he replied.

"Lilac, winter white and brass," I stated.

"Well, that's a strange combination," he said.

I explained the vision I had of how the room should look. One wall was free of door and windows, perfect for building across, creating a walk in wardrobe. Most ladies have more than adequate clothing to hide away and the doors could be of mirrored glass with brass edgings and shaped the same as the patio windows. There was no actual dressing table in my picture, just a large glass shelf supported by dainty brass clawed brackets and situated above this, a decorative mirror. The old four poster could be replaced by an oval ended king sized bed with suitable headboard and similar bedside shelvings styled the same as my modern version of a dressing table. Winter white and lilac decorated walls tastefully defined by patterned borders and furnishings of subtle lilac shades but definitely not flowers. Finally, to finish off, thickly padded satin bedding in rich, almost creamy, winter white.

"Different," he said in a patronising manner. "Not what I expected at all from you."

"Well, you did ask," I replied.

"Yes I know," he said. "But don't you think that's a little bland for a woman?"

"No, not all of us want clutter."

"I know, but the type of room you describe depicts a shallow emptiness," said Andrew

"Well, that's what I like, everything in its place. Anyway each woman would add her own individual touch," I said.

"You may be right, I might just submit it as an alternative," he replied. "See what reaction it fetches."

"Good, you may get a surprise," I said, laughing.

When we arrived home, we found Sabrina up and about feeling much better and within minutes, Jonathan followed us through the door. He was in a triumphant mood, he had intentionally lost at golf and managed to secure a business deal that involved several dealings nationwide.

The day had been hot and a freshen up was called for. Meanwhile, Sabrina volunteered to make dinner. It wasn't very often she cooked so I was looking forward to trying her efforts for a change.

Sabrina had made some fresh pasta and served it with a light cream sauce containing mushrooms and shallots with a hint of cheese, it was exceptionally good, obviously she had learnt something from mother during her younger years. A compliment was in order and I hinted that from now on, she could cook more when we returned to university.

After dinner, Jonathan jubilantly explained his good fortune. The company with whom he had just negotiated such a super deal had several small outlets throughout the country. They specialised in health food products which were sold in retail outlets also owned by the company. Jonathan had secured all the legal work that arose and now they were looking to expand and wanted

Jonathan to handle all necessary dealings. This made opening the second office very urgent. He would need to contact James and arrange to view again some of the properties that he'd short-listed. Andrew also wanted to show off his talented efforts at the castle he had renovated in Scotland so we agreed that when arrangements were made to visit the properties, we could all journey together.

Jonathan had to work the next couple of days at his office in London, that left the three of us to our own devices. Sabrina and I, being female, needed time to decide what to pack for the trip, something if it was warm, something if cold, something if wet, the list was endless. If we had taken everything we thought we needed, we would need a trunk to get it all in. We finally decided to take only a change of underwear, night-clothes, a good coat and welly boots, we would make do with jeans, a couple of T-shirts and jumpers for the main. Andrew, on the other hand, had a very methodical attitude when putting his clothes away, would just grab at various items in the wardrobe, his packing done in the space of ten minutes.

The remainder of his time was spent producing various sketches. I found it fascinating to watch him work, his pencil streaked across the paper unguided, but these random markings soon developed into an image, perfectly proportioned. If I'd tried, it would have looked more like something created by a one-year-old who'd gained possession of a crayon. My opinion on each was taken as positive input rather than a criticism, the final of five versions was of most interest, my design.

"What do you think?" asked Andrew. "Am I close?"

"Yes, almost," I replied.

"Tell me what needs changing," he asked.

"Just the edges to the shelving, they're too sharp, I think they should be rounded off," I replied.

"OK," he said. "Like this?"

"Yes, that's good," I said looking on as my image became a reality.

"I want to get these designs delivered before we leave, so I'll drop them off now," he said grabbing his car keys. "Won't be long."

He was gone longer than expected but when he did return, he was extremely pleased. The lady in question had been at home and wanted to discuss the designs immediately. After a few minor changes, she had chosen the one she preferred and had handed over a cheque in part payment.

"Which one did she finally pick?" I asked.

It took a while for him to answer. "Eh...your's actually," he replied. "Of course, she did make one or two changes."

"Of course," I said smugly turning away, not wanting him to see the smile on my face. "That's only natural though."

His pride must have taken a bashing even if only slightly. I think I would have felt the same if my professional creation had been rejected in favour of an amateur proposal but although he didn't mention the fact, I thought it best not to push the subject and would make no mention of it again unless he did.

Jonathan was late that evening. He'd been delayed by the hire company in supplying the car he'd picked, a large saloon that had plenty of space in the rear. Three of us had to share and wouldn't appreciate being cramped together on such a long trip. Jonathan's own car was a two seater sporty number quite incapable of transporting such a large quantity of people.

Jonathan, or rather his secretary, had booked us accommodation for the first two nights, after that we would stay as and where necessary until we reached our final destination

Andrew had contacted his new found friends at the castle who were so delighted we'd decided to visit that they insisted we stay with them as long as we wanted. He did try and decline the offer, it was a little unfair to impose five strangers upon them but verging on the point of upsetting his female host, gratefully accepted their invitation thus solving our need to seek further lodgings.

CHAPTER 5

The first couple of days of our trip were taken up mostly travelling, apart from when Jonathan and James left us to conclude their hunt for the most suitable office. One of the locations was fairly near the coast so we negotiated a lift to the nearest resort for a few hours. Andrew spent the time posing on the beach and chasing each and every desirable young lady his eyes fell upon. Sabrina and I went shopping first, we may have to dress for dinner at the castle which was something we hadn't planned for. Sabrina had that nice little credit card with her so it wasn't long before we'd found two lovely dresses that were just begging to be bought.

We strolled along the promenade toward the point where we had deposited Andrew earlier. There was no problem in spotting him, he was standing in the middle of the sand where two rather well developed young kittens were swooning from his attention.

"Good, he hasn't seen us, watch this..." said Sabrina. Quickening her pace, she sped down the steps onto the sand. I followed but at a slower pace, whatever she was up to, I wasn't sharing the blame.

She bombarded her way through the two girls and stood, hand on hips.

"What's going on here!" she said, in a raised voice. "I manage to get mum to mind the kids for a couple of hours so we can be alone and what do I find when I return, you playing the field."

Andrew just stood unable to utter a word, I stood back. Sabrina would be in big trouble when his ability to speak returned.

"Unless you want him and the five kids, I suggest you make yourselves scarce," she said turning, but the girls were already making a hasty retreat. Well, they'd soon find another hunk to drool over.

I could see Andrew was red-faced and it wasn't from the sun. Anger and embarrassment had brought this ruddy colour to his cheeks. I think the words 'bitch' also formed by his lips but I couldn't be sure. Seconds later there was an outburst, in Italian, with arms waving, each responding to the other. I, and most of the nearby bathers, watched with keen interest. Even though this charade was in a foreign tongue, the subject being debated in this heated outburst was just as plain as if discussed in our native language.

When there were no signs of the conflict abating, I considered it best to intervene. I moved a little closer, staying just far enough away to avoid body contact and tried with a polite 'excuse me' to attract their attention. But they were too wound up in the argument to hear, this left me with no other option than to raise my voice above theirs.

"Shut up!" I shouted, loudly.

This had the desired effect, both silenced in mid stream.

"That's better," I said. "We have to go now, Jonathan will be here to collect us shortly."

The match was not over, it was purely half time. They gathered their belongings together and we all marched off the beach in a neat, orderly line with me at the helm. I resisted the urge to watch the surrounding faces as we left but I knew we were under close scrutiny. The weather was hot but the watching eyes were hotter.

Andrew and Sabrina climbed into the rear of the car in utter silence. I had been ushered in between them which, under normal circumstances, would be perfectly acceptable but on this occasion, I was a little concerned incase the second half started and I was in the middle of the pitch. Fortunately, they both sat stony faced each looking out the side windows. Jonathan must have felt the tension emitting from behind, after all they both usually had more than their fair share to say but at this precise moment, not a word passed their lips. Jonathan gave me a glance in the mirror, I responded with a slight shake of my head as a gesture to say nothing. He obviously understood and drove off towards our hotel.

I was glad it wasn't too far as the atmosphere inside the car was uncomfortable. After we checked in, I steered Sabrina away from Andrew towards our room, better to keep them apart for a while so they could both cool off.

"Oh Carol, how about joining me for a drink shortly?" asked Jonathan.

"I'd be delighted, give me ten minutes and I'll be ready," I replied.

"Fine, I'll knock the door," he said as Andrew and he entered the room next to ours.

The bar was empty, plenty of room for us to sit in comfort. We chose a table by the open windows, this side of the building was shaded and a cool breeze flowed through the room.

"So what happened?" asked Jonathan.

"What, between Andrew and Sabrina?" I said. "In a nutshell, Sabrina took a fancy to embarrassing Andrew and she succeeded."

Jonathan had tried to question Andrew as to what was wrong but he was still angry and impossible to get any sense out of. I therefore described that morning's events.

"Ah," he said, "that's what the argument was over."

"They'll both calm down eventually," I replied, "otherwise, it's going to be very peaceful for the next couple of days."

"Sabrina shouldn't have done that," he said. "She wouldn't have liked it if the positions had been reversed."

"I know but that's Sabrina for you," I replied.

"She should apologise to him," said Jonathan.

"Good luck in your endeavour to convince her of that fact," I said.

The day was mellowing and we were both more than content to stay put until the others joined us for dinner. The conversation was strained but at least Andrew and Sabrina were managing to grunt at each other which was some improvement.

The property matters apparently were now completed, quicker than anticipated but to the full satisfaction of both Jonathan and James. There was also a flat above the premises they would rent which had been negotiated into the deal. James was in luck, his work and home were to be in one and same place. There was no urgency for either of them to be back at work for another three days so we could all now relax and take full advantage of the remaining time to enjoy ourselves.

By the end of the evening, relationships were pretty much back to normal and as we parted company that night to retire, Andrew accepted a good night kiss from Sabrina.

We were on the road reasonably early the following morning. We still had a fair distance to travel and we also wanted to do a little sight seeing on the way. The scenery was outstanding with the landscape changing by the mile from mountainous hills to forest to deep lush green fields.

As the afternoon wore on, it was decided we should make tracks for the castle, after all, it would be easier to travel while still light especially on strange roads.

Andrew navigated our way from the main highway. We drove for several miles down a narrow, twisting lane lined with dense shrubbery. I remember remarking that I hoped we didn't meet a vehicle coming the other way as there were very few passing places. Luckily for us we didn't, and finally the bushes ceased, the road widened and we could now see the turrets of the castle framed against the evening sun. At first sight, it reminded me of those old scenes from a Dracula film.

We were met by the butler dressed in full regalia who showed us in and arranged for our baggage to be taken to our rooms.

The entrance hall typified the visual image I had

created of such a building, old carved wooden chairs were scattered about and the traditional suit of armour stood in a far corner. We were ushered into the drawing room where a fire blazed in the grate, even though it was summer, the night air was chilled. We were served drinks and informed our hosts would join us shortly. We'd been waiting only a short while before two middle-aged people entered the room. He was tall and well rounded, obviously a sign of good living, she, in contrast, was shorter and much slimmer but she obviously took great care of her appearance. They introduced themselves as Max and Helen Trent and upon hearing the broad accent with which they spoke I deduced they were clearly of American origin.

Helen went somewhat overboard with her greetings, hugging Andrew as though he was a long lost son before proceeding to extend the same treatment to each of us. I dodged behind Jonathan in an attempt to avoid her attentions but my plan was unsuccessful and suddenly arms were wrapped around my chest and I felt discomfort as they tightened. Mr Trent was similarly overbearing but gratefully was not into such bodily contact. He preferred to shake your arm off for a brief moment, more interested in supplying copious quantities of drink before eagerly leading us into the dining room to eat. Being unsure of our arrival time, they had prepared a cold buffet. I was hungry so while the others made polite conversation, I just ate.

After dinner, we returned to the drawing room where we were spoilt with a large glass of Max's finest malt whisky. Helen had been deeply impressed with the work Andrew had done at the castle and I had to admit, if the other rooms were as good as the one we were in, he had indeed done an excellent job to keep the decor in contrast with the surroundings.

Some friends of the Trents had recently purchased two semi-detached cottages and at present were having them renovated and combined into one. Once done, they'd asked if Helen would mind asking Andrew to cast his professional eye over their property, they'd been so taken by his transformation at the castle that they wanted him to carry out some design work for them. Andrew, of course, was only too delighted and with a quick phone call, Helen had arranged for him to visit the following day. Although there was still building work to be done he could at least get some feel of what would be needed.

When we finally retired to bed, I realised why they had given us the whisky. The bedroom, although clean and fresh, felt cold and I was glad that I had to share with Sabrina. Mind you, the mattress on the four poster bed was old fashioned and full of feathers so as soon as you lay on it, it cosily wrapped itself around you like an outer skin. It was not long till sleep took over.

When Sabrina and I descended the following morning, the others were already at breakfast so we swiftly took the two places left for us. Max and Helen had kindly planned some activities for during the day, Andrew would make his visit as promised, Max was to take Jonathan and James fishing, hopefully to catch dinner and Helen was to take us riding to show us the scenery not visible from any road. I'd never been on the back of a horse before but I was willing to give it a go, it was a good job we had decided to wear jeans.

Unfortunately, with modern communication systems

we were contactable. I could hear that familiar ring from Jonathan's mobile phone. The new client had run into some problems with the documentation regarding the lease of a new building they were about to rent and Jonathan needed to check the legal implications. He would therefore have to forgo the fishing and meet the client, who luckily wasn't too far away.

His trip was to take him to Hawick, about sixty miles away. As he departed, he made his apologies to our hosts explaining this line of business had far reaching potential and therefore he couldn't really say no. The Trents quite understood and hoped he would be back for dinner that evening. What a shame, I think Jonathan was actually looking forward to trying his hand at catching a fish. But I suppose business must come first and if it wouldn't have offended I'd have preferred to go with him rather than face the daunting task of my impending relationship with a four legged animal.

At the stables I was confronted by what looked like a rather large cart horse; it had a broad beam and shaggy hair at the base of its legs covering its hooves. I was not short but looking at this monster made me wonder how I was ever going to hoist myself upon its back. Sabrina's horse was smaller and more sleek. I voiced my concerns but Helen soon reassured me that she had chosen this particular horse because I'd never ridden before and although it looked threatening, had a lovely nature and was not at all skittish. With a helpful lift, I managed to slide into the saddle and sort out the stirrups. I felt very unsafe perched so high and hoped that the land was not too uneven, otherwise I could see me and the ground making contact.

We had not trekked very far before we started to enter a more rugged and hilly area. Walking across the craggy slopes at a slow pace, my main aim was to hang on as the horse's body twisted from the roughness of the terrain. Helen was right, the views from the higher ground were delightful. Looking out across the lower lands below sparsely inhabited by cattle, the clouds shadowed the ground as they passed across the sun but although it looked very inviting now, I imagined that during winter with snow on the ground it would be a very bleak and inhospitable place.

We stopped for a short rest near a small brook so the animals could drink. The cook had made us some sandwiches and a flask of tea which we were all grateful for. My appetite has always been good and inspite of eating a hearty breakfast, I was ravenous.

My limbs had started to ache and stiffen and I was not relishing the ride back even though I was enjoying the day.

While we rested, Helen explained that she and Max had bought the property with the idea of semi-retirement. They had owned a cattle ranch back in the States but had found as their years advanced, it became more and more difficult to manage due to its size. Having lead such an active life, they were at a loss as what to do once they'd sold the ranch. It was only the fact that a cousin of Max's had been over to Scotland on business and was so impressed by its beauty that finally convinced them to visit, resulting in them buying a farm here. They had managed to buy the property from a farmer who was struggling to find the funds to continue.

The Trents bought the business and the farmer who'd

owned the land was now merrily running it on a joint partner basis. This suited both parties, they had the cash to support and the farmer was doing what he was happy and good at. Once a week, he would visit the Trents for lunch to update and advise how things were running. Meanwhile Max kept busy by handling all the paperwork side.

It was time to make tracks back and I was grateful for the use of a large fairly flat boulder to assist me once again to mount my transport home. The pangs of pain I felt as I again raised my leg over its back were a clear signal of the suffering to come.

I could not describe my pleasure when I finally slid out of that saddle and my feet touched the ground. I must have stood for ages trying to get my legs to work and straighten. A couple of lads appeared and took charge of the horses, leading them off to be untacked and fed while I struggled to walk back to the house without looking as though I had lost something. I quickly made my excuses so I could sneak upstairs and take over the tub before anyone else.

The water was hot and as deep as I could possibly get it. A quick search amongst the various jars that lined the edges of the bath resulted in the discovery of a soothing mixture to ease my distressed limbs. It was lovely, I stayed immersed for ages and it was only Sabrina knocking on the door hinting that she also may like to bathe that made me finally but grudgingly muster up the energy to climb out.

I returned to the bedroom where I dressed and sat myself in an armchair. My muscles, although relaxed by the warmth of the water, weren't ready for too much action. I stayed sitting until Sabrina was ready and we descended for dinner. I was a bit surprised that neither Jonathan or Andrew were in the drawing room when we entered.

We had just been served with an aperitif when the phone rang, it was for Sabrina. Jonathan's business was taking longer than anticipated so he'd decided to stay at a local motel for the night. He assured us that he would return early the next morning in plenty of time to collect us for the journey home. The disappointment of his intended absence must have been apparent on my face as Sabrina put a comforting arm around my shoulder in an attempt to cheer me up. I had taken a strong liking to him and was already beginning to miss his presence.

The Trents were excellent hosts and it was unfair of me to display my unhappiness to them, so a smile and lighted hearted conversation was called for.

It could only have been ten minutes before the phone rang once more, again it was for Sabrina, this time it was Andrew's turn to make his excuses. He waffled on about needing to get a real feel for the property, this he felt could only be achieved by staying overnight to catch its true beauty in the dark hours, aiding him to create the perfect image. What a load of rubbish! He, like Jonathan, promised to be back shortly after breakfast the following day.

We later discovered that the people Andrew was visiting had a daughter about the same age and once described sounded a perfect catch for any young man. It was obvious, therefore, that Andrew was fishing. If the bait was cast in his direction he just couldn't help himself, he had to chase after it but most of his catches turned out to be purely momentary infatuation. Like a kitten chasing a ball of wool, once caught, the interest was lost to the next adventure.

With this knowledge, I found it impossible to believe that he could ever adhere to the promise he'd made to me that day by the river. Oh, he'd have sincerely tried, but eventually some passing beauty would be too much for him to resist and he'd be a lost cause once more. No, I was sure that was one offer I would decline to take up. Maybe when older and Andrew had finally fed his hunger for unending quantities of female followers, he'd make a faithful companion for the right girl but she'd not be the sort that he normally dated. The chosen one would probably be plain, not a raving beauty but pretty and shy. After all, he could never pick a person that could outshine him or that he'd constantly need to watch, fending off a procession of rivals.

The human species is no different to the rest of the animal world, female blandness appeals more to the vanity of a male when hunting for a life long mate. The woman possessed of exceptional looks is often only chosen as a show piece and to boost male ego in front of his friends, not for love or affection.

Sabrina made her brother's apologies to our hosts who immediately dismissed it as forfeits of building a successful business. The rest of the evening was uneventful. We dined on the fresh trout that Max and James had caught earlier during the day, at least something had worked according to plan. Dinner had been delayed till late waiting for Jonathan and Andrew so by the time we'd finished eating, I was more than ready for bed. Once I felt that a suitable length of time had elapsed, I excused myself and returned to our room. Thoughtfully, a fire had been lit, the heat of which struck as soon as the door opened.

I changed and snuggled up in one of the armchairs in front of the fire. I hadn't been there long before Sabrina came through the door. She was as pleased to see the flames that flickered in the grate and soon joined me to take advantage of its warmth. Watching the fire was relaxing and I found myself unable to stem the tide of yawns that overtook me. We turned out the lights and climbed into bed, a cosy glow hung over the room which must have lasted until well after we were asleep.

As promised, both Andrew and Jonathan were at the castle by ten o'clock. Jonathan had brought with him a very large bunch of flowers and Swiss chocolates for Helen and cigars for Max. They were partly as an apology for ruining their plans and a thank you to reward the kindness extended in accommodating us. We had a final cup of coffee and as we left, the Trents were most insistent that we visit again whenever any of us wanted. I wonder if they'd mind if Sabrina and I made their castle our venue for the next summer break but maybe six weeks would be overstaying our welcome.

CHAPTER 6

On the way home we stopped a couple of times, on the last to have a meal, arriving back at the house by early evening. After dumping our bags in the bedroom each of us collapsed into the nearest comfy chair only mustering up enough energy to drag ourselves to bed later that night.

The trip had worn us out, the unanimous decision was to rest for a couple of days. Jonathan had to go to his office in Mayfair just to catch up on any correspondence but would only be gone a couple of hours and Andrew would have to spend some time drawing plans for the renovation work for his second new client. A major task as it wasn't just a room this time but the entire house. Like the castle, everything had to be in contrast inside and out. Meanwhile Sabrina and I would do nothing more than was necessary, as it was nearly the weekend, we would invite our local friends to join us on Saturday for a swim and barbecue.

The following day while Jonathan and Andrew worked, Sabrina made the necessary calls to invite everyone, but her phone call to David brought disappointment. He said he was leaving later that day for Birmingham; due to large numbers of the force being on holiday all areas had been asked to supply extra men and women to cover a large and potentially violent football game that Saturday, he would not return until Monday and therefore would have to miss the gathering. Sabrina was a little worried and distressed but I managed to cheer her up assuring her he was very capable of defending himself and he would only be gone for a short time. Anyway it would be something she would have to get used to and accept if their relationship was to continue.

Saturday was hot, very hot. I was glad I'd brought with me some long cotton dresses which I wore with the intention of giving my body some protection, I was a little jealous of the others as the strong sun seemed not to have any effect on them. Angela wore one of the tightest bikinis I had ever seen, she really had developed a full but perfectly proportioned figure. Sabrina and I just glanced at each other as she cast off her tiny wrap like a model on the catwalk trying to create the maximum impression. It worked, Andrew's eyes nearly popped out and his face was sporting a grin from ear to ear. He obviously liked what he saw but so did the other lads and he proceeded to spend most of the day fending off their advances like a knight in shining armour. She loved it. I thought if he was ready to be caught, that this was the baited hook.

Actually Sabrina and I found it amusing and it kept us entertained for most of the afternoon. The only male unaffected by the whole scenario was Jonathan who, when not taking a dip, had his head buried in a book. With his total disinterest of the young females floating around, I might have considered him gay but due to our recent encounter I rejected this thought, maybe he was just very choosy and preferred older women.

We didn't notice Andrew and Angela disappear, it was only when food was nearly cooked that they were missed. I had to fetch the salad from the kitchen so gave them a call.

They were obviously engrossed in what they were doing not to have heard me enter, the house was quiet and my footsteps silent due to the absence of shoes. I called but received no answer.

Andrew's bedroom door was open and I could hear voices. That's where they are, I thought. I pushed the door slightly and was faced with Andrew's nude back, it was now obvious that the noises I had heard were those of pleasure not chatter. At the head of his bed hung an ornamental mirror in which I could see his face, the light from the window behind me must have caught his eye and for a split second our eyes were locked together through the glass. He was unmoved at being spied upon and continued his rhythmic advances to the pretty creature he had enticed and lured into his clutches. I pulled the door over and retrieved the salad before joining our friends once more. Shortly they both reappeared, he with that look of satisfaction at his achievement and she giving a somewhat triumphant smile of entrapment. How wrong she might be.

Most of our guests sat out in the sunny areas whilst I retreated to a choice spot back towards the house in the shade to rest and eat. Andrew instantly joined me, I briefly glanced up and gestured silently for him to sit beside me. Obviously he was unsure of my reactions to what I had witnessed in his bedroom. I would like to have said I was surprised, but I wasn't. It was his first and maybe only opportunity to speak to me without the others being around. Angela came across and I could see the frustration on his face as he made an excuse of being hot and told her to go back and join the others. I caught her whispers to him suggesting they get hotter together again later as she wiggled away.

"I hope what you saw didn't offend you," he said. "I thought everyone was outside in the pool."

"No, no offence taken, what you do in your own room is your business and I suppose I should have knocked before entering," I said playing down the situation.

"Angela had obviously come here with the intentions of tempting me, making me jealous of the other lads. You only have to look at that bikini she's barely wearing."

"You don't have to justify to me what you do, it's none of my business who you want to have sex with," I said in a raised voice.

"Shush, they'll hear... Anyway she got what she deserved," he said in a sarcastic manner.

"Just because she dresses in a skimpy outfit doesn't automatically mean she wants you to screw her."

"No but it wasn't only that, the whole time we were in the pool she clung to me like a limpet, rubbing her body against me and her hands groping down the front of my trunks enticing a reaction," he said. "She started the game I only finished it!"

"Fair enough, then she did get what she wanted but as I said before, it's nothing to do with me," I replied.

"You won't say anything about it to the others will you?" he asked.

"My lips are sealed, OK?" I said.

"Thanks," he said. "Remember, if you ever change your mind, you know about us, I'll drop Angela or any girl for you, I mean it."

I glanced up with a smile on my face. "I'll remember," I said. I couldn't believe his cheek in expecting me to take him seriously whilst during the time it took me to make up my mind, he felt it reasonable to bed any lady that he fancied and virtually in my presence.

I couldn't believe what was happening. I was wanting a man that had taken very little notice of me since our first brief encounter, only to have a man I didn't want literally throwing himself at me. Life can be very complicated, not always taking the direction you'd wished.

After consuming vast quantities of food and several bottles of wine the lads suggested going bowling which Sabrina and Andrew eagerly agreed to. I, however, just wanted to stay put. The weather was turning humid and I didn't fancy any activity to raise my temperature further, anyway it was too warm to be stuck inside so I declined the offer. Jonathan just peered over the book he'd had his head stuck in most of the day and said a short, curt, 'no thank you'. They all grabbed what clothes they'd brought with them and within minutes they had left, it was so peaceful.

"I've just got to make a phone call to check some papers with James, he should be home now," said Jonathan out of the blue before disappearing into the house.

Great! I'm stuck with the washing up, I thought. I struggled with a stack of plates into the kitchen and proceeded to see if I could break the time recorded of getting dishpan hands but the ordeal was over fairly quickly and I once again spread myself on one of the patio loungers to read some magazines.

It was getting quite dusky before Jonathan reappeared dressed in some shorts and a T-shirt and carrying two glasses of brandy. His eyes were soft when he looked at me and there was a difference in his mood, that disinterested stare had gone. Although I had drunk only a couple of glasses of wine with dinner the heat was making me light headed but another drink wouldn't hurt. We just sat and talked for ages about all different subjects, I felt so at ease with him I would have been quite happy to sit on that patio forever more.

"It's so warm tonight and this brandy is making me warmer," I said giggling as it was starting to take affect.

"Yes, very warm," he replied. "Maybe you would like to swim, the water should be warm after the heat of the day and it would cool your body".

"Hm... that would be nice," I said trying to stand up but losing my footing and slipping back onto the lounger giggling.

Jonathan came towards me. "Let me help you," he said stretching out his strong hands for support.

As I rose he pulled me close to him. "God you're so beautiful Carol," he whispered shocking me into silence. He gazed into my eyes and kissed me pulling me even closer so I could not escape and as with our previous encounter, I didn't want to. His embraces were full of passion, teasing every nerve ending his lips touched. Finally he released his grasp allowing me to pull away.

"Shall we swim?" he said.

"Yes, I'll change," I replied in a breathless voice.

"Oh," he said gently as he slipped off his clothes standing naked in front of me. "There's nobody around to see and the others won't be home for ages, who needs clothes, you're not shy are you? Come...come." His voice was intoxicating my mind far more than the alcohol as his hands again reached out, this time unfastening my dress, letting it drop to the floor. I was a little hesitant when he turned his attention to my panties but there were soft words of reassurance. "It's OK, I won't touch or do anything you don't want me to. Relax."

He took my hand and lead me to the steps of the pool, the whole area had subdued lighting, enough though for me to have a full view of his manly stature as he stood aloft. He really did have a superb body. Jonathan lay back in the water as I entered the pool. I felt his eyes were drinking in every line of my body. He was right, it was like stepping into a warm bath, not shockingly chilled as earlier in the day. It was so refreshing and we both floated letting the water take us where it willed.

"Do you feel better now?" he asked.

"Yes much," I murmured.

Once again he pulled me to him, our lips touching, his hands gently caressing my body arousing my passions and I liked his touch.

He was a clever lover raising me to a height of pleasure that made me hunger for more of his attention.

We left the pool and Jonathan softly rubbed my body dry with a towel before leading me to the grassland by the trees.

He spread the towel on the ground and urged me down, he sank to his knees in front of me, his kisses more intense as his fingers ran across my breasts and down my hips finally finding their goal between my thighs. My dampness conveyed my state of excitement as he tenderly stroked my most inner sanctum while his lips gently nibbled at my hardened nipples. I was at the point of no return and completely under his control, never had I been in such a situation.

He laid me on my back and I could now see he was fully aroused, I reached up and touched him, his eyes closed as my hands provided him pleasure. Letting out moans of desire, he eventually returned from solitary indulgence and smiled as he spread my knees apart giving him easy access to my inner body. I raised my knees slightly as he entered and placed his hands above my shoulders to support himself. I cannot describe the intense joy I felt at that moment as we moved in unison to our ultimate goal. I knew the time was close as Jonathan increased the speed of his rhythm and as I reached my own summit of intensity, I felt him thrust one final time before emitting a long, lingering groan.

After catching his breath Jonathan finally pulled away. He lay down beside me, both of us incapable of speech relishing the ebbing pangs of our union.

I'm sure we would have lay there till morning but our tranquillity was disturbed by a police car travelling up the lane at high speed with lights flashing and siren blasting.

We retreated to the sanctuary of the house, a wise decision as we felt the first large spots of rain, the threatening storm had arrived at last. The rain was heavy and it was not long before the air blew cooler and we could smell the earth giving off its scent of thanks.

I put on a long T-shirt and Jonathan pulled on some shorts, just enough for decency as we weren't sure what time the others would be back although we knew it would be after midnight as the bowling club didn't shut till then. Jonathan sat on one of the stools virtually in the same spot as when we first met. I moved about the kitchen making us some coffee, the whole time his eyes following my body, it was like standing with your back to the sun, you couldn't see it but its warmth heralded its presence.

I sat down opposite, lost as to what to say and trying to avoid eye contact. I suppose I was shy or possibly a little embarrassed but I shouldn't be, I had just shared the most ultimate contact a woman can ever have with a man. Eventually I plucked up courage to glance across at him, he just smiled and stretched out his hands towards mine gripping them tight, all the time his eyes meeting mine.

We had finished our coffee before he finally spoke.

"I want you to know that I really am very fond of you, Carol."

At that moment my immediate thoughts were, oh no, here comes the brush off, the words uttered by so many after the final ebbs of passion have receded and minds have returned to the cold reality of life.

"I think I'm falling in love with you," he said in a very calm and subdued voice. "When I'm alone with you I feel so relaxed and content, when I have to be away from the house on business I find myself wanting to rush back as soon as I can to be near you. I have never felt that kind of urge for a woman before."

"I'm sure you say that to all the girls," I said light heartedly, not knowing how to react.

"Don't be silly Carol, that's not the sort of comment I would expect from you," his voice scolded me and he was right. "You should know by now that I don't say things I don't mean, you are a beautiful, intelligent woman whom any man would be proud to have share his life."

This really was getting serious, at last I was hopefully on the brink of capturing the heart of the only man I had ever wanted or desired. It looked as if my wish was about to come true and it was my turn to be truthful.

"The first time I saw you I wanted you, you stirred feelings in me that I had never felt before with a man," I said. "It wasn't just sex for personal pleasure it was for making love which I believe is totally different, do you understand what I'm trying to say?"

"Yes...I've been with other women but have never felt the bliss I did tonight. Come here," he said pulling me round towards him. "Kiss me."

Our lips met with the same excited passion and his grip just as strong. I found I could not resist letting my hands run up and down his back stroking the contours of his strong hips, my lips seeking and caressing every inch of exposed chest. It was only the noise made by the others returning that broke our embrace, we managed to adjust our clothing before a key turned in the door and in bounced Sabrina and Andrew.

They both stopped in their tracks and stood looking in our direction.

"Eh...Sorry did we interrupt something?" asked Andrew giving me a cheeky but somewhat quizzical grin.

"No, actually I had something in my eye and Jonathan

was taking a look," I said the first thing that came into my head.

"Did he find anything?" asked Sabrina.

"No nothing, I must be tired," I answered.

"Hmm... maybe you should go to bed then and get some sleep," said Andrew. "What do you think Jonathan?"

"That is normally what one does when one is tired but Carol's a big girl now and I'm sure she can decide for herself," he said dismissing Andrew's obvious play of words.

"Yes I can see she's a big girl," he said giggling, he was obviously making reference to my lack of attire.

"That's enough now," said Sabrina who had brought a large bottle of lemonade from the fridge and poured us all a glass full. "Stop teasing and leave them alone, anyway you can talk after tonight's little fiasco."

Something had happened and I was eager to hear.

"Oh yes, what's all this then?" I asked eagerly awaiting a response.

"Well," said Sabrina, "we had all been enjoying the game up until the last few bowls. Oh, I neglected to say that we had teamed up in pairs. I was with Steve and Andrew was with Angela. Anyway, there were only two points between us and Andrew kept on bullying Angela to make sure her last throw scored as many points as possible."

"I didn't bully her, I just tried to emphasise the importance of her throw!" said Andrew.

"As I said, he bullied her, she was so intent on pleasing him by knocking down all the pins that she put so much thrust behind the ball and although she let go, she could not stop herself from falling forward. Now if you remember there was only a straining bikini top trying to contain her ample chest and with all that stretching and bouncing the back strap broke. There she was flat on her face with bust almost fully exposed," giggled Sabrina.

I must admit I was finding it most amusing and could not help but join in the laughter.

"But that was not the worst," said Sabrina. "Andrew being the perfect gentleman..."

"It wasn't my fault, I only tried to help," said Andrew butting in.

"Shut up a minute," she said. "Andrew helped her up, dusted her off and proceeded to use his hands to cover her embarrassment, so there they were, Angela blushing and Andrew with a bosom filling each hand. Well I had to take pity on the poor girl, I grabbed one of the lad's shirts and helped her slip it on, needless to say I literally had to prise Andrew's hands away to allow her to button up the top."

"I was trying to stop people staring," he said.

"Listen, everybody had had a damn good look well before your hands arrived on the scene," stated Sabrina, "In fact the lads talked about nothing else. We of course left at this point to save her feelings"

"Is she alright now?" asked Jonathan.

"Yes, Andrew used his utmost charm to calm her down and help her indoors."

"She won't live that one down in a hurry, will she?" I replied. "Well I'm going to bed, see you in the morning."

"Good night, Carol and sweet dreams," said Jonathan in his low, sultry voice.

"Yes, good night," replied the other two giving each an inquisitive look.

As I lay back on the bed I was unable stem the contented smile on my face, his emotional confession of love had left me happy and fulfilled. I closed my eyes and tried to recreate every second of the evening over and over again in my mind, not wanting them to fade and when I slept I wanted to fill my dreams only with him.

CHAPTER 7

I awoke the following morning in a very jubilant frame of mind, singing to myself whilst lying in the bath. It's amazing the effect love can have on the human brain, when administered correctly it acts like a drug, stimulating and exciting. I chose my outfit carefully, now I had his interest I didn't want to lose it.

Andrew and Sabrina were lazing in the front room reading the papers and watching TV, Jonathan was already out on the patio with his head stuck in that same book just as the previous day, so I decided to join him. I said good morning and sat down waiting for a response. Eventually he did mutter.

"Morning," he said raising his eyes briefly from the pages.

"Would you like some coffee?" I asked cheerily.

"No thanks I haven't long finished a cup," he replied with a look that told me I was obviously disturbing him. Great!

It was becoming quite clear that Jonathan, although a very loving person, was the one who would decide when and how he would express affection to those around him and this was not one of those times.

"Is everything alright?" I asked

"Yes, why do you ask?" he replied.

"You're very quiet, that's all."

"That's because I'm trying to read." He sounded annoyed at my intrusion into the private sanctum into which he had withdrawn.

I went back in the house grabbed a cup of coffee and skulked off to the solitude of my room feeling down and rejected. What game was he playing? Definitely not one that I'd ever had to participate in before which probably explained why I didn't understand the rules. Or maybe it was a test, yes, a test of my loyalty and strength. Isn't it strange, you can feel love for a person and want to be with them but at the same time have no notion, or ever expect to, as to how their mind thinks, (makes that phrase 'my wife doesn't understand me' quite feasible.) I sat trying to figure it all out when there was a knock on the door and Sabrina made her entrance, obviously she'd glimpsed my long face when I returned from talking to Jonathan

"Is everything OK, you know between you and Jonathan?" she asked.

"Yes, as well as can be expected I suppose," I said. "I'm finding it very hard to understand him, one minute he is so loving and thoughtful, the next he's cold not wanting you around."

"I know but he's always been that way, he finds it very hard to drop that invisible guard. Even as a child, if he grazed his knees while playing he would put up a strong front never running to mum for comfort."

"But last night he said he thought he loved me yet this morning nothing," I said with a note of dejection.

"We made love, you know, but I'm sure you've already worked that one out."

"Well, I thought as much, Jonathan told me that without even speaking," said Sabrina.

"How do you mean?" I asked

"Last night while we all chatted he listened to the conversation but his eyes very rarely deviated from you," she replied. "Don't worry, if he said he loved you he meant it and it wouldn't surprise me if it's the first time he's ever said it, so cheer up because I think you're just perfect for him."

Sabrina was a very frank person who would never knowingly lie to me, our chat made me feel better and I agreed to slow down and let our relationship steer its own course. I was hungry, tea and toast were called for so I made some and sat down with Andrew and Sabrina to watch one of those mundane breakfast programmes, the sort that bus in an audience for discussions on the rights and wrongs of some obnoxious subject, only interrupted by adverts for nappies, washing powders and women's things.

I wondered if there was some underlying message that these TV companies were trying to get across because I couldn't see any purpose for the repetitiveness of such programmes; depressing, flogging the same old subjects time and time again about divorce, redundancy, unemployment or some other well chosen suicide inducing topic. Some of the people watching programmes at this time of day were possible casualties of one or possibly all so it's just what they needed, to be reminded every morning, of failure in one form or another.

I wasn't really taking much notice, actually I was

trying to complete a five minute crossword which operated under the guise of the 'quickie' version but I had been working on it for more than half an hour when the programme broke for the news. The newsreader's first headline made me look up and pay attention.

A girl had been found murdered in the north of the country, not an unusual occurrence these days but when reference was made to police concerns as to the strange circumstances in which the victim was found and their suspicions that it may be linked to an earlier killing, this unexpected revelation prompted my curiosity. Could that case be Jane Downing?

I just couldn't wait, I had to telephone Jennifer. When I finally got through to her, she sounded unsurprised to hear my voice, infact she'd expected my call. Apparently there was a slight chance that this murder was the work of the same person. An officer from Scotland Yard had been assigned to investigate and that person was Jennifer.

She was leaving that night by train to reach the borders the next day and I couldn't believe my luck when she suggested I tag along to keep her company, but I was under strict instructions not to interfere in anyway. I wasn't suppose to be there at all but I would agree virtually to any demands just to be allowed to go. Under normal circumstances it wouldn't have been possible. However, that very morning her trusty aid, sergeant Pat Mallon had kindly taken upon herself while in the course of her duties to trip and topple down a flight of stairs finally landing at the bottom breaking a leg in the event. Jennifer was very picky in her choice of companion, no one else currently available matched up to her sergeant Mallon's standards therefore she'd decided to go it alone, much to the disappointment of the up and coming fledglings.

I had to meet her at 10.00 o'clock that evening, suitcase in hand, and if for any reason I was late she'd leave without me. With my fevered activity and gibberish chatter Sabrina only needed one guess to know something was afoot.

"So, what did you find out?" she asked.

"Not much yet but Jennifer has been assigned to the case and seeing as there's a spare place she's offered to take me with her tonight. I must pack," I replied, rushing around as if I hadn't a second to spare.

"Slow down a minute," said Sabrina as I rummaged through the bottom of the wardrobe in search of my one and only tatty suitcase, "And just how was this spare seat made available?"

"Well normally Jennifer would have be accompanied by Pat, you know, sergeant Mallon."

"Yes, I know that," replied Sabrina in an agitated voice.

"Well apparently she's had a nasty accident this morning, broke a leg in two places and has plaster fitted from foot to hip," I said. "Jennifer doesn't warrant anybody capable of taking Pat's place and has decided to work alone, fantastic stroke of luck, don't you think?" I continued. "Well, for me anyway."

I wasn't much good to them for the rest of the day, even when Jonathan finally decided to be sociable I basically ignored him. Well, two can play at that little exercise, anyway I'd almost forgotten that niggling problem, I could sort it out when I returned. Although they never said it, I'm sure they were all grateful when they finally deposited me at the station that evening. Their last view was of me anxiously pacing up and down the platform constantly referring to my watch for the time as I impatiently waited for Jennifer to appear. She was late, in the distance I could see her dashing towards me at a very fast past with two young chaps trotting a few steps behind. As she came closer, her hand gestured to me to get on the train which I obediently did.

I stood in the passage way and waited. I could hear her dishing out various instructions as to what was expected of them while she was away. Some notes and a few questions later, Jennifer boarded.

She had cut it fine and seconds later I heard the whistle blow and felt a judder as the train lurched into motion. We were taking the sleeper service, there were two beds in each cabin and as the compartment had been reserved for two she, in a moment of misguided pity, decided to let me make use of it. There wasn't much time to chat before dinner, however she did make one thing clear, if anybody asked who I was, I should say I was part of the forensic team, that would be a valid enough reason for being around.

Jennifer looked tired so after dining I suggested bed, I had purchased some magazines at the station so I was contented to relax and read. Of course, I ended up in the upper bunk, but once in it felt safe enough. I scanned the pages of my chosen publication while Jennifer checked through some of her paperwork. Naturally, I chatted away to deafened ears but didn't mind, she must have been tired because when I glanced down a little later Jennifer was asleep and the papers on the floor. I must admit the gentle rocking as the train journeyed to its destination was inducing drowsiness in me so I turned off the light and snuggled down.

The early night did us both good. We'd just finished breakfast as the huge engine gently pulled us into the station.

A uniformed officer was patiently waiting with a car ready to collect and transport us to the scene of crime, no time wasted, their office had been set up in the grounds of the nursing home where the latest victim had been discovered. As our car came to a halt we were approached by the officer in charge who courteously opened the door and introduced himself as sergeant Mallory. He gave me a wary glance but Jennifer just motioned her hand as a sanction for my presence, she was of higher rank than he so her authorisation was accepted without question. I walked a few steps behind but was able to clearly hear some of their conversation. From the snippets I did catch, I made out he was explaining the basic facts so far, so what did reach my ears was informative.

The second victim, a young Scottish lass named Sarah McDonald, suffered her fate in her room at the nurses home where she lodged. She too had been strangled. As before, Sarah was neatly laid out, clutching a red rose, her message read, *TOUCHED BUT ONCE...* However, the police felt after close examination that the 'loving touch' bestowed on the first victim was lacking on the second. Her night-dress was of plain linen, not fancy and expensive as the first, and although her hair was brushed it lacked presentation. Again sex had taken place just before death but the police concluded that who ever had committed these crimes would appear not to have felt the great love for this lady as he had the first, only respect or time dictated such limited attention

Jennifer was shown to the room where the murder took place, the area was cordoned off with that familiar blue and white tape and uniformed men barred any uninvited intrusion. I tried to comply with Jennifer's wishes and went no further than the doorway, inside was their domain. The body had obviously been removed and the forensic team and finger print people had already searched the room for any possible clue, again filling their little plastic bags with such things as strands of hair, fabric samples and of course, they had completed the customary dusting of every surface just in case there were the killer's prints. As Jennifer and Mallory talked, I took an inventory of the room.

Sarah must have been a very plain living person, there was little finery on show. The contents of the dressing table amounted to a cheap bottle of toilet water, a box of hankies and what appeared to be an old silver backed hair brush, the sort of heirloom that is passed down from mother to daughter. The wardrobe door was open exposing its contents to all, a few cotton type dresses, a couple of skirts and blouses hung limply on hangers. There were no daring mini skirts or snazzy tops. The bed clothes, although touched by many hands, were still fairly neat and some kind of cuddly toys lay at the end, a dog and rabbit, I think. The only other items visible were a couple of pairs of flat shoes and a cross hanging above the bed. He obviously wasn't watching over her that night. Everything in the room summed up a picture of a quiet, reserved, even sheltered girl with an inbred religious trait, not the sort you would expect or who would deserve to be found in this situation.

When their inspection was over we left. Jennifer was eager to view photographs and any information that was already available, this necessitated a visit to the mobile office situated in the car park.

As we made our way to this office, Mallory explained that the police had carried out some preliminary interviews with the other girls at the home which had furnished them with snippets of information. One thing was clear, although none would openly admit to it, boyfriends were often smuggled in. For Sarah, this would have been a simple task, her room was at the back of the house on the ground floor, the entrance was masked by shrubs which obscured the visibility of anyone coming or going, that and very dim lighting would only aid someone wishing to go unnoticed.

The two girls whose rooms were either side had tried to befriend Sarah, chatting to her whenever the opportunity presented itself. Sometimes she acted pleased to talk but often they got no more than a half hearted reply as she retreated to the loneliness of her room. From the little knowledge they'd gained they thought her a shy, homely type person, always dressed in clean but simple clothes and never seen to wear make-up. Sarah had not been one for discussing her personal life like many of the others, but about a week ago and much to their astonishment, she suddenly blurted out that she had met a man and been invited out for dinner. She seemed unable to contain her excitement of the fact.

The impression gained was that whoever he was, he hadn't been around for very long, but long enough, unfortunately, for poor Sarah. The girls had decided that he must be an extremely unique person to have gained her confidence so quickly, one of them had hinted that he may be a religious chap, a vicar possibly. One of the girls, Sandy Keaton, had loaned Sarah a dress for the occasion, nothing too risqué, a small sleeveless black dress that fitted to the waist with a flared skirt. After a few finishing touches with a little make-up, Sandy had to admit that Sarah looked good. Just as she was fastening a little gold chain around her neck, a car horn sounded. Sarah grabbed her things and shot out the door, too quickly for Sandy to catch sight of her date. All she could say was that he drove a large car, dark in colour but as mentioned before the lighting was so bad it was hard to make out.

Sandy had fallen asleep before Sarah had returned that night but when she'd been disturbed, just after midnight, she could hear music and laughter from Sarah's room. With the thought that she was enjoying herself, Sandy had turned over and gone back to sleep, not waking again until her alarm clock buzzed.

Sandy knew that Sarah was on the same shift as her the following morning so was surprised not to find her milling around the kitchen as normal. She'd made a joke with a couple of the others as to what might have happened to cause her to oversleep but knew better. She made some coffee and set off towards Sarah's room with the intention of shaking her lazy bones. It was only after bashing on the door for several minutes and receiving no reply that she became concerned and sought help.

Eventually she found the administrator who took care of the home and dragged her along to open Sarah's door with her pass key.

At first Sandy thought that Sarah was asleep, only when she touched her did she realise otherwise, the coldness of the body instantly told her that this person was un-wakeable.

The shocked administrator mumbled as she left to telephone for a doctor and subsequently the police. Sandy waited, for some strange reason she felt Sarah might want her to. She sat at the foot of the bed, compassion and pity took grip as a tear trickled down her face, what a god awful waste of a life. The dress she'd borrowed had been put on a hanger and hung against the open wardrobe door so as not to crease, most would have discarded it in a heap until morning but not Sarah. The dress didn't hold the same appeal anymore, once the police had finished with it she'd dispose of the garment to some charity shop.

A doctor and the police had been called and with their arrival bureaucracy took over. She found herself being ushered away but as she left she loudly voiced her departure to Sarah's dead soul. This provoked some odd looks from surrounding persons but Sandy didn't give a care to their opinions of her.

Unknown faces were to-ing and fro-ing for most of the day, some in uniform some not.

Sandy, under doctor's orders, had been dismissed from her duties for the time being so she sat in the kitchen overdosing on caffeine between bouts of police questioning. When they'd eventually finished with her services, she took pity on herself and spent the evening in the local pub with a couple of friends.

Mallory had managed to cram in a lot before we reached the little mobile office, a bare room with a solitary desk in one corner which was covered in a disarray of paperwork. There were a couple of chairs that could quite easily have come off the local rubbish dump and, of course, the customary tea pot and kettle, a solid reminder of that old British custom; whenever there's a crisis somebody makes the tea.

He shuffled and rearranged each pile before handing them to Jennifer, her eyes furtively scoured the pages absorbing every detail but there was nothing further to be learned other than what she already knew.

The photos were of particular interest, Jennifer spread them across the table. I think this was done for my benefit, I could see them but they'd not been handed to me, maybe it made her feel better about the situation.

Most were of Sarah from different angles, the others were of the room itself. Her face was definitely not the sort that would stand out in a crowd, straight dark hair framed a somewhat chubby, sallow looking face. Any make up she'd worn that night had been cleaned away before her death, even the marks around her neck enhanced the black and white image.

I whispered to Jennifer about the little chain Sarah had supposedly worn that night. What had happened to it? Mallory's hearing must have been good, he explained that even though a thorough search had been made, the necklace hadn't been found.

With the inspection done the next step was to view the body.

Sarah had been taken to the nearest hospital mortuary, there her body would be examined in great detail, all discolouration noted, each nail content removed and every crevice checked. I followed the others down the corridor unsure how I felt about seeing a dead body. Jennifer took me to one side suggesting I wait outside, but I needed to face the cold harsh reality of death, after all, I'd only ever experienced the pleasure of new life. The coldness of the air gave signal that we'd arrived at our destination. A man wearing a white coat met us and showed us into a large room where the walls were white and every working surface was of stainless steel. Jennifer whispered that if I wanted to leave now would be a good time as Sarah's body was being pushed through the door.

The sheet covering her was pulled down exposing a small white frame, the attendant was busy relaying various medical points and conditions of the body which to my untrained mind meant very little. However I could clearly see the bruising around her throat. It was a slender neck marked from hairline to shoulder, a sign that the killer must have fairly broad hands. At first sight her bland appearance mirrored that of the photos but the longer I looked, the more her natural beauty stood out. Her body and skin although sullied by the effects of her departure were well cared for, she must have been to the hair dresser recently as her hair sported that just cut look. She was no stunning beauty but she had full lips, a slim nose and long curling eyelashes. With a little attention and the right make-up she would have held her own in most company. The only thing missing was that aura of the living and my mind no longer recognised this as a human being, all it saw was a lump of meat laid out for inspection as though in the butcher's window.

This was the true face of death and I praised the people who found the courage and summoned up the heartlessness to deal with it every day. I must have turned a little pale because Mallory who'd stood opposite asked me if I felt OK. I mumbled my assurances blaming the coldness of the room, mind you, it was like standing in one of those walk-in cold rooms, the type designed to house dead carcasses, well described I thought. I moved around hoping to stimulate circulation to my feet while using the short span of time to mentally proportion this tragedy.

As we walked back down the maze of corridors I was invisibly patting myself on the back, no tears, hysterics or rushing for the nearest sink to deposit the contents of my stomach but would I have coped so well if it was a loved one there on that cold slab?

It was now after midday and Mallory suggested that we find somewhere for lunch and Jennifer agreed. They wanted food? Oh well, the dead shouldn't hinder the living. He took us to a little pub which served excellent home made food, as I perused the menu I noticed home made steak pie which I love but under the circumstances felt unable to order, I opted for fish. I did note that both Mallory and Jennifer didn't suffer with the same affliction as both had a large, rare steak. The conversation over lunch was light and informative with Mallory doing most of the talking. The way he enthused about the area in which he lived, pointing out its finer qualities as opposed to southern regions, meant he was obviously proud of its heritage. Jennifer and I sat obediently listening, allowing him a brief moment of glorification.

There was one more visit to make before we left to get the return train that evening and that was to the police station assigned to handling this murder. Luckily it was situated on the edge of a small town and at this point I was happy to leave them to their business while I strolled and did some window shopping, only checking before parting company what time to be back.

The town was unspoilt by the invasion of the supermarket type outlet, the shops were mostly small specialising in their different wares and it made for a refreshing change not to see the same item repeatedly in each window. I found myself compelled to purchase some of the local goods such as sweets, biscuits and cakes. There was only one thing left to buy and I was standing in front of the shop that sold it; a bottle of malt whisky for Jonathan, I wanted to surprise him. Unable to carry anymore I made my way back and sat down on a bench opposite the station. It was too nice to go inside and I'd bought a newspaper to read.

I kept looking at my watch, the business was taking longer than anticipated but I wasn't concerned. Eventually Jennifer appeared at the doorway looking for me, I gave her a wave and crossed the road to join her. Seconds later a car pulled up, Mallory was driving, he was providing our lift to the train.

I had to admit I was much more sedate and withdrawn on the journey home not mentioning the case at all much to my companion's relief. I believed that Jennifer had taken me with a purpose and that was to make me understand that solving crime wasn't an excitement but a necessity, to realise and experience first hand death, the result of that irreversible action, murder. Her plan had worked to an extent but it had not dampened my intense interest or desire to understand.

It was early morning when the taxi dropped me back

at the house, Jennifer had gone on to her office in London while I continued my journey home. All three of my hosts were sitting at the table which was strewn with the remains of breakfast, each totally wrapped up in their own little world. Jonathan reading the newspaper, Sabrina buried in one of her girlie magazines and Andrew scouring the pages of his little black book, obviously he was feeling the need for further female company. Of course the observance of manners ensured each ceased their activity and displayed pleasure at my return. While I showed them the wares I had purchased Andrew made me some coffee. Jonathan was delighted with the whisky I'd chosen, expressing that it was one of his favourites which in turn pleased me.

A loud knock on the front door put an end to our chattering and Andrew rose to answer it.

"Eh...it's for you Carol," said Andrew, "A rather large chap of eastern origin."

Oh no, not the prince! I thought, I'm not really in the mood for entertaining.

It wasn't the prince, it was a diplomat from the Saudi Embassy, Prince Ahmed had requested he contact me and make the necessary flight arrangements for my visit. The child was due within the week and he was insistent I be there. I felt I had no choice but to agree, however, as I was a female, the prince had made provision for another person to accompany me as chaperon. As I turned round Sabrina had a grin from ear to ear, dashing my immediate reaction to invite Jonathan, which one?

The decision was made for me, Andrew made some comment about being unable to take all the attention the women would give once they caught sight of him and

Jonathan just said he couldn't handle such a long flight or donate the time, so Sabrina it was to be. The dusky envoy would telephone when he had made the necessary travel plans and would send a car to collect and take us to the airport.

No sooner had he gone than Sabrina was dashing about in frenzied excitement, rushing to her bedroom to pack, and as normal taking everything out of the wardrobe a dozen times before deciding. It would take her hours. I sat back down to finish my coffee still slightly stunned at the whole affair. I'd just returned from one unique experience only to be faced with the onset of another, it truly was from one extreme to another, this week death next week life.

Jonathan really could talk with those eyes of his, an unspoken message had passed to Andrew as momentarily he mumbled some feeble excuse to leave. My face must have displayed my feelings of disappointment.

"I know," he said quietly, "you'd have preferred to take me."

"What makes you think that?" acting at first as though it didn't matter, but then I repented. "Yes I would, we could have spent a couple of days seeing the sights and being alone," I replied.

"I think it's better that Sabrina go with you, she'll enjoy it tremendously and anyway they frown on men and woman who are not married sharing isolated time together, it wouldn't embarrass you but I'm sure it would displease the prince, you don't want to offend their strong Muslim beliefs." For a brief second it was as if listening to my mother who used to tell me not to do what I wanted but what was right.

"I'll miss you," I said grasping his hand.

"I rather hoped you would," he said leaning across to kiss my forehead "Now go and rescue my little sister from the mountains of clothes she must already be sitting under."

Sabrina had her head buried amongst the hanging garments in her wardrobe when I entered her room. She'd already managed to devastate the contents of every drawer in her efforts to pick the right underwear but after much deliberation the catches were snapped shut on a bulging suitcase. She did offer to help me but I assured her I could cope quite adequately by myself.

It didn't take long for the flight arrangements and I duly received a telephone call from my dusky visitor that evening. We were booked to leave the following day at eight in the morning, a car would collect us at 5.30am. I suddenly realised that my passport was still at my parents house so Sabrina and I whisked away in her car to collect it.

Mum was surprised to see me. After introducing her to Sabrina I tried to cram in as much news as possible before our hasty departure, nearly forgetting the one reason for my visit.

Mum and dad were overwhelmed when I explained the need for my passport causing them some excitement in their mundane lives and I knew before we'd reach the end of the road that the phone line would be red hot, calling everybody they could think of to boast that their daughter wasn't just any old midwife but one chosen to deliver the children of royalty. The little cul-de-sac they lived in would never be the same again.

We had supper and both retired for an early night, but excitement had taken over and I found it difficult to sleep only managing to doze. I was aroused by a knock on the door, it was Jonathan, he was going to bed and noticed my light still on.

"I can't sleep, the butterflies in my stomach won't let me," I said laughingly.

"That's alright, just because we get older doesn't mean we shouldn't still have the pleasure of excitement," he answered. "You deliver that baby safely and have a wonderful time in the process, I want to hear all about it when you return. I'll miss you every minute you're gone," he whispered as his lips briefly touched mine before he departed. My immediate impulse was to invite him to stay but with the prospects of a long tiring journey that would have been stupid, enjoyable but nevertheless still stupid.

I had watched the clock most of the night not wanting to oversleep and rose at just after four. I crept around not wanting to wake the others but gave up when Sabrina surfaced. I must admit I'd never noticed how noisy she was at our flatlet, but maybe that was because of all the other activities going on in the house.

The car arrived exactly at 5.30 as we stood outside waiting, checking we had everything. The only job remaining was the exchange of currency, a simple task that could be effected upon reaching the airport.

The limousine in which we travelled was luxurious and provided us with a very comfortable ride. Our charming guide chatted in his native tongue to the young assistant who sat behind the check-in desk, who listened attentively to his ramblings before producing our airline tickets and tagging our baggage. I couldn't get this more than helpful chap to understand that we wanted to visit the exchange bureau, every time I mentioned it he just waved his hands in some form of gesture, none of which made any sense to Sabrina or I. No matter, we could make some other arrangements once landed.

As he bid us goodbye he handed over an envelope that I presumed contained our tickets but as we sat waiting to take off I opened it to find not only our tickets but a wedge of money. I wasn't sure how much was there all I could see was a bundle of notes, the prince had indeed taken care of everything.

CHAPTER 8

The flight was long and boring but the prince had generously provided us with first class seats and, of course, with these came all the other little luxuries. People say there's no difference in the service but there is, it's a whole new world the other side of the curtain. I'm not into westerns so I gave the in flight movie a miss, instead I plugged myself into the music and Sabrina read between sleeping bouts.

Once through customs we were met by a woman who introduced herself as Dorothy Summers and as we drove to the prince's home she told us a bit about herself. She'd been born in Surrey but had lived in Saudi for some years with her husband who was a freelance architect. One dark, dismal winter's evening he'd come home and voiced his total boredom with his job, the company and all the drudgery that was created by it. She'd jokingly said to him words to the effect of tell them to stuff it and upon his return the following evening he proudly announced that was precisely what he'd done.

Her first reaction was that of devastation with instant images of them surrendering their more than plush home to that now, not so nice man from the mortgage company and moving into a designer cardboard box. These were rapidly eroded away by the contented and ecstatic smile on her husband's face, something that had been missing for years but she'd only just realised

Luckily Dorothy had not lost all of her marbles and the money she earned from her secretarial job kept them going, just, admittedly. It had proved a trying period in their married life but they'd managed to survive. Simon, her husband, hadn't sat around waiting for opportunity to come to him, he'd purposely gone seeking it and by the time dark had given way to light and cold to warmth, he had secured himself several freelance projects that would pay healthy returns.

Dorothy thought he was satisfied with his new found quest in life but no, there was to be a further surprise in store. It took a couple of years and a lot of hard work but he'd reaped the rewards, stashing away enough funds to chance another leap into the unknown. This time Dorothy wasn't so shocked in fact she was full of encouragement.

Simon had been doing regular work for a company who had building interests in the Far East , a lunch time rendezvous with said client had conveniently provided the key to open the next door of his career. The client had been so impressed by Simon's work that when he mentioned a whim to move on, they eagerly suggested Saudi. They had several plots ready for expansion work and felt he was the man to fulfil the task.

Within a matter of weeks they were firmly installed in their new abode. With the expedience of their departure they'd not sold their house, only rented it out, this would provide income and an escape route home if required. Necessity made them learn the language which she managed to pick up fairly well but it wasn't long before the pangs of boredom set in, and being unblessed with children Dorothy felt the urge to work. Naturally her scope was limited and it was by pure luck that she was offered the job as personal secretary to the prince, she was to handle his western affairs, the position suited her perfectly.

I guessed her age to be around fiftyish, she had taken great care of herself but was unable to completely banish those tell tale lines that appear with time. When questioned whether she would prefer to live back in England, her reply was adamantly no, her husband's business had flourished beyond even his expectations and she had become accustomed to her new lifestyle enjoying it to the full.

Eventually our conversation veered to the reason for my visit, the mother to be. Dorothy described her as a timid creature of slight stature and the last few weeks of the pregnancy had proven to be a severe strain, she'd taken to sleeping for a couple of hours during the day to preserve her strength. Her last comment concerned me somewhat. Nadia, the princess, had been complaining of backache for several hours. Although I was grateful that the car was air-conditioned and unsure how long I would be able to bear the intense heat, I found myself urging the driver to hurry. In my professional opinion it was possible our little princess was already in the early stages of labour.

We were shown to our rooms upon our arrival, the prince would be back shortly, he had to attend an unavoidable business meeting. His house, and I use that term loosely, was magnificent, marbled floors and walls to reduce the heat, hand-crafted blankets and finery in deep silk colours adorned the chairs throughout and pure crisp white sheets lay upon the beds. The bathroom was a picture, a swimming pool sized bath sunken into the floor, every tap and plug being of gold and an array of heavily scented oils imposed their heady aroma throughout the room.

Once settled in Dorothy returned to make sure everything was to our satisfaction. I'd just taken a quick shower and my only covering was a small towel, one look at my exposed skin prompted her to ask that we observe their stringent dress code, that meant keeping our bodies covered. I could take my choice of the pure silk gowns which had been made available for my use and were hanging in a large ornate wardrobe, the only concession was not having to cover my face. I suddenly started laughing and Dorothy looked at me rather strangely, a rapid visit to Sabrina's room was needed otherwise cropped shorts and a plunging top might appear in the doorway! All those revealing clothes Sabrina had mulled over were of no use at all, we both might as well have come with empty suitcases.

I dressed, eager to visit the expectant mum. The princess had tried to rest but the pains in her back made her uncomfortable and when I entered the room the girls were flapping around her trying to massage the problem away. Dorothy introduced me to the princess and although her English was limited we managed to converse fairly well. I wanted to examine her so asked that the others leave, their presence was not needed at that precise moment.

I was surprised, the prince had listened well while

we had sat together in the judge's garden, as every necessary piece of equipment had been supplied. Firstly I checked her blood pressure which was slightly high but not serious, the baby's heartbeat was fine and a small internal examination and feel of her tummy confirmed that she was in fact in early labour. I suggested that she no longer lay but sit up or walk around as much as possible, this would help the baby to manoeuvre down the birth canal naturally.

I had just finished when the prince returned rushing to greet me, full of apologies for being absent upon my arrival.

"Well it's a good job I'm here," I said jovially.

"Why?" he replied. I thought under the circumstances it was a stupid question.

"Your wife's in labour, that's why," I told him.

"But the child is not due for another week."

"Babies don't run to a timetable, they decide when to arrive," I said.

I told him what I had advised and that her ladies should call me when there was any change. In the meantime I was hungry and I expected Sabrina was lonely left alone in her bedroom. Her face was a picture when I collected her, she'd attempted in her own sweet way to jazz up the sack hanging from her slim body with a long silk scarf which she'd wrapped around her waist and tied off.

"This is awful," she said. I just shrugged my shoulders, what could I say?

After the introductions we all sat down to eat. The prince had especially imported foods for our nourishment and the chef had been ordered to tone down the spices used in cooking to ensure our poor, uneducated mouths didn't suffer. I tried the strange new dishes strewn about, I hadn't a clue what I was eating but they tasted lovely and plenty of fresh exotic fruits were furnished to complement our meal.

It was hot but with evening setting in the temperature was dropping, hopefully this baby would be born during the night helping both the princess and myself to cope. Thankfully we had finished our food when a man servant entered the room and whispered in the prince's ear.

The princess was in need of attention, the second stage had progressed quicker than expected and the pains were coming every few minutes, it wasn't going to be long. I instructed her ladies to make her as comfortable as possible in a seated position, I have always been adverse to laying a woman down to bear her child.

I quickly checked my charge before speedily returning to inform the prince of progress asking him to join me. I was not ready for the reluctance he displayed. In this land men didn't normally attend the birth of their children, women's work, you know. Sabrina could see I was becoming annoyed at his insistence not to participate in the event, she hastily bid us goodnight and retired to the sanctuary of the bedroom.

"Look, if you don't come and encourage your wife and share in the pleasure of this birth then I refuse to move from this spot, she'll have to cope on her own," I said in a raised voice taking a seat. I could be very stubborn when required and he must have realised as he begrudgingly consented to be present.

"Alright," he said finally. "But I think it's unfair of you to put me in such a position."

"I'll remember that next time someone insists I deliver their baby."

The ladies were more than shocked to see the prince follow me into the room as they busily whispered to one another. His discomfort showed as he hovered in the background trying to appear inconspicuous constantly fiddling with his clothing.

"OK, all of you out, you don't need to be here," I said and Dorothy ushered them all away closing the door behind her. Although I didn't understand the language it was clear they would prefer to stay but their words of objection fell on deaf ears.

The princess was as uncomfortable as the prince but I was determined that he enjoy this happy event. That was another reason for disposing of all those unnecessary floating females. At least he could relax a little not having to promote a macho male image to an all woman audience.

"Take your jacket off then and pull up a chair by your wife," I ordered.

This he did without speaking.

"Well, talk to her then, tell her how well she's doing!" I could see the distress on his face from this last command, I relented for a moment. "You have to, I can't , I don't speak the lingo remember?" That hadn't helped. "Look just tell her you're translating for me, OK?"

He nodded and started to chat to this poor creature who was trying to be so brave in front of her husband.

"Right, let's have a look then at how we're doing."

I raised the sheet covering her lower region and could see that the baby's head was already visible. Good. As unpleasant as he may find it, I wanted him to see, to somehow feel the pain she felt. Her contractions were more rapid and the time for real work had arrived.

With the non-existence of any anti-natal teachings and it being her first child, guidance was needed and I had to constantly remind her to pant after each push to ensure the baby was born with the least stress for both of them. The more imminent the birth became, the more involved the prince became, clutching his wife's hand, wiping her forehead and whispering encouragement.

Even now the temperature was still warm, the blanket of sweat that covered her body was evidence of the immense effort needed to expel this new life from within her. With the next push the head was fully exposed, that was the hardest part over.

"You're doing fine Princess, one more should do it," I said. "Come on Prince, come and see your baby make his or her appearance on the face of the earth."

He moved further down the bed, I knew the child was alive as it was already crying its disapproval of sudden repulsion from the safety of its mothers body.

As the next contraction gripped I urged her into the final thrust, the shoulders cleared and the baby slid from between her thighs.

The child possessed a healthy pair of lungs, I was sure its strong cries could be heard thoughout the palatial home.

I placed the child on his mother's stomach for a few moments before cutting the cord, her face beamed with delighted as she realised she'd produced a boy.

"Congratulations Prince, you've got a son!" I exclaimed. "And a noisy one at that."

After severing the final bonds of connection and cleaning him up, I wrapped him and handed the boy to his mother who immediately held him out to his father. The smile upon his face needed no words of description. I however, still had work to do, mother still needed my attention.

When my tasks were finished and the princess had been taken care of the prince opened the door. Most of the household had gathered waiting for news, he strutted through the courtyard like a peacock, proud of the tiny bundle cradled in his arms.

I allowed him a few moments of glory before dropping a gentle hint that maybe mother would like to hold her baby, after all, she was the one who'd done all the work.

There was a momentary glance of resentment at this prospect as he handed her the child but he relented as he left his new family to revel in the admiration of the army of staff who all vied to be the first to shower him with their words of congratulation.

"Come on Prince," I said clutching his arm dragging him away before he drowned in self praise. "In England we always wet the baby's head, so I think a drink is in order."

Disappointed or what, there wasn't a single drop of alcohol in the whole place, we had to toast the new arrival with iced water which just didn't produce the same effect.

I was tired and as mother and baby had no further need of my services I retired for a well earned sleep.

The heat woke me but I'd managed to catch a few hours. I took a long cool shower, dressed and went to check on my wards. No need, people were dashing to and fro catering for every conceivable eventuality. Sabrina had surfaced earlier than I and was already half way through breakfast, I could see that the prince was also at the table and by the look of distaste on Sabrina's face, relaying every detail of the previous night's event.

"Ah, good morning Carol, I hope you slept well," said the prince in jubilant form.

"Like a log thank you," I replied. "I've checked your family this morning and they're just fine."

"I know, a very handsome boy indeed," he said grinning. Then came those well spoken traditional words, "Looks like me, don't you think?" That question I left unanswered.

"You both have things to discuss so if you'll excuse me I'll see you later," said Sabrina. I could see the relief on her face when I had appeared, as yet she had no appreciation of the joys of birth.

"Perhaps you ladies would like the use of the pool later?" he asked as Sabrina rose from her chair. "It's completely private so clothing restrictions are not upheld."

Sabrina's face lit up. "Oh that would be great, just let me know when, I'll be ready."

Tea, the prince had imported tea for our breakfast, how thoughtful. Fresh fruit had been chopped and only needed the addition of some yogurt.

The prince had been overwhelmed by his experience and I had to admit that even I was glad to get away from him as soon as I'd eaten and that swim did sound rather tempting. What a pool, it had been built in a disused house which I later discovered had been redesigned and constructed by Simon, Dorothy's husband. The outside had been restored to its original beauty with all the white stonework cleaned, repaired or replaced where necessary. Inside had been totally revamped, walls removed with marbled pillars installed for support, all the walls and floor were also in marble of contrasting colours, producing a cooling environment.

The pool varied in depth and its shape followed the contours of the building with several points of entry and at one end you could actually walk in as the floor sloped away like the sea shore. Various white loungers were scattered across the available floor space interrupted only by large green foliage some heavy with fruits. Large arched changing rooms had been incorporated in areas that provided no other use and pristine white robes and towels lay symmetrically folded at sporadic points throughout. It was such an idyllic surrounding that we stayed there most of the day and it was only the arrival of one of the princess's attendants that made us aware of how long we'd been gone. The royal couple had become worried and had despatched a scout to check on us.

Sabrina and I spent the next couple of days being chauffeured round the sights by Dorothy, visiting the local markets. Anything we wanted was paid for by the prince and if we weren't reducing his bank balance, we were swimming in the pool of perfection, this was one part I'd definitely miss.

What a fantastic time we'd had but all good things finally have to come to an end and not wanting to abuse the more than generous hospitality of our host, felt it only right to return home.

On our final evening just before eating I couldn't resist one more visit to that purpose built oasis. Sabrina declined the invitation, I think maybe too much walking had worn her out, either that or the stress of spending money. Surprisingly, the prince asked whether I would permit him to join me, which drew a raised eyebrow from Sabrina and a look that said 'oh yes?' It would be impolite to say no but an approving smile from the princess came as a great relief.

"Sure I don't mind, but does custom allow it?" I asked slyly. My question drew a silent response.

Even though it was not far to the pool-house a bodyguard would always be a few discrete steps behind but on this occasion as we left, the prince raised his hand and the huge hunk stayed still. What was he up to? I'm sure I'd find out sooner or later.

I changed into my costume but on this occasion I felt somewhat embarrassed at my lack of attire. Although it was a one piece swimsuit it had a plunging neckline and the leg section was high cut and modesty prompted my use of a robe. As I removed this outer covering the prince stared for a moment before removing his wrap, his costume was classic and well concealing.

"Is there a problem?" I asked.

"No, no problem, shall we?" came his reply as his hand gestured towards the water.

We spent a couple of hours enjoying each other's company laughing and chatting mostly about the future plans for his son and during this whole time he never came closer than arms length until we prepared to leave our watery home for the last time. He sidled up close, I was shocked and for once at a loss as to what to do.

"Don't worry Carol," he said quietly, "I don't intend to do anything dishonourable."

What a relief.

"I am very fond of you, you're so refreshing to be with," he said. "I love my wife and respect the traditions by which we live but you emanate that western independence that is forbidden to our women, having your own views of life and not afraid to say so."

"Of course" I said not knowing what he wanted me to say.

"I want to be serious, just for one moment, look at me, I know it would be breaking with our tradition but...well if you could ever consider becoming my wife you would do me the greatest honour." What a bloody stupid suggestion, to comply would mean suppressing everything he admired in me and was he so naive to believe that being educated to condemn bigamy that I'd accept second billing or any competition. And what about love, where did that fit into this scenario?

I was speechless, I turned away and left the pool. I'd dried myself and put on the robe before finally finding the words to reply. Overcoming my instant anger that he'd given thought to categorise me as a person ready to consider or accept such a profound offer, I decided the best method of dealing with this unprovoked request was to discard it as a joke, laughing away its serious implications.

"Thanks for the offer, Prince," I said with a whimsical note in my voice, " but where I come from men only take one woman I couldn't be second choice and besides I'm not in love with you." At that very moment they were the simplest words I could summon to express my feelings.

"I understand, maybe if I had met you first I would only have taken one woman," he replied, his voice sounding a little dejected.

"Let's go and dine," he said changing the subject entirely and I gave a silent sigh of relief.

Nothing further was said on the matter, the evening passed jovially and even the princess joined us for the feast.

Once again we were travelling in the air conditioned limo but this time we were accompanied by the prince who was adamant in ensuring our smooth departure.

The chauffeur helped Sabrina check in our luggage which one of the ladies had kindly packed for us. We'd also had to acquire another case to carry the additional items we'd purchased.

"You take good care of that baby now and don't forget to send me pictures as he grows!" I said, turning to the prince as we left the check in desk.

"I promise. When I come to England again may I visit you?" he asked.

"I'd like that."

"Of course, if I am in need of your professional services again I will send for you," he grinned.

"Not too soon I hope!" I laughed as Sabrina and aid reappeared.

"Goodbye then Prince and thanks for a lovely holiday," said Sabrina.

"The pleasure was all mine," he said with a slight bow of his head.

"Wait... I nearly forgot, I have a gift for you, Carol." His hand disappeared into his pocket and he withdrew a small velvet bag from which he drew a ring, identical to the one he wore. I could see its magical sparkle as he thrust it in my direction, gesturing for me to take it.

"No...I can't take it, it's very special and..."

"Yes! You are special, a true friend and you have done me a great service, you must accept or I will be offended!" he insisted.

I took the ring and slipped it on my middle finger, it fitted perfectly.

"If you ever need my help or you change your mind about my offer just let me know," he said.

There was no time for further objections on my part, the final call for our flight was being announced.

"Goodbye, Prince."

"Until we meet again, Carol."

As we boarded the plane Sabrina was full of questions but I managed to dismiss them, any relationship I had with the prince was purely personal and not open for discussion.

CHAPTER 9

The travel home had taken its toll on us both, we'd managed to sleep a little but were still very tired. I was certainly grateful to see Andrew's familiar face waiting for us as we trundled our trolley through and out of the various official channels at the airport. It was supposed to be Jonathan but he had some sudden business to attend to and would be back later. A bubble filled bath and a long nap were called for and as we both disappeared to the beckoning comfort of our beds, Andrew agreed to wake us in time for dinner.

"Come on lazy, Jonathan's eager to see you," said Andrew. "Dinner's ready." And it was, a lovely salad with cold meats, cheese and fresh bread, all washed down by a large glass of red wine. While we ate I left Sabrina to relay our adventure, of course her main topic was how much we'd managed to buy and very little about the reason for being there.

There was one item though that Sabrina hadn't mentioned purely because she'd missed the presentation of that fine gem and as soon as the prince was out of sight I'd removed the said item and placed it into the safety of my bag.

"I've got something to show you," I said as I went and retrieved the ring.

They were speechless as I flaunted this large gem that, as the light bounced off its surface, created beams of mesmerising beauty.

"Where did you get that?" gasped Sabrina.

"A friend," was my only reply, I really didn't need to say anymore as they passed it amongst themselves each admiring it's deep ruby colour.

"Very nice," said Jonathan. "But I'd suggest you find somewhere safe to keep it."

"Yes I will but I don't know where."

"There is a small safe fitted in my room if you want me to lock it away for now," he replied.

"Yes if you wouldn't mind," I said wrapping it in cotton wool and placing it in a small box that had held some cheap earrings I'd purchased.

"Oh by the way Sabrina, David phoned while you were asleep, he wants to see you," said Andrew changing the subject.

"I'll give him a ring after dinner," replied Sabrina.

We decided that a stroll to the inn was in order. Sabrina telephoned David who said he'd join us there in five minutes. Angela had just arrived and as usual immediately drew the attention of Andrew by wearing such a tight skimpy top that her bust had no option other than to spill out.

David had good news while we'd been away on our jolly jaunt, he had got the transfer to the plain clothes brigade so wanted to have a little celebration. We were all for that and a pleasant evening was had by all.

When we returned to the house Jonathan opened

some wine but I drank too much and didn't remember much more of the evening. The next thing I knew was being woken by the telephone. I put a hand out and grabbed it, just wanting to stop that ringing.

It was Jennifer, and her news brought me to my senses. Another victim, but the body had only just been found. If I wanted to go with her she could pick me up first. What a stupid question, of course I wanted to go, I had half an hour before she'd arrive.

A movement in the bed told me I was not alone, Jonathan popped his dishevelled head from below the covers to enquire who had phoned. I quickly explained and disappeared into the bathroom while Jonathan offered to make some coffee. When my mind was functioning properly I ventured a question about the night before to which I received a short reply. I had dragged him to the bedroom, had tried unsuccessfully to remove bits of his clothing and then passed out, so he just cuddled up beside me.

I was not the only one who had company that night. David had just emerged from Sabrina's room sporting a pair of boxer shorts and judging by the noise, two were 'tangoing' in Andrew's room.

Moments later I could hear the horn of a car, Jennifer had arrived.

As was normal, the victim's house had been cordoned off with the familiar bold blue and white tape. There was such a flurry of activity that no one questioned who I was but I still tried to portray an air of professionalism whilst discreetly following Jennifer closely.

The third body to be found was that of Sammy Nielson, she was totally different to the other two girls not what I'd expected. Lying motionless on a garden lounger, she'd been noticed by the next door neighbour while he was surveying the garden from his bedroom window.

She was dressed in a skimpy, short see-through dress reminiscent of the 60's, her head and body had been turned on one side as if flaunting the extensive heavy bruising to her neck that signalled Sammy had not been such easy prey. Her knees were bent and parted with one arm resting on her hip while the other was extended with her hand pointing upwards. In it lay a rose, gently encased by a slim hand with long painted nails. Her shoulder length, artificially curled hair was splayed out to cushion her face which was heavily made up and although slightly smudged. It had been effected with great care. I noticed that she wore no shoes nor were there any on the ground, not unusual, but the soles of her feet were clean not what you'd expect if she'd walked around the garden barefoot. There were also some kind of markings on her ankles and wrists which I was unable to see clearly.

It was only when the body had been moved that police discover the crumpled piece of paper trapped beneath her. Written upon it, were the killer's final words for poor Sammy. He must have rearranged the body after its composition, it read, FOREVER A TEMPTRESS IN MAN'S EYES, not the terms of remorse or innocence as bestowed on his previous victims. As I bent over her to take a closer look, the face that confronted me wasn't as young as I'd first thought. She had chosen her foundation well, almost succeeding in concealing the lines of age around her eyes. I estimated she must have been in her late thirties or early forties, she had a trim muscular body, an indication that possibly she indulged in some form of exercise.

The house only mirrored the scene outside, unimpressionable mismatched furniture cluttered throughout and although not a posh residence all the rooms were tidy, except for her bedroom. Various items of clothing lay scattered on a chair stuck in one corner and an old wooden dressing table under the window was bowing under the weight of bottles and jars that contained creams and perfume. The remaining space was taken up by a large wicker basket that overflowed with brightly coloured items of make-up.

There was a set of drawers to one side, on the top sat a gaudy box which was open, the contents were a selection of beads, bangles and plastic earrings. She was either unable to afford or had no desire for better quality decoration but the bulging wardrobe was evidence as to where her passion lay. Short dresses gave way to long flowing skirts and floppy blouses, none I would call modern in style, she obviously dressed to her mood. The copious pairs of shoes also showed the same pattern from stilettos to canvas sandals with string ties, most of which had seen better days.

Interviews came next and Jennifer asked me to wait in the hall but with the door conveniently left ajar, I could hear their conversation. The first interviewee was Simon, one of the chaps from upstairs.

The gist of the story was that Sammy shared a converted house with two men, they lived upstairs and she down. The deal suited them all quite amicably, Simon and Rod, the second of the duo, were clearly only interested in men but had found her a great friend. Sammy had worked as a secretary in a large distribution company where she came into contact with more than her fair share of the male species thus providing her with company any evening she chose. Simon said he and Rod took great delight in eyeing up any man Sammy brought home with her and would tease her by asking for the phone numbers of the ones they fancied, but it was only done as a joke, they respected her friendship too much for it to be any more.

They had shared the place for over seven years and during that time, Sammy had helped them out on more than one occasion, even when they'd suddenly found themselves both out of a job and unable to find rent money. For two months she'd struggled and scraped together enough funds to pay it for them, she was a true friend and they loved her.

Jennifer asked him where he'd been the previous day, Simon told her that he and Rod had been invited to dine at a friend's house, he had been at work all day and had picked Rod up after work at about sevenish and gone straight there, not returning until after 2 am the following morning. Simon said that Sammy had mentioned she was to have one of her very special dates that evening with a handsome hunk. Upon their return that night they'd noticed the usual subdued lighting from Sammy's bedroom and presumed she must still be entertaining.

When asked if he knew how long she had known her mysterious visitor and how often she'd gone out with him, Simon was vague. He was pretty certain that the relationship hadn't been going on long but as to the frequency of their dating, maybe three or four times but possibly more, he couldn't say for definite. Had he ever seen him? No, he'd not been so fortunate, somehow fate had ensured that neither he or Rod were ever around during his visitations but they knew he'd been, the presence of fresh flowers on show in the living room window were evidence of his recent presence and Sammy was always in jubilant mood afterwards. When Jennifer suggested that maybe Sammy bought the flowers herself, Simon dismissed that explanation, these weren't your cheap bunch from the market stall, no, these were roses, dozens of them. Sammy would never have considered spending that kind of money on flowers.

I moved around to try and glimpse the window through the crack of the door. Sure enough, there in full splendour was a vase tightly packed with deep red roses buds bursting open as if they were another deadly advertisement to the giver's existence.

The interview with Rod only paralleled the facts given by Simon, the only additional item he mentioned was Sammy had been keen on working out, often visiting the gym once or twice a week. If the killer was as strapping as she made out, that's where she may have met him.

The final guest was the neighbour who called the police. I'd say he was aged around sixty to sixty-five, he was slovenly dressed in faded attire dotted with the tell tale marks of previous meals stained into his shirt. I couldn't help thinking that although he tried to create the image of being a morally clean minded person, he reminded me of the type who would burn himself to a crisp on the beach rather than give up ogling the bare chested beauties, a very slimy and creepy character. He stated that he was a bad sleeper, often waking in the early hours of the morning, he would sit at his bedroom window to watch dawn break and listen to the birds heralding its approach.

The previous morning had been no different to any other except that when he opened the curtains, he could see Sammy still lying out there in the garden. He'd noticed her there at tea time the previous evening but thought nothing of it. Sammy often spent many hours in her garden, but it was too early to contemplate sun bathing so he opened the window and called to her but received no answer, she just lay there motionless. He knew something was wrong so he struggled downstairs and into his own garden, again he called but nothing, he'd already started to suffer with the pangs of pain from the arthritis in his hip joints so was unable to climb up and look over the fence. He'd tried waking the lads shouting as loudly as he could but due to the effects of a late night and the vast consumption of alcohol they never heard him, the only thing he could think to do was call the police. The rest we knew.

Had he ever seen Sammy's mysterious lover? Unfortunately not, he said he had no interest in the procession of men who passed through her hands but he had heard them, well, her; he recognised her laughter. As to his movements the previous day, he had stayed at home as usual watching the television. His evidence could tell us nothing more so Jennifer dismissed him, asking a constable to ensure he got home without any harassments.

With nothing further to be gleaned from this place, I knew we would be leaving soon but not before the body.

The silent crew had already done their job, ensuring nothing was missed, like marching locusts seeking out every spec of greenery.

Jennifer had let me attend one autopsy with her so I couldn't see a problem with this one, also she hadn't the time to drive me home till later, so I was on a fairly safe bet. When she suggested lunch I readily agreed. If I'd mentioned waiting till after our private viewing in case I threw up, she would definitely have refused to take me.

Cold air blasted from an old noisy conditioning unit designed to keep the room at a constant, chilled temperature, just right for dismembering bodies and thus ensuring the meat wouldn't rot before finishing the task. Luckily, the doctor had not long finished his preliminary inspection and as yet had not had time to take a scalpel to Sammy. With her body stretched out and de-clothed she was remarkably tall, more slight of build than I originally thought and with all the make up clinically removed, her face was plain and not particularly pretty. The doctor confirmed, of course, that she'd been strangled and unless further investigations found anything different this would be his judgement as to the cause of death. His opinion of the additional markings to her wrists and ankles and the bruising to her sides was that they may have been caused in her struggle to fight off her attacker. Jennifer's suggestion of kinky sex and handcuffs brought a raised eyebrow from the old doc but previous victims who'd been shackled at the point of death always bore much deeper, wider bruising and often broken wounds caused by harsh, un-giving metals.

I had opened my mouth before my brain took control.

"Tied to the bed," was my muttered comment.

Jennifer gave me a sideways look. "The doctor's just explained that she wasn't cuffed to the bed."

"I know," I replied a little indignantly, "but could those marks be made by some softer restraint?"

"Yes, very possibly but nothing wide or hard such as a strap or belt, they would produce near enough the same wounding as some kind of cuffs," he answered.

"How about ribbon?" I asked.

"Ribbon?" said Jennifer looking puzzled.

"Yes, if you remember on each corner just under the brass domes on the bed stead was a ribboned bow, maybe not decoration as I originally thought," I said, turning my mental observation into words.

"Would such an article be strong enough for such a purpose?" asked Jennifer.

"Oh yes, cheap ribbon is made of man made fibres such as nylon and although thin, quite strong, unbreakable almost but of course it would give or fold with force," replied the doctor.

"But if the ribbon had stretched surely she'd have managed to free her hands and fight back?" suggested Jennifer.

"Maybe, but what if by that time her strength had gone, and she was already at the point of taking her final breath?" I said.

"Even if she was secured she still must have put up a tremendous fight, look at the extensive bruising to her neck, he would have had to strengthen his grip to stop her moving," said the doctor.

With my mind in overdrive I butted in once again. "Let's say she was tied down, to get even pressure on either side of her throat he would need to have been over the top of her body, otherwise the bruising would be less severe on one side," I suggested.

"Quite correct young lady," said the doctor.

"If that was so could the grip of his thighs have caused the other bruising to her sides? After all, if she was as fit as people have made out, he would have needed to control her lower body movement as well." There, how was that for a theory I thought, silently notching up a point for me on some kind of invisible score board.

"Who's the policewoman here, me or you?" said Jennifer.

"Sorry, I'll shut up," I said apologetically, time to back off and keep my place.

The doctor stated that she had had sex within the last 12-24 hours but with more than one partner which would complicate matters.

The doctor promised to have the report ready by the following morning and with nothing else to be revealed by this poor unfortunate carcass, we left. I didn't need to question when she headed the car in the direction from which we'd come, Jennifer wanted to return to Sammy's house and take a further look at those ribbons, such innocent items but possibly tools used by a murderer. There, as before hung those inoffensive bows, gold in colour using the brass as camouflage but now their presence shining, almost calling out to be noticed.

Jennifer had to agree that although noticed they'd been quickly dismissed as of no importance but if my theory was correct and the killer had touched them then he could also have touched the metal shafts they were tied around. This discovery could also change where

Sammy met her end, not in the garden as originally presumed. One phone call and the place was again crawling, for a much more thorough job this time on that bed.

Jennifer had been summoned by her superior and with the uncertainty of how long she would be I decided to catch a train home. This suited me, I was tired and the journey would be relaxing.

The rhythmic clicking and rocking of the carriage along the track soon provided the desired effect and my eyes closed for rest but with this darkness, my mind kept resurrecting clear images of faces, places and death. Using this bank of knowledge I tried to figure out what sort of person this man was. For a start, he was obviously rich, enabling him to lavish the best on his victims. The sleek black car was not the sort chosen by too young a man, most men mirror their choice of vehicle. Its fine lines and power would signal to me that the owner was between thirty and forty, physically fit and well groomed.

I had listened to the constant repetition of the generous and thoughtful way he had treated each girl when alive, this lead me to only one conclusion, he was either a very devious scheming heartless bastard or, one of society's poor creatures unable to follow the correct course of life. But whichever, he needed to be caught and either helped or locked up with the key thrown away. Both would have the same result, his total isolation from his fellow beings.

With no real motive for his killing I favoured the latter excuse but his cunning ability to move amongst people unnoticed was a contradiction and pointed to the first. The girls he had befriended were also puzzling; the first a beauty and independent, the second young, innocent and withdrawn while the third was lively, bubbly, an enjoyer of life. With no pattern as to his chosen victims and the vast distances between them, the chance of a familiar connection became even more remote.

The juddering of applied brakes signalled our imminent arrival and roused me from my pondering. I was surprised to see Sabrina's car waiting outside the station, apparently Jennifer had thoughtfully phoned through and asked someone to meet me. Sabrina and Andrew decided on pizza for tea, so they picked me up on the way. Loud rock was booming from the stereo, dismissing the possibility of conversation. I was contented to just sit silently in the back of the car, Sabrina was chattering away but, unable to hear, I nodded when I felt it appropriate.

I would have much preferred to have disappeared to the sanctuary of my bedroom once home. I had eaten more than sufficient during lunch and indulged in a rather large bar of chocolate during my dreamy journey quashing any pangs for further nourishment. I just nibbled at a small slice of the amply topped pizza as I divulged the basic facts of my day. For some eerie reason, I felt they were feeding from the information I was readily giving, a strange situation, intense eyes looking as if to know the words not yet formed by my lips.

Unsure of the motive for their insatiable curiosity, I held back most of the secretive details, only parting with generality, nothing they couldn't hear or read through media. Anyway, I don't think I could have put into words what my own eyes had viewed of late, how do you describe your thoughts as you look down at a lifeless being and the feeling of overwhelming despair that one human found it possible to inflict the premature end to another, taking away the only natural gift one is given, the gift of life. No, my ramblings would express nothing and command little more emotion than as if read in a newspaper, a moment of pity before turning the page.

A change of subject was called for and I easily managed to manipulate the conversation, giving the impression of interest in how each of their days had developed. With the subject touched they chatted amongst themselves leaving me to sit back and just listen, looking on as if a stranger. I found it amusing, Jonathan leaned back in his chair, quiet and thoughtful whilst in contrast Andrew and Sabrina with elbows on the table did battle for verbal space. I did notice, however, that on one or two occasions Jonathan was staring straight at me, studying my face, as one would study the fine lines of a painting, picking out every changing detail. I found his desire to look at me pleasing, full of warmth which I was delighted to bathe in.

It was about tenish when Jonathan stood up.

"Carol and I are going for a stroll." I looked up in surprise.

"You don't mind do you?" he said.

"No...no I'd like that," I replied.

Caught unawares by Jonathan's unrelated comment Sabrina and Andrew fell short of words, all they managed was, "OK, see you later."

I rested a cardigan on my shoulders, as I expected the night air was chilled for once, not muggy as had been the norm lately, most refreshing.

"I don't know about you but those two can certainly talk," he said as we passed through the gates.

"Yes, I had noticed," I replied.

"It's more peaceful out here, cooler tonight, which would you prefer, grass or road?" he asked.

"Hm...grass I think!" As we headed across the soft green carpet beneath our feet.

"There is the pretty stream further down if you'd like to go, not that you will see much in this dusky light," said Jonathan.

"Beauty is not governed by light, you know," I replied gently scolding him.

"True," he agreed.

We were in no rush to get back and with my affections for him growing I took pleasure in our solitude, his hand had wrapped around mine urging me to follow as he guided me into unexplored territory. As our eyes grew accustomed to the dark, we found it easy to navigate through the bushes that lined the water's edge and once through followed its course along a natural corridor. It must have rained at some time during the day, the ground was slightly damp and fresh smelling.

"It's lovely," I said.

"I'm glad you think so, I've only been down here once before and that was during the day," he replied. "And you were right about the beauty bit, look down at the water."

Night had taken full grip, the sun had disappeared, dusk had turned to blackness and the moon was shining strongly, bright and alluring. Its image was bouncing off the mirrored waters of the stream, creating light that illuminated our surroundings in varying shades of grey to black. I knelt down and thrust my hand into the water causing a ripple effect that distorted the mirror for a few moments before it finally pieced itself back together to perfection.

"You seemed a little apprehensive at dinner tonight, was everything alright today?" he asked.

"Yes fine, I'm tired that's all and I think I'm still suffering from the effects of last night," I replied again. I had no willingness to discuss the matter further.

"So the police found nothing?" he quizzed.

"No, nothing," I answered.

"Not even a finger print?" he asked.

"I just said they found nothing," I replied, my voice a little raised. What was this sudden interest? Normally he and the others would play down my passion for the subject.

"OK...OK, just curious that's all!" he said.

He put his arm around my waist giving me a playful hug as we walked silently on, the only noise was that of the night creatures going about their rituals; working, eating and communicating with each other.

As we came to the next large clearing Jonathan stopped, pulled me towards him, the passion emitting from his kisses was familiar. He was in the mood for love, but his luck had run out tonight, it just felt wrong. The closer he got, the more I pulled away, pushing hard against his chest making my reluctance clear.

"What's the matter Carol? he said gently.

"Nothing, as I said before I'm tired and I'd rather not," I said.

"As you wish," he said in a cold voice as his arms dropped away. "You don't have to do anything you don't want to." The way he spoke and his tone gave off strong signals of indifference, I found it hard to believe that someone could change so quickly.

"Can we go back now please, I'm getting cold," I asked.

He nodded and we reversed direction cutting across land but this time there was no holding of hands or linking of arms and I was more than glad when the house came in sight, my rejection to his advances of affection had struck deeper than I first imagined but he would have to accept and get over it.

To my surprise, both Sabrina and Andrew had already retired for the night and with the current mood I thought it might be wise to follow suit. Jonathan obviously had different ideas and before I could speak he asked me to have a drink with him before bed. We needed to talk, clear the air, I had not intentionally set out to hurt his feelings and I wanted him to understand that fact. Avoiding the cosy restraints of the sofa I perched myself on one of the stools where Jonathan joined me.

"Jonathan, I didn't mean..." I began to say trying to excuse my earlier behaviour.

"I know...it was my own fault," he said apologetically. "I can't expect you to always give into me."

"It's just...well it's been a long day, I must be more tired than I thought, sorry." I replied.

"Look, I have to entertain some clients tomorrow evening, how about coming with me?" he asked changing the subject.

"The people you mix with are very posh, what if I embarrass you?" I replied.

"Don't be silly, anyway, I want to show you off." he said jokingly.

"I'm not an animal to be shown like a prized possession!" I felt a little indignant.

"No, it's not like that. I'd really like you to meet some of the people I know but the real reason is I like your company and want you to be with me," he explained.

"OK but I don't have the right sort of clothes here unless Sabrina has something suitable," I said.

"I'll take you into town first thing and we can go shopping," he said. "Afterwards, I can pop into the office, you don't mind waiting for an hour or so do you?"

"No I wouldn't mind," I answered.

"I'll book the restaurant and a hotel," he suggested.

I gave him a sly glance which he quickly read and addressed.

"Separate rooms of course."

"Fine, agreed then." There wasn't much conversation after that and I was ready for bed and a kiss goodnight provided an acceptable parting.

CHAPTER 10

I was awake earlier than normal the following morning. A shower and then breakfast was in order; I loved shopping and knew it would be several hours before a stop for lunch. If Jonathan wanted to show me off, as he put it, he'd have to foot the bill for the privilege; some feminine clothing, shoes and accessories sounded reasonable to me. The whim of indulgent selfishness had taken grip which Jonathan had more than ample funds to satisfy.

The shopping went well and by the time we were ready to partake of refreshment, I had managed to amass several items. I had decided on a dress, the long, plain, flowing type. Being tall meant I could show it off to full advantage. Though he said nothing, I got the impression that Jonathan would have preferred something more skimpy but that was precisely why I chose differently; high heels, jacket and bag finished the ensemble. We had been walking for hours and I'd dragged him into every shop trying on more clothes than I wish to mention. I was secretly relieved when we sat down for some lunch and by the look on Jonathan's face, so was he.

The next adventure was a visit to his office. This was part of a large converted house and although on a main road still managed a well kept look, no peeling paintwork or shabby blinds hanging at the windows. As we entered, I noticed all the highly polished brass fittings including the name plate secured to the door, impressive so far.

They had one half of the downstairs which consisted of three offices, one being Jonathan's, the second...his new partner's, who was out, and the third and largest housed their secretary and her assistant.

"Ah, there you are Miss Simpkins," he said as a mature lady emerged from his office. "Please meet Carol, a very special friend of mine," he said with a wide grin.

"Pleased to meet you," she replied stretching out a frail, well lined hand to shake mine. "Jonathan has spoken of you. Would you like some tea?"

"Yes thank you, if it's not too much trouble," I replied.

"Not at all," she said. "Sally, please put the kettle on and make some tea for Jonathan and his young lady, we can have ours now as well."

"I'll sit over there on the couch if that's OK?" I asked.

"Of course, would you like something to read?" asked Miss Simpkins.

"No, I brought a couple of magazines with me thanks."

"I have laid out the necessary documents you need to deal with today Jonathan, I'll just have a cup of tea and then I'll come in to take notes if that's alright with you," said Miss Simpkins.

"Yes, when you're ready, no hurry," he replied. "Carol doesn't mind waiting, do you?"

"Not at all, take what time you need, I have plenty to read," I said reassuringly.

Sally placed the tea tray on the table in front of me. She could only be about sixteen or seventeen, a tiny looking creature who still possessed her childlike features and stature. She must either have had a sheltered upbringing or her teenage hormonal outbreaks suppressed, her dress was more like that sported by a mature woman, skirt down to the knees, blouse buttoned to the neck and flat, uninteresting leather shoes. There was also no trace of make up on her baby skin or paint on her over trimmed nails.

As I smiled and thanked her, I received a momentary glance and a nervous half-hearted smile as she scurried away from her mission before finally returning to her desk and a large pile of papers that nearly obscured her from view.

Miss Simpkins was an entirely different character, of the old secretarial school I would say, in her late fifties maybe early sixties. She was neatly dressed in a classic skirt and a long sleeved blouse, a modest pair of court shoes upon her feet and the traditional pearl necklace finished off her couture. Her hair, now grey, was wavy and brushed back from a face that bore just a modest hint of lipstick and powder.

She was as good as her word, as soon as she put down her cup she stood, gathered a couple of pencils and a notepad before disappearing into Jonathan's office to perform her professional duties.

I had read most of the first magazine before she re-emerged clutching several files. It was apparent even in the short time of my visit that she was the hub that kept the wheels of the company turning. I didn't have to wait too long before Jonathan surfaced, then we said goodbye and left. As we drove to our hotel, I couldn't help but smile to myself, Jonathan must have noticed because he asked me what I found so amusing.

"Sorry, it's just they weren't what I had imagined," I said.

"What, Miss Simpkins and Sally?" he asked.

"Yes, I had pictured your secretary to be more...well..." I started to say.

"A bimbo you mean," he said.

"Well... not quite a bimbo, a nail filer actually!" I couldn't stop myself from laughing.

"Listen, when it comes to business you employ for the qualities and professionalism that are offered not the outside packaging!" he said indignantly. "Miss Simpkins has vast knowledge and skills which I am more than grateful for, her presence at the office allows me to continue business without being tied to a desk. I just hope she doesn't retire on me too soon."

"I agree, she's a lovely lady but I think Sally could do with a little encouragement, bring her out of that large shell surrounding her," I said.

"You're probably right there, she is very shy. I'll speak to Miss Simpkins about her, maybe letting her answer the telephone more or sending her out on errands will help let her think for herself instead of being told what to do all the time," he said.

The rest of the day and evening took a sharp downhill turn, most disappointing. The hotel was very stylish with its rooms of uniformed design but the atmosphere was cold, forced smiles and pleasantries as you travelled the conveyer belt of the establishment's business.

Tonight Jonathan had decided on French cuisine, apparently the preference of the people he had invited to dine with us. We arrived at the restaurant slightly late, my fault as I got the time wrong. His guests had already assembled and were chatting and drinking at the bar. My first impression was what a bunch of good looking chaps but towards the end of the evening my views had changed, they were really most boring. Being the only female in the group they spent most of the time showing off to me or trying to impress. Obviously the mere sight of a woman had induced a boost of testosterone in these shallow creatures. They seemed to think a high falluting job title, racy sports car and the famous people they confessed to knowing would do the trick.

The more they drank the more pitiful they became with their well used chat-up lines and supposed sexy looks across the table. At one point, some insipid looking guy even attempted to play footsie under the table. Looking across with a forced smile, I felt obliged to return his advances, raising the heel of my shoe just under the leg of his trouser ensuring it dug in deep on the way. His pathetic grin changed instantly, the pain now portrayed on his face signalled my message had been transmitted and he quickly removed his leg and repositioned himself in his seat. That was him sorted.

After what seemed like an eternity we eventually left the restaurant, Jonathan had drunk too much red wine and was stumbling about which made getting him into the waiting taxi very difficult, but I managed. I was more than grateful when at last I pushed him onto his hotel bed. He was in one of those silly moods, grabbing at my hands, trying to pull me towards him. I conceded to his slurred pleas and lay down beside him. This turned out to be the right choice because within a short space of time I heard the tell tale signs of sleep. I struggled to undress him and throw the bed covers across him before switching off the light and heading for my own room. I read until my eyes became heavy and I, too, gave way to invading slumber.

Jonathan was more than worse for wear the following morning and only managed some toast for breakfast which he found great difficulty in swallowing. I, on the other hand, was famished and tucked into a hearty plate full of eggs and bacon. I think the smell of all the food wasn't helping either and Jonathan was relieved when I had finished. My offer to drive us home was readily accepted, he sat quietly in the passenger seat covering his red puffy eyes with sunglasses.

Once home Jonathan sought the comfort of his bed and slept till late afternoon when he looked much better and more capable of taking the jibes thrown at him by Andrew and Sabrina.

It was around six when the telephone rang, Jonathan answered it, it was his mother. From the topic of conversation it was apparent something was wrong, he had initially spoken in Italian before reverting to English but even in a foreign tongue it was easy to detect the sombre tones. His final words were of assurance, he would book the next available flights and be there as soon as possible.

It was bad news, their maternal grandmother had died that morning. She was a frail old lady who had been unwell for a long time before her heart finally gave up beating. Although they were not close, the news was saddening and they felt the need to be with their mother at this time to provide the support this loss would demand.

Jonathan spent the next hour on the phone making

reservations, the first available flights were the following morning which meant they would have to be at the airport very early. I suggested I drive them there but Jonathan said he would take his car and leave it in the long stay car park because of the uncertainty of when they would return.

My hosts' moods remained sullen during the early part of the evening, none taking much interest in doing anything apart from skulking around.

Andrew and Sabrina had arranged to go bowling later with some of the lads, they thought it disrespectful but Jonathan practically insisted they go, just because one life had ceased to be didn't mean others should suddenly stop enjoying themselves. I agreed, they would be better in company, it would take their minds off of the mourning to come.

The telephone rang again, this time it was Jennifer for me, her call came somewhat as a surprise but was warmly greeted. She had some news and suggested I pay her a call, they had found a print from Sammy's bedstead, just underneath one of the bows. In a vain hope, they were in the process of trying to match it to prints they already had on file, a long shot but one that had to be taken, they could be lucky. Jennifer didn't normally suggest I visit so there had to be an ulterior motive, she'd never admit it but I think she found me an ideal person to discuss and bounce her ideas off , and I was sure my comments in the autopsy room had also provided good grounding for my continued inclusion on this case.

"Who was that?" asked Jonathan.

"Jennifer, she wants me to see her tonight, she thinks they've found a finger print that may help," I replied.

"But I thought you said they didn't find any?" he asked.

"That's what I thought, but it would now appear different, I'll find out later," I said. "Oh, that would leave you on your own tonight, I could change it if you'd rather me to stay."

"No, you go, I have to go out and draw some cash and fill up the car so I'll be out for a while myself," he said reassuringly. "In fact I 'd better go."

"I should be back but if not can you let Sabrina know I've borrowed her car," I said following him out the door. "I promise not to stay out too long." I would try and return a little earlier, maybe provide a little company for the latter part of the evening.

Jennifer expected to be home shortly after seven so I attempted to coincide my arrival with that time, but unfortunately even the best laid plans often fail as did this one. I had to sit in the car until well after eight thirty. Jennifer's car came to an abrupt halt as she hurried over towards me apologising profusely for her lateness but she'd been caught by her boss just as she was about to leave and, by all accounts, he did like to talk. Never mind, at least she was home now. I was starving and Jennifer had no desire to cook so we drove to the local Peking restaurant to eat.

The food was good but my interests were more concerned with what she was about to tell, with the idea that the ribbons had been removed during the killer's visit. Jennifer had one of the forensic team re-visit the house and remove them for investigation. It was not long before the excitement of discovery took hold, they'd found a thumb print, not complete, only half, the other part was smudged but even with the little section they were able to eliminate all known parties. The computer came up with several thousand possible people by matching the small section it had, but it was soon clear that no conviction could be gained on this small, incomplete shred of evidence. Once more they had been stumped.

Our conversation went on longer than I had anticipated and after explaining my reasons for a hurried retreat, Jennifer promised to phone me if anything else surfaced. With that, I left for the journey home.

As I entered through the gate onto the patio I was suddenly confronted by Jonathan, naked and wet, he just stood staring at me, obviously he hadn't heard my return.

"Oh, you startled me," I said. "Here, you'd better dry yourself or you may catch a chill."

He grabbed the towel from my outstretched hand and quickly rubbed the water from his body before wrapping it round his waist. Under the lights within the house I could see Jonathan had started to shiver with the cold so I insisted he put on a robe for warmth. Meanwhile I made some coffee to provide heating from the inside.

He seemed a little apprehensive, avoiding conversation as though I had burst into something personal.

"Bit late for a swim," I suggested.

"True but I'd suddenly remembered I wanted to check the pool, it had completely slipped my mind until about half an hour ago," he said. "And I didn't want anything to go wrong while you're here on your own."

My puzzled look gave rise to further explanation.

"With all the rain we've had lately, water's been gushing into the pool like a flowing river. I was a little concerned the banks would not hold the volume even though its pouring out rapidly, I just wanted to make sure, but it seems to be coping well," he said with his hands wrapped round the cup for warmth.

"Has it flooded before then?" I asked.

"Yes, a couple of years ago," he said. "Made an awful mess in the house. When we investigated we found that a build up of leaves and loose bracken just below the water level had narrowed the exit so now when we have a heavy down pour, it's easier to check."

"Much better to be safe than sorry, eh?" I replied.

"Something like that."

"Well, what did she have to say?" asked Jonathan changing the topic of our conversation.

Not wanting to bore him with my waffling I didn't go into detail, in all fairness I should be listening to him, offering what condolence I could.

"Not much really, they have found one print but as yet haven't been able to match it," I said.

"It wasn't that of the girl who was murdered then?" he quizzed.

"They're still checking but it's not confirmed yet. Jennifer said she would let me know how it develops," I replied. "Anyway that's enough on that subject, you should get some sleep, tomorrow will be a busy day."

"Yes, you're right I think I will turn in, good night Carol," he said standing up. I went to kiss him but he turned away, almost with the intent of rejection, I again put it down to the day's events. "Don't you rush out of bed tomorrow either, you sleep on, there's nothing you can do."

"Goodnight Jonathan and safe journey, I'll miss you," I whispered as he disappeared into his room.

I had just washed up the cups when Andrew and Sabrina returned. The evening hadn't been a great success, when they arrived all of the alleys were in use and they'd been double booked with another party who were already playing. This meant they had to sit and wait till fairly late before starting their game. They would have given it a miss but it would have disappointed the others, so they stayed.

I offered to make them some supper but they declined, they were also in need of some rest. I finished the dishes and turned off the lights as I disappeared to my room.

They must have crept around the house the following morning because I never heard them leave, infact I slept until late morning.

CHAPTER 11

This holiday had been hectic from the start, not the peaceful one I had originally anticipated. I'd been places, met people from all classes of society and had even gotten myself involved in the intricate solution of murder but I must admit that up to now it had been exciting and was as yet unfinished. What else was in store, I wondered.

They'd be away in Italy for probably a week or so and I was grateful of the time, I needed to relax and pull my mind back to normality before returning to university.

I intended not to venture out for a while, just laze on the patio, eat, read, watch TV or sleep, an easy plan to follow. Sabrina had asked David to keep a watchful eye on me while they were away, so apart from his telephone call, I saw or spoke to nobody, perfect peace. This time reaped its rewards, amazing what a little pampering can do. I was soon refreshed and ready to get out and about before my self imposed solitary confinement turned to boring loneliness. The weather was still fine but cooler and I decided a walk would provide gentle exercise. I put on some flat shoes and a woolly cardigan before setting off. I had taken a fancy to that stream I had visited with Jonathan, wanting to explore it during daylight hours.

I was in no hurry, strolling along breathing in the fresh air. This was a beautiful area to live, Sabrina and her brothers were very lucky with their parents finding such a place and everybody so friendly, not like most people these days, who don't see or don't care about others.

Pushing through the hedgerow that lined the riverbank, I could hear the water and I was faced with a vastly different picture to last time. All the rain we'd had lately had found its way down to this lower part of the stream and was flowing well, churning up the bottom as it went, making the water heavy with mud and unpenetrable to the eye. Further on the land flattened, here the water was much deeper but less hurried. I ventured near the edge in an attempt to see if any of its natural inhabitants were in residence but the foaming bubbles created by the rush and its murky depth obscured my view. There was something further down the bank nestled in a clump of trees which looked unfamiliar. Choosing my footings carefully, I manoeuvred my way down the sodden bank. I was certainly not prepared for what I was about to discover.

I thought at first I spied a wig floating, there was what appeared to be hair lodged against one of the riverbank trees. I smiled as I bent down to grab this strange, displaced item but once touched, I knew it was more and I felt a cold shiver down my back. A light tug should have dislodged it from its moorings but from the resistance offered, I instinctively knew it was still firmly attached to what I could only assume to be a head .

I ran as fast as I could across the field and down the

road that lead to the police station. I wasn't in top physical condition so by the time I arrived, it took a few minutes for me to catch my breath. I think the officer on duty thought I was the one in need of help but finally I managed to gasp my desire to see sergeant Long. It was a couple of minutes before he appeared and this delay provided the much needed time to revive myself. I garbled to him that I may have found a body and within minutes, I was leading him and four burly, uniformed officers to the point of discovery.

Its retrieval from the watery bed wasn't a delicate operation, big feet had to balance on narrow edges as large hands grasped at any part of the body they could. Once a preliminary hold had been established, the body was rocked from side to side to enable disentanglement from it's watery bonds. With sufficient flesh exposed, a few final grabs hoisted it clear before they released their grip, letting the natural weight slump it gradually to the ground.

They then proceeded to drag the limp body upwards and lay it down on the grassy bank. It was a young woman. As the officers moved apart slightly, it gave me a chance to take a closer look, staring at the contours of her pretty face before raising my eyes towards David. From his look it was clear that he had also recognised this poor creature, it was Angela.

Poor Angela.

She was naked, her hair a dishevelled mess, entwined with debris and her skin had the appearance of being in the bathtub too long. The make-up she'd worn was smudged across her face. As blue eye shadow and pink lipstick intermingled, she looked more like some local tart rather than the baby-faced girl she really was. I didn't need any guesses as to how she'd met her end. There, around her throat, were the same markings I'd seen before, that dark purple necklace of death. Was it a coincidence? As the body was uniformly straightened out, her mouth fell open and I could vaguely see some form of life wriggling inside. After all I'd seen and my experiences of late, it was the first time I'd felt repulsion and the sight before me gave rise to an intense desire to vomit.

I distanced myself from the immediate vicinity, moving further up the bank. The police went to work roping off the area waiting for the police doctor to pronounce the obvious. It took him a while to arrive and minutes to carry out his official duty. Then came the photographer, forensic expert and finally, men scouring the grass, bushes and water's edge for any glimpse of a clue, but they found nothing. Shock must have taken over, I found myself rooted to the spot unable to move as my mind built an invisible barrier of protection. My eyes looked on as if watching the scene of a play, being there, but not taking part.

Once David could do no more and the body was removed, he came over to me and suggested he take me home. When we arrived back at the house, David insisted he sit with me awhile which I was grateful for, my mind was still trying to cope with this tragedy. I poured myself a very large brandy and joined David on the settee. We talked for what seemed hours before I finally reassured him I would be alright and he should get back to his work. As he left, he asked me to come to the station in the morning as they would need an official statement.

Once alone, I sought the relief that tears bring, not those of hurt but of sadness. God, what about poor Andrew? He'd be absolutely devastated. Who was to be the bearer of such unhappy tidings? I couldn't settle, roaming from one room to another, watching the day ebb to night through the large bay window and wishing Jonathan was here to wrap his arms around me and make everything right again.

Although I didn't sleep well that night, I woke the following morning with more peace of mind. I washed, dressed and had some breakfast before walking to the station.

It was all very proper, David and a fellow officer interviewed me making sure every detail was recorded on tape. Something that I may have noticed or seen may mean nothing to me but could be a vital clue to them. Most of the questions posed were simple enough to answer, however, the other officer's inference as to my involvement in the affair angered me. I curtly clarified that my one and only part in this sordid affair was that of an unfortunate person discovering the body of a friend. David could see that this line of questioning was distressing me and brought the interview to a speedy and somewhat abrupt conclusion, much to the disappointment of his colleague. The young man appeared at first as if to push the subject but a quick glance from David, his superior officer, forced him into silence.

Once done, David wanted to make sure I was alright so took an early lunch saying a walk would do both him and me good. I agreed, anyway I wanted to talk about what had happened. I needed to comprehend what had occurred.

The police's first impressions that she was killed near where she'd been found were soon proven wrong when an examination of the soft earthy ground provided no unaccounted for footprints and no unnatural damage to the surrounding plant life or riverbank other than that created by the investigating police. The professionalism of these large, burly creatures was inbred; even though the choice of footage had been limited with regards to the water's edge, each had instinctively used the same virginal passage in and out so as not to obliterate any evidence that may be present.

If she had been murdered or dumped even at that exact point there would be some evidence of a struggle had she put up a fight. The ground was damp and in perfect condition to yield any visible signs of movement. Angela was a buxom lass but blessed with a slender foot, much smaller than my own, and her prints would definitely stand out from those of a man.

No, she had to have met her fate further up stream and her progression downwards had only been stopped by becoming caught up in the roots of the tree that sprouted out below the water line. The medical examiner who'd first examined her body believed that she had not been in the water for more than 10 to 12 hours max., but he would be more precise after he had done the post-mortem.

"Do you think that Angela's death is related to those others?" I asked.

"I don't know," said David. "There's a chance and the fact that she's been strangled makes it more probable."

"Who the hell could have done this, David?"

"If I knew the answer to that, I wouldn't be sitting here," he replied. "The trouble is she liked to play the field, so to speak, and could have attracted unwanted attention."

"What do you mean?" I asked.

"Well, it's not unusual for a jealous lover to kill," he said. "Did you know of any rivalry?"

"Not really, I knew that she and Andrew had a tiff but nothing serious," I replied. "Didn't Sabrina tell you about it?"

"Yes, she did mention something about him disliking the way she teased the other lads. What was the outcome?" asked David.

"It provoked the obvious," I said. "She wasted no time in being seen with as many men as she could, knowing full well the effect it would have on Andrew."

"And did it?"

"Have an effect?" I questioned. "Oh yes, he stomped around the house for days in a bad tempered mood."

"Did they patch it up?" he asked.

"Not as far as I know," I replied. "Maybe when he returned from Italy they may have got back together."

"I need to get back to the station, do you mind if we go?" asked David.

"No, that's fine...don't want to stop you working," I said as we left the pub.

There was no point in discussing it further until the police had done more extensive research, hopelessly trying to piece it all together with absolutely nothing to go on. Our topic of conversation changed during our walk home to general chat, mostly about Sabrina, and when David left me at the foot of the drive, I asked him to let me know of any new developments and suggested it might be worth having a chat with Jennifer.

The next couple of days were quiet, I was happy to stay put hoping that David might call with more news. I relived the events of that tragic morning over and over in the faint hope of remembering something I'd missed, mentally mapping out the time I left the house starting with my decision to take a walk and explore the woodlands on such a beautiful, fresh morning.

I pictured myself picking up the waters edge just below where it exited the pool and following its journey down past the station and into the woodland where the land levelled out slightly, then strolling alongside at a somewhat leisurely pace as it slowly meandered down towards the village in the distance. The trees lined the banks of the stream like an avenue and bushes had sporadically sprung up as they pleased among the grassland. I noticed that the water was much deeper here and stopped every now and then just in case I caught a glimpse of a fish.

I remember questioning Jonathan about the fish that had to find their way into and out of the pool. Apparently, when the hollow was constructed, a fine mesh channel had been provided along the far side that ran parallel with the edge. Any fish that entered the pool were supplied with safe passage along the channel until they swam out the other end. The inside of the mesh had been bonded to a plastic lining thus stopping the plant life entwined on the far side invading into the cleaner water, this filtering also prevented the presence of leaves and twigs. Any poor, isolated fish that did find itself stranded on the wrong side was soon rescued with the aid of a net and set back on its pre-destined route.

My visual recall continued on the journey. Further on, I came across a lump of trunk that had on some past time fallen. A little human intervention found it relocated in a more suitable position, creating an ideal seat where I sat to take in the peace and beauty whilst watching life pass by. Eventually, I continued on my timeless voyage only to shatter my tranquillity with the discovery of Angela's lifeless form.

I tried to think whether I'd noticed or met anybody else but I hadn't, the only life I had encountered up to that point was that of the birds and creatures of the land and I was sure they weren't the purveyors of this death.

My reminiscing was broken by the telephone, it was David asking if he could come round later as he now had the results from the autopsy and thought I might like to know. Of course I wanted to know. I suggested he join me for dinner, only a salad, nothing too involved. He said thanks as it would be a nice change, even during this hot weather his landlady still served up a copious hot meal which he felt bound to eat rather than watch the distress that invaded her face should he not tuck in with full gusto.

He arrived just after six looking hot and bothered. I teased him that if he wasn't shy about being alone with me in the house, he could freshen up in Sabrina's room. He eagerly jumped at this opportunity while I waited on the patio for him to emerge.

I had laid a tray with various items of chunky salad, fruit and cheese alongside assorted dips, warm weather has always made me a lazy eater and being able to pick seemed the easier option.

I left David in peace to stem his hunger only encroaching on the subject of his visit when he slowed the pace of his eating.

The post-mortem had only confirmed what had been visible at the time. She had been in the water for no more than 12 hours and she'd been strangled. There were no other markings about her body to indicate a struggle although there were two or three bruise marks but they were not representative of those normally found on a battered victim, too small and spasmodic, nothing that couldn't have been inflicted during daily life.

The revelation that during the last 24 hours of her life she'd also had intercourse but with no evidence of rape gave rise to familiarity between Angela's death and those of Jane, Sarah and Sammy. The only difference was the state in which the deceased had been abandoned, causing some doubt as to whether the police were in fact looking at victim number four or a coincidence killing.

"Did you manage to speak to Jennifer?" I asked.

"Yes, only for a short while but she managed to give me brief details of the girls she is investigating."

"Do you think there's any connection to those three girls?" I asked.

"Some similarity but that's all, it's possible I suppose," said David. "But this victim was just left, not like the others."

"Hm...maybe," I said unconvinced "The distance I'd walked was only short, did you find anything during your search?"

"No, absolutely nothing, as you know the ground was soft and would have shown any movement but the only footprints found were yours and those of my men," he said shaking his head.

"We just can't fathom out how the killer managed to leave no tracks, the only other possibility is that the deed took place much further up the hill but then the body would have jammed at the inlet of your pool."

"So what now?" I asked.

"Start again, there's got to be something we've missed. I've arranged for a couple of policewomen to do a house to house tomorrow, there's a slim chance somebody saw her or her killer," he replied.

"What about that chap in the silver car, did you check him out?" I asked.

"Him!" David said laughingly. "He turned out to be a salesman for a garden accessories company selling forks and spades. I hoped by pure chance that we'd got a connection but after we pulled him in for questioning he had firm alibis for the time of each murder."

"What was he doing parked up in that lay-by all the time?"

"He was having an affair with one of the ladies in the village so he'd park his car there and cross the field where he could see her house. Her husband was working the night shift and when the coast was clear, she'd put a statuette in the window as a signal it was safe," said David.

"I thought I hadn't seen him or his car lurking about recently," I said.

"I don't think you'll see him again especially after our visit to the woman to collaborate his story," he said. "Her hubby insisted on staying when we spoke to her, poor bloke, knocked him for six when he discovered what his wife got upto during the lonely evenings."

"Oh well, that gets rid of one suspect."

"I am afraid to say this but our main suspect at the moment has to be Andrew. I know he's out of the country now but he wasn't when she was murdered," he said looking across for my reaction. " I've got no choice but to have him picked up immediately he returns next week and I have to ask you not to contact him or divulge any knowledge about this if one of them contacts you."

"Surely you can't suspect Andrew, he wouldn't hurt anybody. Anyway, I know he hasn't seen her since their tiff," I said defensively. "They argued, he told her not to be so childish, she took offence to this remark, stormed off and he hasn't heard from her since," I said.

"But how can you be certain? He could have arranged to see her without anybody knowing."

"Andrew's not like that, he'd leave it for a while and then lure her back, he likes to play the field and give everybody the appearance of disinterest but he really has...sorry, had a thing for her. I was getting worried I'd have to fork out for a new outfit. God knows how he's going to take this news."

"But what if he had met her, they'd argued again and he got angry and killed her?" he asked.

"Use your common sense, if you had just bumped somebody off, would you leave the body so close? You might as well have a neon sign on the top of the house with 'killer lives here' written on it," I said almost laughingly.

"Anyway, he and Sabrina were out bowling till late the night before, if he'd murdered her it would have to have been in the early hours of the morning," I said defensively. "This house is very quite at night, all movement is heard and Jonathan's such a bad sleeper he'd definitely have noticed if anyone tried to sneak out."

"Yes, I understand what you're saying but we have to face facts, I have no choice but to treat him as a suspect."

"Well, if you look at it that way we're all suspects, even me, and I didn't bloody kill her!" I shouted.

"Calm down, Carol, take it easy. I'm not accusing you, anyway, you're not strong enough and your hands aren't large enough," he said. "The pressure applied and the finger span tells us that it's most likely a man."

"Yes, OK," I said still angry at his intimations but his conclusions were logical. "You're right, of course, you must do your duty as they say, let's drop the subject," I suggested, cutting short the discussion. "Would you like a cold beer to wash down your tea?"

"I'd love one."

David didn't stay long after that but promised to pop in tomorrow when they had made a second search of the area.

When I opened the curtains the following morning I could see the police had already started their grisly task further up stream. They must have been at it for some time because they were half way down the hill towards the lane. I made some coffee and sat watching for a while but I didn't see any sudden activity indicative of discovery. The day was cool and the clouds were starting to build, rain was on its way which would not help matters. Suddenly I heard a whistle blown in the distance, they'd found something.

I passed the time watching TV but after a couple of hours of stereotypical programmes designed for mothers, babies and the older generation, I picked one of the many videos that sat on a shelf above the television. I chose a thriller and what a thriller it must have been because I woke up four hours later, the video had rewound and cartoons had taken its place. With that, the telephone rang, it was David, he had mentioned to his landlady that I was alone so she had insisted that I have dinner with them. That suited me as I didn't feel like getting a meal myself. After all, if she was as good a cook as David said, then I was in for a treat.

He introduced his landlady as Mrs Burcott, she was in her 60's, plump but homely. She made me very welcome and we sat at the large farmhouse kitchen table where a meal of shepherds pie and vegetables was served. It was superb, I struggled but managed to finish the lot. Proud of my efforts I sat back. Only then, and much to my distress, did Mrs Burcott whisk out of the fridge an enormous trifle. I didn't want to offend her so accepted a tiny portion. I offered to help with the dishes but she said no and insisted that David and I go through to her parlour and she would fetch us some tea while she busied herself in the kitchen.

"You found something today, didn't you?" I said. "I heard the police whistle earlier so I knew something was going on."

"Actually, it was an old trainer. It gave us a few minutes of excitement before we realised that it could only fit a child's foot and had obviously been there for some time, green mould had grown over it," he said. "Apart from that there was nothing above or below the house, no footprints or distinctive markings, I can tell you we're really stumped. How can a body just appear with no signs of its arrival? I just hope the house to house we're carrying out will come up with something," he replied in a dejected tone.

"I wish I had seen something, I feel I should be able to help but I can't, there was just nothing except her."

We finished our tea and I thanked Mrs Burcott for dinner, complimented her on her cooking and suggesting I might come and gather a few tips at a later date. I had obviously pleased her as she was most adamant that I visit again. With that David walked me home.

CHAPTER 12

Nothing much occurred over the next couple of days except I had one of those summer colds making me feel poorly so I retired to my bed, I've never worked out yet how people manage to catch colds in summer. I surrounded myself with magazines, drinks and a never ending supply of tissues but I soon became bored as my self pity diminished and I started to feel better, once again my mind wandered back to Angela. How on earth could she have ended up in the water if she'd not entered via the riverbank? I fixed in my mind a vision of its course from the top of the hill down to the pool and then on down where I had walked.

The sudden bitter coldness of realisation numbed, like the penetration of cold steel unexpectedly thrust into the warmth of human flesh, blotting out every thought except its damaging presence. The solution was simplicity itself. I don't know why it had taken so long to realise, I lay back seeking the motherly comfort of my pillows as the shock of this potential discovery took effect. How had the police missed what now manifested itself so clearly? If her body hadn't entered the water from any natural bank then there was only one feasible place left, the pool. If it were true then David could be right, Andrew may have killed her. What a ghastly thought, but I couldn't possibly see how he had the opportunity.

I jumped out of bed and telephoned David.

"Can you come over straight away?" I said in a tense nervous voice.

"What is it Carol, are you alright?"

"Yes...Yes just get here!" I said.

He must have run, no sooner had I replaced the receiver than he was banging on the front door.

"What's the matter Carol, what's happened?" he asked.

"Sit down David, I think I've sussed it."

"Have you found something?" he said excitedly.

"No, nothing material, but I have thought and thought about it and the only logical alternative I can come up with is: if Angela's body didn't enter up stream or down, the only logical place left is the pool," I said looking for his reaction.

He sat silently for a moment. "Christ, you could be right but we'd dismissed it as getting through the barricades of this house would take inside knowledge of the grounds and the ability to break in without it being noticed," he said.

"Who has access to the house?" he asked.

"As far as I know, I am the only person outside the family to have keys to the house and gates which are always kept locked," I replied.

"But could somebody somehow have got in, dumped her body in the pool and left without your knowledge?"

"I suppose it's possible but as I said before, it's so quiet we would have to have heard them, especially breaking open the gates, they're heavy enough to move when unlocked. And if someone was just dumping her body, one of us would have to have seen her in the pool especially with her natural buoyancy aids," I said.

"We've had some heavy downfalls lately, could her body have been carried in the swell and fallen over the edge?" asked David. "Maybe that's what the killer intended."

"That would mean knowing the place extremely well. Anyway I'm sure the exit would still be too narrow for a body to slip through, somebody would have had to give her a helping hand and that would mean getting in the water..." Frozen shivers invaded my body as the second stab of cold steel struck leaving me momentarily paralysed, unable to speak as those once vivid images of that tragic night now crowded my mind again with crystal clarity.

"It couldn't be..." I muttered under my breath.

"What have you remembered?" asked David .

"Well, the evening before, as you know, I had been to visit Jennifer. Andrew and Sabrina had gone bowling and were late returning. Jonathan had been out during the day but I don't know what time he actually got back, it couldn't have been that late though," I said trying to follow the thread closely. "I came in just before midnight. As I crossed the patio, I fumbled with my keys as normal trying to find the right one to unlock the front door when I was suddenly confronted by Jonathan, naked and dripping wet. I must say he did give me a fright."

"Go on," David said coaxingly.

"As I said, he was naked but he did like to swim with nothing on when alone. I thought it a little chilly to take a dip so late but the excuse he gave seemed quite reasonable. He said he was concerned that the banks of the pool would not hold the excess water and was checking them."

"Was he scratched or bleeding?"

"Don't know, but he was definitely cold. I could see him shivering, so he dried himself quickly and put on a robe. The house was dimly lit so unless he was badly hurt, I wouldn't have noticed," I said.

"Did he seem different in any way?" asked David.

"A little withdrawn perhaps but that could have been due to tiredness plus the shock of his grandmother's death."

"I need to go to the station to fetch some papers. Does Jonathan keep a diary?" he asked. "Also, I'd like to ring Jennifer, I think she should be in on this as well."

"Yes, I'll look but normally he carries his diary, " I answered. "Here's Jennifer's mobile number if she's not at the office."

"Would you mind taking a look around just incase? I won't be long," said David as he disappeared out the door.

If Jonathan had left his diary, it could be anywhere. I had a quick scour of the living room and dining area before trying his bedroom. I didn't feel very comfortable about rummaging through his personal things but this was a serious matter and something in his diary may help. I was just about to give up when I noticed his briefcase tucked away behind a chair in the corner.

I picked it up and laid it across the arms. It had one of those combination locks. As I pushed the levers I was convinced it would be locked but to my surprise they both popped open, what a stroke of luck. Inside were various documents which I tried not to disturb as I carefully filtered through. There at the bottom of the pile was his diary. After its removal I closed the case and returned to the living room where I waited for David to return.

I made some coffee and watched TV trying to pass the time but it was just noise in the background, I wasn't paying any interest to what was on. He was taking his time, perhaps he'd got involved in something else.

When eventually he did return he had Jennifer in tow. They both came with an armful of papers, these were all the available case notes relating to the dead girls Jennifer was currently investigating. It was apparent now that they were hoping for a link and maybe there was sufficient information to make some kind of match.

I silently perched myself on the edge of the sofa whilst they furiously but systematically scanned every piece of paper; they were most interested in dates and times as each entry in Jonathan's diary was scrutinized.

The pattern evolving from exhausting cross-referencing showed he'd been in close proximity at the time of all but one of the murders. Not only that but also on occasions just before. I was astounded by Jennifer and David's behaviour as they crawled around the floor from one paper to the next, it was reminiscent of a pack of hounds jostling around a newly discovered fox hole.

Finally they sat back gathering each file together, closing it and piling them to one side.

"Well, it could be him," said David.

"Yes," replied Jennifer. "But what about Sarah McDonald, he couldn't have killed her."

"Why's that?" I asked.

"Don't you remember?" she said. "You were all together in Scotland at the time."

"He wasn't with us all the time," I spoke quietly not wanting to reveal such information.

"What do you mean?" asked Jennifer.

"The night Sarah died Jonathan was supposedly staying at a motel. He'd been to see a client and had rang through to say he wouldn't be back until the following morning."

"Do you know where he went?"

"Haven't a clue and I hadn't really been interested enough to ask," I replied. "Wasn't there anything in his diary?"

"No, nothing," said David. "But your trip was for pleasure not business, he probably left it at home."

"So that's it then," I suddenly spurted out, almost arrogantly, "Jonathan's your man."

"Don't be in such a hurry, we have only established he is a suspect," said David.

"Oh, so you're not sure then?" I asked.

"Without some proof to link him, he just joins the ranks of others out there that could have had equal opportunity," replied Jennifer.

"What about the fingerprint?"

"Not good enough," said Jennifer, "there's not enough to use in court, a lawyer would dismiss that idea immediately. But we will take a sample of Jonathan's prints before we leave. If the bit we have got doesn't match, it will at least help one way or the other."

"I see, so this was just an exercise was it?" I said.

"No, Carol, we take this matter very seriously," said David. "What's got into you? After all the interest you've shown over the past months, I find your change of attitude strange."

"Sorry, it's just that I don't like scheming behind people's backs," I replied turning away so as not to show the first furtive signs of my discontent at being involved in this sordid affair.

"We're only after the truth, nothing more. I know you're very fond of Jonathan and I'd rather it not be him either. It affects my relationship with Sabrina as well, remember, so if I can clear him from this mess I will, OK?" said David in an assuring voice.

"I'll have them re-check the hire companies again in more detail for that yellow sticker and see if they can provide us with a list of names and addresses of all those hiring a black saloon style car around about the time Jane Downing was murdered," said Jennifer.

"Have you been to see Angela's body?" I asked Jennifer.

"Yes," was her short reply.

"Would you say the killer was the same person?"

My second question was met with an awkward silence. At first, I genuinely thought she'd not heard, but her reluctance to reply or maintain eye contact supplied me with the answer.

"In my opinion and it is only my opinion, the answer has to be yes," she replied.

"So, how do you proceed from here?" I said.

"We'll wait for the results from the lab on the prints and from the hire companies. Once we have those we can decide how to proceed, alright?" she said.

I just nodded, overcome by the sadness that seemed to well up from the very depths of my body fuelled partly by pity and partly anger, my sub-conscience repeating the same question, why him? He seemed too nice to do such a thing but, I know people are not always predictable, history has proven that.

"I'll arrange to send somebody along to do the necessary," said Jennifer. "Don't fret I'm sure it's not him," she said attempting to sound convincing but it hadn't worked and both she and I knew it.

When they had gone I just sat and cried, cuddling a cushion as a child would hold a teddy bear for comfort. I was unable to pacify myself, moping around the house for the rest of that day in my pyjamas. Finally reading in bed, I hoped I'd tire myself enough to sleep. In that at least I was successful.

The following morning a man appeared at the door, suitcase in hand. He needed no words of introduction. I just let him in and showed him to Jonathan's bedroom. After he'd finished, I took a cloth and polish ensuring I cleaned every inch of exposed surface removing all traces of the stranger's presence. There was no way I wanted Jonathan returning to inches of white dust, a major giveaway of my deception. With my deed nearly done, I made sure his diary was replaced exactly where I had taken it from, recalling the precise position where his briefcase had stood, matching it identically to the impression it'd left in the carpet.

Unable to relax I continued to busy myself deciding to give the rest of the house the same treatment, polishing and scrubbing my frustrations away. I had just finished washing the kitchen floor when I heard the doorbell. A momentary glance at my watch told me how late it was. As I opened the door, the solemn look on David and Jennifer's faces told me the news was not good.

The results had been quick in coming back, the section of print they had had matched perfectly with that taken from the house and on comparing the two, I could not deny this damning fact. The police had successfully discovered the hire company who used the infamous yellow sticker and immediately gained access to the company's records. Jennifer produced a faxed copy from her briefcase and showed it to me. There, in black and white, was Jonathan's name and home address on a hire contract for a large BMW car a couple of days before Jane was murdered.

"This evidence makes our case against Jonathan very strong Carol, and we must pursue it," said Jennifer in her calm but firm voice. "Do you understand?"

"Yes, I understand perfectly," I replied.

"We need to do this carefully though. If it is Jonathan we don't want to frighten him off or let him know we suspect him before we can gather enough to charge him. If it's not him then we would rather he never knew of our investigations and leave individual friendships intact," she said. Her quick glance at David showed signs of her concern for him too. He, in return, just smiled.

"How are you going to prove it?" I asked.

"Basically, we need a confession," said David looking directly at me with a hardened shell-like face.

I studied the two strangers that now stood before me. They'd got scent of a possible catch and nothing would deter them from chasing it. It's true what they say, you have to be bred of the right attitude to succeed as a policeman or woman, capable of suppressing all feelings of compassion, no matter how closely it impedes into your personal space. I wasn't sure whether I envied their strength and dedication or reviled for what they'd become; whichever, my opinions would have no bearing on what may happen. I reasserted the defensive stance I'd portrayed previously.

"Oh yes, I can hear it now. 'Jonathan would you mind telling us, did you kill these women? You didn't, oh good, just forget we ever mentioned the matter then, alright?'" I said. "How do you think that sounds, because apart from an outright confrontation, I can't see any other way you could achieve it," I said almost mocking their suggestion.

"Don't be stupid Carol, you know that's not what we mean," said David.

"Well, explain it to me then, I'm sure I'll find it quite informative," I replied.

Whatever devious plan they may concoct would almost certainly involve me. Nobody else outside of blood kin would get close enough to penetrate any barriers that may arise, but I wasn't going to make their task any easier.

"We thought you might help us," said Jennifer. Now how did I know what she was going to say?

"In what way?" I asked giving the impression of willingness to become a player in their game.

"Maybe you could chat to him about things, he knows you like him and wouldn't suspect you," suggested Jennifer.

"Just chat eh...what about this one then? 'Oh

Jonathan, the police suspect someone at this house murdered Angela, you didn't happen to leave her body lying around anywhere?'" I said. I knew I shouldn't spurt out these stupid and totally irresponsible comments but I just couldn't stop myself.

"You're being silly now," she said. "This is not the sort of reaction I expected from you, Carol."

"What sort would you like?"

"A sensible, adult response would have been sufficient," she said.

"Right now I don't feel that way," I replied. "It's unfair of you to put me in this position."

"I wouldn't have asked if I didn't know you so well. You've always been so definite in your judgement that people who hurt others should be caught and punished but it would seem your views have changed, maybe we should forget it. I think David and I should go now," said Jennifer turning towards the door.

She'd struck a cord. She was right, I was running away from the truth, not wanting to get hurt, hoping it would all vanish but this was the real world and things had to be faced up to despite the consequences. My spurious replies ceased and were replaced by a somewhat submissive silence.

"What if it had been your sister lying in the morgue, would you feel different about it then?" Jennifer's final words were well chosen. "If you change your mind call, will you?"

"Yes," was the only answer I gave.

David had the final say. "Remember, if any of them call you mustn't mention anything about this to them, do you understand?" I reluctantly nodded my agreement.

Funny, the enthusiasm to clean had ebbed and died. I poured myself a rather large scotch and stood staring out of the window at the setting sun as it dipped below the trees. The telephone disturbed my admiration of such a natural delight. It was Jonathan. This was to be my first test.

He had just phoned to check everything was alright and to let me know the funeral was the next day. He said that the house was full of close and distant family. He must have detected my despondent mood because he asked if anything was wrong. I made an excuse of feeling lonely, missing his company. He, in turn, promised to make it up when he came back by taking me to one of his favourite restaurants. After a few minutes of general conversation he rang off.

I took a deep breath, poured myself another large drink and returned to my position at the window. The sun was now a final sliver of light on the horizon and the black branches of the trees pointed like crooked fingers to the heavens against the rusty sky. My mind was battling with itself for the right answer, morality doing battle with emotion. Jennifer was right, of course, it would be different if it was my own flesh and blood that had been snatched away.

If a loving relationship was ever to flourish between Jonathan and I, it would have to have solid foundations, any rifts could allow our union to be marred and the doubts I now had could create those first but unnoticeable cracks. Was it possible to override the discipline that had been entrenched since the age of understanding? Maybe I could suppress it for a while but sooner or later it would consume me and then it would be too late to change my mind. In this short space of time it was clear that I had no real choice other than to seek the truth, no matter what. I knew that I could accept no less. I poured myself yet another drink before picking up the phone. Jennifer was quick to answer, perhaps she knew me better than I knew myself, she'd obviously been waiting for my call.

"Hello, Jennifer," I said.

"Hello, Carol. Are you alright?" she asked with a minimum of concern in her voice.

"As well as I can be, I've decided to help, if you still want me to," I told her.

"Oh course I do, but only if that's what you really want," she replied.

"I must."

She must have noticed a slur in my voice. "It sounds as if you've been drinking," said Jennifer.

"Just a couple, that's all," I told her.

"You're not agreeing under the influence of alcohol are you, how many have you had?" she asked.

"Not enough to fall over but sufficient to numb," I replied.

"What made you change your mind?"

"Why ask, you knew bloody well I would," I said.

"I'll come and see you tomorrow. I'll ask David to make provisions for a room to be available so we can talk, alright?" she said.

"Fine, whatever, not too early though, say midday?" I suggested.

"That suits me. I'll see you then. Oh, don't have too many more will you?"

"No, I'll be good, see you tomorrow. Goodnight," I replied putting down the receiver.

No, I wouldn't have too many but just one more should do the trick. This ultimate comforter I took to bed but I never finished it, it was still there when I awoke the following day with a headache.

It was a good job I had suggested such a late hour for our meeting. I needed some time to recover but it was nothing a shower, hot coffee and food wouldn't cure.

My somewhat slower than normal stroll to the station was pleasant and the fresh air cleared away what cobwebs were left. The constable on the desk had been notified of my arrival and he ushered me into a side room where I waited, my only company being a plastic cup of coffee, readily supplied.

CHAPTER 13

Jennifer was punctual as normal, David had also joined us. Clearly they had worked hard since our last meeting face to face planning various methods of snaring a potential culprit. All but one had been dismissed as feasibly impossible, leaving the main and favoured version which included me and my anticipated co-operation.

I listened while they explained their ideas with a strong sense of enthusiasm, admittedly the course they had decided to follow sounded the only possible one to take; using me to try and milk some kind of confession from him, not an easy matter but one that needed undertaking. When the session was over Jennifer instantly changed, her once serious tone now light hearted as she suggested we go for some lunch at the local. Jennifer was about to throw the invitation open to David but he'd perceived the notion and his comments of pressures of work were sufficient to be accepted as a genuine excuse. Personally, I felt he'd rather leave us two alone for a while.

We sat at a far table in the corner of the pub that was

subtly positioned for privacy. I knew that sooner rather than later, Jennifer would once again broach the subject of our meeting. I didn't have to wait long.

"Are you sure you still want to go through with this? You don't have to you know," asked Jennifer. "We could find other ways to catch him."

"Oh yes, which ways are those then?" I said with a slight sneer in my voice. "You admitted yourself you've no evidence against him."

"None, but we would keep digging, eventually something would surface," said Jennifer giving me yet another chance to back out, but the overtones of her voice emitted different signals.

"Are you nervous?" she asked, but she'd decided to answer her own question. "Stupid question really, there would be something wrong if you weren't," she said.

"Petrified I think would be a more apt description."

"I know I've helped set up this type of operation before but I've always been distant from the people involved, no personal feelings to hinder...oh, it's not very easy to get across what I want to say," she hesitated for a moment. "...It's like the scene of a fatal accident, they're just another statistic, don't get me wrong, there's a certain amount of auto-reactive emotion but when you look down and it's a face you know, a colleague, friend or even a relative it completely changes your vision. The death then becomes personal leaving you unable to deal with the situation in a logical manner, am I making sense?" said Jennifer.

"Yes I think so," I said. I knew exactly what she meant and it was a while before either of us spoke again.

"I love him, you know," I said quietly, sounding almost matter of fact.

"Oh God, Carol," replied Jennifer with a huge sigh. "I knew you were very fond of him but I hadn't realised it was that serious, why didn't you tell me before?

"Love has strange ways of manifesting itself, my feelings have only intensified over the last few days with just the thought of him being taken from me and it hurts," I said. "I love him and whatever the outcome I'll lose him." I looked down towards the table as the tears welled in my eyes, I knew it was too late for emotion to rear its head, I had made my choice. Jennifer took her time before speaking again.

"If you feel so much for this man and he's not the person we're looking for, why jeopardise any future you may have with him? Of course this changes everything." Once again she was unlocking the door for my escape.

"But what if he is a killer, how can I continue to love a man I don't trust?"

"People have lived together for years thinking they know and trust each other only to discover they're rapists, molesters, wife beaters or even worse," said Jennifer.

"Yes I know, but up until the point of discovery they had probably never been given cause to suspect or even doubt but I do, I would always be watching over my shoulder incase I was the next victim," I said raising my voice slightly. "No, I've made my mind up, I must do this, I must know."

At that moment, as if to create a natural distraction, lunch headed towards us carried by a large lady whose hurried, red-faced pace signalled that the kitchen was hot and extremely busy.

We both struggled to keep the topic of conversation on other themes while we ate and Jennifer made no further mention of the matter until she dropped me home but I could tell by the relief on her face that my decision to continue had pleased her.

"I'll see you tomorrow afternoon then," said Jennifer. "We can go over the details again and answer any questions you may have thought of."

"Alright," I said trying to sound cheerful.

"And don't worry, it'll all go like clockwork, you'll see," said Jennifer as I shut the car door.

She had only driven a few yards when she halted the car and jumped out calling towards me. "I almost forgot to ask," she shouted. "Have you spoken to any of them yet?"

I couldn't deny it. "Yes, Jonathan rang last night." I saw the distress on her face that my positive answer caused.

"Don't worry, I didn't say anything," I said. Her visible relief was expressed in a huge sigh and her body seemed to shrink as the air was forcibly expelled from her lungs.

"Did he say when they'd be back?" she asked. "Only I want to make sure we keep a watchful eye on them."

"No, he wasn't sure when they'd be home, I expect it would depend on how things went," I replied.

"Can you let me know if you find out?"

"Yes OK," I shouted as she climbed back into her car.

I waved to her as she drove away then turned back to look up at the house. It no longer looked the same as when I first set eyes upon it, now it's sight chilled me. Distrust, falsehoods and death shrouded its beauty.

I grabbed a drink and stretched out on the sofa

listening to some music. Suddenly the door burst open and the three of them trotted in, an unexpected return.

"Hi, we're back," shouted Sabrina. Obviously. "Did you miss us?" she asked.

"Tremendously," I said.

Sabrina went on to explain that after the funeral, mother wanted to get rid of her many house guests and return to a quiet and peaceful existence. They would have stayed longer but mother had insisted she could manage and they should leave. Luckily, they'd got a flight home mid-afternoon and everything was arranged so quickly there was no time to ring.

In one way I was pleased to see them, in another wishing they had stayed away. I disappeared into the bedroom to ring the station without their knowledge. Hopefully I would be in time to catch Jennifer before she left for London or if not, at least David would be around. Someone had to tell them and I didn't feel it was my place. I thought the devastating news should come from the police, more official, and I wasn't sure how they would all react to their home being a potential murder scene, especially Andrew.

"They're back already?" said David.

"Yes, just arrived out of the blue," I replied, almost whispering in case one of them was in ear shot. "What shall I do?...I think you should come over."

"I'll be there, just keep calm and for God sake don't say anything OK?"

I returned to the lounge. Luckily, they were busy milling around shuttling suitcases to bedrooms and filtering through the mound of mail that had launched through the letterbox since their departure.

I slipped unnoticed into the kitchen in the guise of putting the kettle on, not attempting to get involved in any conversation until David arrived. Luckily, I didn't have to hold out too long, he was there in minutes, even before I'd made some tea. It's supposed to be good for shock and that's what they were about to receive.

Sabrina greeted him with a huge hug and a wide smile but he pulled her away much to her puzzlement, he then asked them to sit down. At first there was silence as David, in the usual Yard manner, explained about Angela. I poured and handed them a large brandy which each numbly accepted and gulped. When the news had sunk in then came the questions which he attempted to answer. I, by now, had retreated once more to the kitchen. David must have decided it best to leave them for a few moments and joined me. I wanted out of the house for a while and made an excuse that I needed to get some milk due to their sudden return, so would walk to the local shop.

I took my time, cowardly really, not wanting to rush back to sorrow and I hoped by the time I eventually returned any major reactions would have reared and calmed slightly.

I walked up the drive and entered the gate. Andrew was sitting out on the patio, his face devoid of expression, just staring into space.

"Are you alright, Andrew?" I asked.

He suddenly snapped back to reality, "What...yes I'm OK. I didn't hear you come in," he replied.

"Has David gone?" I asked.

"Yes, a short while ago."

I know he played down his affections about Angela

to others but I knew deep down he had loved her. The news of her death had come as a big blow to him and he was struggling to try and come to terms with the brutality of her departure. Loss is hard to cope with even under normal circumstances even when its your own loved one's mind and body that ceases being of this world. He needed to talk to somebody, anybody to relieve some of the pain he was feeling, maybe if we walked he might just talk to me.

"It's a nice afternoon, how about a stroll?" I asked.

"No, I don't really feel like it," he mumbled.

"Come on, it'll help. I'll just pop this milk in the fridge," I said coaxingly.

"Oh alright then, I'll slip some sandals on," he said dragging himself out of the patio chair like an old man.

We took the lanes down to the village below. I spent most of the time talking about anything; the trees, flowers, bushes, just something to break the gloomy spell that had besieged his mind. He, on the other hand, said very little but politely acknowledged my ramblings from time to time. We stopped in the village at the tea shop for a cup of coffee before continuing our walk.

"Which way shall we go now?" I asked him.

He said nothing for a moment, then, "Would you take me to where you found her?"

"Yes, if you really want to go, but do you think it's a good idea?" I said trying to discourage his request.

"Please Carol, I think it would help me to deal with this," he pleaded.

We headed out of the village across the fields to finally meet the stream as it flowed down the hill. It was a steady climb through the woodland which became more dense the higher we went. As we approached the spot, the grass was churned up, evidence of the many large police boots that had recently trodden over it and the foliage showed signs of damage inflicted by bodies that had waded through in search of that vital clue.

"There," I said quietly, pointing to the tree at the water's edge, "she was by that tree."

He moved forward and crouched down letting his hand feel the water as it flowed through his fingers. He stared into its depths as though peering at a crystal ball seeking an answer to his questions. I waited silently for him to retrieve whatever he felt he might find. Eventually he stood up and started to walk on, I followed a couple of steps behind. As we carried on up the hill, we came across the tree stump I had found before. I made an excuse of feeling a little weary and asked if he minded if we stopped for a while and sat down.

I slipped off my shoes as my feet were hot. I gently massaged them, attempting to attain some relief whilst continuing to chatter. This was only broken when Andrew suddenly muttered, "Why?"

"Why what?" I said quietly.

"Why did it have to be her?" his voice slightly shaky.

"I don't know. It's a question people repeatedly ask, why?" I wanted him to talk but not look to me for answers I was unable to provide.

He hung his head down, his hair falling over his face but it was unable to conceal the tears that were running down his cheeks. When women cry it's acceptable for them to receive that arm of comfort but for men, I don't know, I had never seen a man cry before. Natural reaction urged me to hug him, to share his pain but I didn't want to threaten his male standing.

I sat for a while contemplating what was best before gently slipping an arm around his shoulder. He came to me, he turned and put his arms out looking for consolation like a child who falls and grazes his knees looks for his mother's enveloping arms to make it better. This expression of grief would help to give him the relief he needed and I would be there for as long as he wanted. It seemed ages before he finally pulled away, fumbling for his handkerchief to wipe his tears. His face seemed less tense, relaxed even.

"I'm sorry about that," he said.

"That's alright," I said reassuring him. "We must all grieve in our own way."

"I know, but it's not the done thing for grown men to cry."

"Everybody cries at some time in their lifes, it's a natural emotion much needed for our sanity," I said, hoping to make him feel more at ease.

"I was very much in love with Angela, you know, although I never told anyone, not even her and now I wish I had."

"I think most of us realised but were waiting for you to make known your feelings," I said.

"I feel so angry with myself, I keep thinking if I hadn't argued with her she would never have gone off and if I had patched it up quicker she would still be with me now. Instead I pushed her away and paved the way for someone to snatch her from me," he said, his voice now stronger.

"It happened and you can't change it, so you'll have to learn to accept what will be." I tried to crush the guilt he had imposed upon himself.

"I wish I knew who did this to her, I'd rip him apart," his voice expressed anger. "The police are useless, they should have found this maniac by now."

"That's not fair Andrew, the police are doing their best but with so very little to work on it's very difficult for them," I said.

"I know...I know..." The change in his voice signalled the trouble he had controlling the deep anger that was rising from within. "You would tell me if they suspected anyone wouldn't you, I mean, if your friend Jennifer told you?" he asked. I felt awkward, I knew who they suspected but was unable to give him the hope he so desperately seeked.

"I don't think she would tell me, well, not until they had him under lock and key with a cast iron case against him. She would break all the rules divulging that kind of information to anyone outside the investigation," I said.

"Yes, it was unfair of me to ask, let's forget it alright?" his voice now sounded more normal.

"I'm feeling better now, shall we continue?" I said.

By the time we got back, Sabrina was making some dinner and Jonathan was taking a quick shower. I was glad when Sabrina told me David had agreed to return for dinner. I felt a little uneasy not knowing what to say and his presence would aid the situation slightly. He must have followed us up the drive because it was only moments before he entered. I gave him a wary glance before disappearing to my room. How on earth could he be so laid back? He was here in this house laughing and joking with a girl whom he'd admitted strong affection for and a man who he was convinced was a killer, his ability to hide or ignore his feelings was quite unique.

I, on the other hand, felt like a spy. These people trusted me, invited me into their home and made me welcome while all the time I was watching and waiting to betray them. What would happen to my friendship with Sabrina? Her feelings towards me would change, inevitable really whatever the outcome. I could just hear her introducing me as either, 'oh this is Carol by the way, the woman who helped put my brother behind bars' or ' this is Carol, she tried to frame my brother for a crime he didn't commit'. What a choice. The trouble was that due to my eagerness to become involved, I was now in too deep to back out. I had no option but to see it through to the end no matter what.

Unfortunately, David was in the same situation as me. He was involved with a girl he stood to lose because of the demands his job thrust upon him to do whatever necessary to get their man.

Life plays nasty tricks on people, Jonathan had or was about to ruin four people's lives apart from his own. Andrew had already lost the love of his life, Sabrina would reject David and her best friend through hatred of their deceit. My punishment for taking part would be the sacrificial deliverance of the only man I'd ever loved and finally, Jonathan would lose not only his freedom but his brilliant future.

After dinner I felt a little hot and bothered. I wanted to take a shower and relax on my bed to watch TV, I just couldn't sit there with them in the same room knowing what I was about to do. I'm sure if I'd stayed I would definitely have reversed my decision to help

Jennifer. I lay on the bed with just a thin cotton night-dress on, I had opened the windows and a gentle breeze was airing the room. As you can imagine, I didn't sleep much that night, my eyelids threatened to close with heaviness but my mind was over-active, refusing to let me sink into depths of silent slumber. I must have eventually dozed off because the last time I looked at the clock it was three fifteen and now it read seven twenty.

Sabrina had managed to wangle some extra allowance from her father while away and was eager to spend it. She wanted me to go shopping with her but I made some excuse about visiting Mrs Burcott, David's landlady, saying I'd promised to visit her to collect some recipes she thought I might like. It would be a better idea to persuade Andrew to go with her, he was so down that a change of scenery might help cheer him up. Sabrina quietly suggested to Jonathan that they could all go for the day and seeing as he had to collect some important documents from his office, the trip would be an advantage to them all. He was happy to join them but insisted he be back early for our very important dinner date.

During my stay at the house, Sabrina and her brothers had spent more and more time away from me, leaving me alone. She felt unhappy about inviting me and not being with me all the time. I assured her that I was enjoying my stay immensely and it was good for us to do our own thing. I had been to stay with Jennifer and we'd had that wonderful week in Saudi so I had been away as much as she and the others.

This was going to be the most difficult day of my life and the more time spent alone the better it would be for me. I did make that visit to Mrs Burcott who made some tea and wouldn't let me leave until I had consumed a large slice of her famous cherry cake. It was nice but I didn't feel very hungry, the nerves in my stomach had been fluttering all day killing my desire for food.

I spent about an hour with her but only in body, my mind was focused on the evening to come and its eventual outcome. I couldn't face just sitting around the house for the rest of the day so I walked, finally returning to the spot where I discovered Angela's body hoping to draw strength, even inspiration, to do what was needed. I must have walked for hours because it was already late afternoon. I had to make one more stop before returning home, that was at the station.

Jennifer was waiting for me when I arrived and she quickly ushered me into a side room out of the view of any locals that might know me. She didn't want anyone or anything to jeopardise the outcome of their finely balanced plan.

"You know we'd discussed strapping a microphone to your body, well we've discussed it again and decided it might not be the best approach," said Jennifer.

"What do you mean?"

"Well, we must take into account that he may touch or hold you. The restaurant he is taking you to is very plush, they have entertainment and a floor is laid on the lawn for people to dance on," explained Jennifer, "you might be wary about letting him too close and we want you to be able to react to any of his advances naturally."

Here I was, about to trap and betray the only man I'd ever contemplated spending the rest of my days with and she thinks I'll be acting normal. Christ I'm not a machine. What about my feelings? I sat for a moment crushing this, wanting to put an end to the whole saga now. I just had to keep picturing in my mind those poor dead creatures knowing that I was probably the only person able to get close enough to catch the man who'd wantonly and heartlessly despatched them from this earth.

"What alternative have you come up with?" I said, pulling my mind back to the present time.

"We can fit a microphone into a bag. I have brought one from home, it's just a small clutch type which you can carry around with you," she said. "It's black in colour so it will go with any outfit you decide to wear and is small enough to be inconspicuous."

She produced a little velvet covered bundle, "What do you think?"

"Fine," I said in a quiet voice. "Any way you want to play it, it's your game, you can make the rules."

"Good, I've had a microphone fitted already and had it tested out, as long as you don't move further than six foot away we will be able to hear every word you say."

The tone of her voice was different to that of normal, it was calm, logical and without feeling. Police life had given her the ability to create an invisible barrier that halted the invasion of any emotion interfering with the ultimate goal. I also needed to summon up this barrier to protect my sanity through this ordeal, allowing me to emerge without too many scars. I took a deep breath and looked across at Jennifer, mirroring her look, stern face meeting stern face, cold eyes reflecting into cold eyes.

"Is there anything else I need to know?" I asked.

"No, everything's set, the rest is up to you. You know how important tonight is, this could be our only chance to trap him," she said. "But...if anything, anything goes wrong, we will halt the operation immediately, we must not mar any chance we may have to try again."

"What should I do then if something's wrong?" I asked.

"Just say something out of context to your conversation that we could take as a signal," said Jennifer.

"Like what?"

"Eh...tell him you are thinking of changing the colour of your hair," she suggested. "Then go to the ladies room where I'll meet you and we can decide how to proceed."

"Alright," I agreed.

"There's nothing more then, just remember to keep calm, stay sharp and we will all come out of this in one piece and with the right result."

What, she might come out with what she wants but me, I could only lose, I thought.

"Oh Carol, do you know what the other two plan to do tonight?" she asked.

"Not sure, staying in probably, they haven't mentioned anything," I replied.

"Good, I'll have a police officer watch the house, just in case," she replied.

As I was leaving I met David who said he'd been in a meeting with the other officers involved in that evening's little escapade.

"Good luck, love, for tonight," he said and I knew I'd need every bit.

Just for one moment, I wanted to scream, letting the world know the hurt and anger I was feeling about the personal sacrifice I was about to make. My dearly held morals meant I had to do it but would I be able to face the possibility that he wasn't, infact, the murderer? I should have tried harder to stem the tears that were now running down my face but I couldn't, I was crying for me.

"Let me walk with you for a while," he said.

"Whatever," I replied as we left.

"You are doing the right thing, you know," said David.

"So everybody keeps telling me," I replied sarcastically. "Anyway, I don't know why you're so eager."

"Sabrina, you mean?" he said. "It's a chance I must take, this job calls for commitment and sometimes that means losing what you most want but I knew that when I joined the force."

"So what's my excuse?" I asked in an agitated tone. "Why should I be asked for that type of commitment, life's so unfair."

"I know how you feel."

"No you don't!" I shouted. "You haven't any idea of my feelings, you're not the betrayer, you've got an excuse for your part in all this, it's your job after all, isn't it!"

David could feel and see the anger that was being emitted with my every move and word. He was good, very good at his job and he knew he would have to calm me down if we were to succeed. There was an entrance through the hedgerow into a grassed area and he suggested we sit and relax for a while. He was obviously hoping if he talked to me long enough I would cool off and take control of myself again. We crossed the field to where a couple of trees stood. We sat down using their heavy leafed branches as shade from the full rays of the strong sun.

I sat for a while just staring across the field, the next time I spoke, I was more relaxed.

"A fine pair we are, aren't we?" I said. "Both sitting here facing the prospects of loosing what we most cherish and both trying to convince ourselves that we're doing what's right, we must want our bloody heads examined."

"I know how much you love Jonathan but could you face life not knowing if he was a killer?" said David, "I know that Sabrina will hate me for trying to snare her brother, that's only natural, we all protect our own when danger threatens," he said.

"Yes but at least you have that spark of hope that eventually she may forgive you. As I said, it's your job but mine's a lifetime sentence, a lost cause whatever the outcome."

"You can back out, say now and it's over, forgotten," he said.

"But you won't give up will you? You'll keep hounding and hounding until you find some scrap of evidence against him," I replied. "Every time there is a knock on the door I would expect to see you carrying a warrant and handcuffs. No, I couldn't live like that."

"You know we'd have to keep searching Carol, you love him but those girls were also loved, what about them?"

"And you would succeed eventually, maybe not

straight away but you would succeed and then you'd come and take him from me."

"I don't know what else to say, it's your decision," he said.

"Yes and I've already made it," I replied. "Would you mind just holding me for a while?"

He moved closer and wrapped his arms around my shoulders pulling me near. His strong grip made me feel safe creating a shield from the outside world. I wanted to stay wrapped up forever but knew it wasn't to be. Eventually he pulled away and I knew it was time to play my part, giving the performance of my life. He kissed my forehead and held my hands tightly before we parted company to go our separate ways.

CHAPTER 14

I arrived back at the house at about five o'clock, the others weren't back yet so I decided to take a long cool bath. I chose a pink liquid which, once combined with the foaming water, created lots and lots of hypnotic, scented bubbles. I picked up a book and submerged myself into the soapy depths.

It wasn't long before I heard the inevitable return of my hosts. Sabrina shouted out and I replied that I was in the bath. I could hear her excited chatter and knew she'd obviously had a good day's shopping. She was a creature of habit, any moment now she'd burst in clutching bags of goodies keen to adorn and display her new finery like a peacock eager to spread his beautiful feathers.

I closed my eyes trying to grasp the last brief seconds of solitude before the bathroom door opened.

"Oh good," I said. "Pass me a towel would you, please?"

"Certainly," came the reply. That wasn't Sabrina, I opened my eyes to see Jonathan standing holding up a towel.

"Oh...I thought you were Sabrina," I said.

"Sorry to disappoint you but I did call, you obviously didn't hear me," he said.

"No." He couldn't have called very loudly.

"Well, are you getting out or not?" he asked shaking the towel.

"Yes, of course," I said standing up. He stood gazing at my dripping body making no move to pass me the towel.

"Towel please," I reminded him.

"Sorry," he said, offering his steady hand as assistance from the bath.

Instead of handing me the towel he grabbed my arm and pulled me close, his passionate kisses covering my body. This was not the time or the place for love and I couldn't allow it to continue. I managed to pull away long enough to mumble a few words convincing him later would be better.

"I've bought you a small gift, come and see," he said in a teasing tone of voice.

I slipped on a robe and went through to the bedroom. On the bed lay a dress, a gorgeous black dress.

"If you don't like it you can take it back and choose something else," he said, "but when I saw it I knew it was perfect for you. Of course, I needed a little help from Sabrina when it came to getting the right size."

I picked up the dress and held it up. It was made of a light velvet material, it looked like it had been moulded, every section was designed to snugly grip each individual area of the body. The bust was shaped with tiny straps over the shoulder, the bodice was fairly straight and it was drawn up on one side creating a kind of side split.

"Do you like it?" he asked. "I suppose I was really thinking of myself when I bought it, please wear it this evening, I want every man that sees you to envy me. Will you?"

"Yes, of course, if it fits," I replied.

"It'll fit, I know it will," he said. "I'm going to take a shower and get dressed, you can join me if you like."

"I don't think so, not with Sabrina and Andrew roaming the house. Where are they anyway?"

"They're swimming in the pool. They knew I wanted to show you my gift first so I asked Sabrina to wait till later to show you what she'd bought."

I sat for a while trying to decide on my underwear. Finally I decided that very little was needed but for modesty, I chose some small lacy black panties that were high cut and wouldn't show below the spilt in th dress.

I had started to put on my make up when I heard a tap on the door and a soft voice asking to enter. It was Sabrina.

"Well?" she said. "Did you like it?"

"Yes it's lovely, I only hope it fits," I replied.

"So do I, Jonathan took a long time in the shop, the poor assistant was so relieved when he said yes he'd take it."

"Actually while you're here, would you do my hair in a French plait?" I asked. "I could try myself but it would be much neater if you did it."

Now came the moment of truth, would it fit? I took the dress off the hanger and undid the zip, I stepped in and pulled it up over my hips, so far so good. I slipped the straps onto my shoulders and bravely asked Sabrina to zip it up holding my breath as she did so. To my delight it did up easily, Jonathan was right, it was a perfect fit.

"What do you think?" I asked Sabrina.

"You look stunning," she said. "He certainly did his homework to pick that dress."

I slipped on a pair of open toed shoes and prepared myself to take that glance in the mirror. The reflected view pleased me, I did look good. His mind must have created a blue print when his hands touched my body.

I made the finishing touches to my make-up just as there was a knock at the door. It was Jonathan asking if I was ready.

As I entered the front room both Jonathan and Andrew stared.

"Wow," exclaimed Andrew, "you look fantastic!"

"Breathtaking," whispered Jonathan who was dressed in a double breasted, long coated suit which was steel grey in colour with a very fine pin stripe. This was complimented by a crisp white open neck shirt and highly polished shoes.

"Hey, Jonathan, if you like, I'll take your place," teased Andrew.

"Not a chance in the world," said Jonathan. "Tonight she's mine." His eyes were fiery, a sign of things to come.

"The only thing is," I said, "I didn't bring much jewellery with me and wondered if Sabrina might have a suitable necklace just to take off the bareness of my neck a little."

"I'll have a look..." Sabrina started to say.

"No need," said Jonathan, "I have just the very thing here in my pocket." With that, he pulled out a small box.

Inside was a necklace and matching earrings studded with stones.

He stood behind me laying the necklace around my throat fastening the clasp. "A lady should only ever wear the best," he said as his lips brushed my shoulder sending shivers down my back.

"Here," said Sabrina, "let me help you with the earrings."

"We knew of the dress but he hid this other little surprise from us well. You must be special. Jonathan has never given a lady diamonds before," said Andrew.

"Diamonds?" I whispered. "Oh Jonathan please, no, you shouldn't, they're too expensive."

"They put the finishing touches to an already perfect picture and nothing is too good for the woman I love," he replied.

Oh God! What was happening to me? I couldn't speak, I just went to him and put my arms around him, holding tight, praying that tonight would never end.

"What's the matter?" he whispered in my ear.

I had to pull myself together. "Nothing, I'm just a little overwhelmed, it's such a wonderful gift."

"Listen, I'll buy you lots of diamonds if you'll hold me like that," said Andrew.

"Shut up!" shouted Sabrina. "Really, you have no sense of occasion, I think it might be a good idea if you take me for a drink."

"I thought we might go later," suggested Andrew.

"No, now I think!" she said with an insistent voice.

"OK, I'll grab a jacket," he answered.

"You two have a great night," said Sabrina as she shoved Andrew through the front door slamming it shut behind them.

I stood waiting for Jonathan to make the next move and it wasn't long before he did. His touch was always electrifying, exciting every nerve ending on my body. He stood behind me kissing and nuzzling my neck while his hands roamed. I had no, nor wanted any, defences that would interfere with our joining.

"Let me make love to you, right now," his voice was almost pleading like that of a child wanting his favourite sweet and I knew I wouldn't deny him. His hands slid up my outer thighs until they met the panties I was wearing, his fingers expertly easing them down letting them fall to the ground. I turned round to meet his lips and return his lustful embrace. He slid my dress up over my thighs as he lifted and pushed me against the wall, my legs wrapped around him and once again we were joined as one. His love making was strong and forceful, bringing us both to the height of passion. We stayed entwined for ages trying to calm our breathing.

"I do love you so much Carol, we are so perfect together," his voice was low and sincere.

As he released his grip my legs dropped to the floor.

"I'll just go and freshen up before we leave," I said.

"Take all the time you need, I'm in no hurry," he replied.

I grabbed my panties and retreated to my room. I had to agree with him, we were perfect together, every time we made love it felt like the first, no lesser passion, lust or love. If this was to be our last night together then I would make sure it was one we'd both remember forever.

It only took me a few minutes, I opened the bedroom door and was just about to leave when I remembered the bag. I turned and looked at the little bundle inconspicuously lying on the dressing table. My immediate impulse was to leave it there, make an excuse to Jennifer that I'd forgotten it but I knew she wouldn't believe me. I took a deep breath, grabbed the bag and joined Jonathan in the living room where he was waiting.

"Ready?" he said. He escorted me to his car and being the perfect gentleman opened the door for me to climb in, closing it behind.

We had been travelling only a short time before Jonathan took a turning to the left. We were on what appeared to be a narrow track, tarmac covered but unmarked and unlit, the trees hung over the road creating a tunnel effect with the reflection from the car headlights. I felt uneasy, trying to control an urge to question where we were going. My mind was going into overdrive with all manner of sinister thoughts racing through it. Did he suspect? Did he know of the police trap?. If he was aware, it could be my death I was being transported to, not dinner.

I was cold but my hands were clammy, an obvious sign of panic. Every now and then he would glance across smiling but saying nothing while I sat only mustering a pathetic grin. The imminent words of question were on my lips when, to my great relief, I spotted lights in the distance. I physically felt my body shrink back into the seat muttering praise to the Lord for safe deliverance. I'm not normally religious but at that precise moment it was automatic.

The restaurant was decoratively illuminated with strategically placed lighting. As we pulled into the car park, I could see a long stone building with thatched roof and small windows dotted along its length. As we approached the door I glanced back, that road was the only means in or out.

"Anything wrong, Carol?" he asked.

"What a strange road, like a tunnel," I replied.

"Yes, but it's the only access and this is such a super restaurant. Come on, let's go in," he said putting an arm round my waist.

We were greeted and shown to the bar. A good looking, dusky waiter brought us a menu along with aperitifs. As I perused the menu, I smiled.

"Oh lovely, how did you know I held a passion for Italian food?" I questioned.

"Sabrina told me actually. It would seem we also share the same tastes," he said as he peered across once again with that enchanting stare. I don't think I would ever find another man that could affect me so much with just one look.

There was a vast selection and I took ages to choose but finally I settled for stuffed pancakes and veal cooked in a white wine and mushroom sauce. I didn't want to eat too much as I had already spied the heavily laden sweet trolley and needed a little room left to sample its delights. Jonathan opted for mussels and strips of beef in a red wine sauce, ordering a bottle of full blooded red to wash it down.

The restaurant was dimly lit, each table had been well situated to maximise each party's privacy, not as usual where they cram everyone together trying to seat as many people as possible. Candles burned on each table with fresh flowers, each posy individually made of different but beautifully coloured petite blooms. It was clear that this restaurant catered for a select clientele that was prepared to pay the cost of the very personal service they received.

Three sets of French windows opened out onto a patio area. A trellis overhead was heaving with the weight of climbing roses that oozed a rich, pungent aroma. Several tables were sparsely scattered and at the far end, on the lawn, a trio played mellow music. Their backcloth was that of shimmering reflections from the river that flowed just behind. If the food was as fine as the setting we were in for a real treat.

Our table was different, a mass of perfectly formed red roses greeted us.

Jonathan noticed my look of surprise. "A beautiful woman should have beautiful things around her," he said in a dulcet tone.

"Thank you, they're lovely," I said as the waiter served the first course.

The food was out of this world and Jonathan's choice of wine complemented it to perfection. The restaurant was full but we managed to remain in our own small world, making idle chatter whilst eating. After squeezing down a more than generous portion of Italian trifle, I knew I had eaten too much, I could feel the restraints of the new dress as I sat back slightly to ease the pressure letting my heavy lids shut in contentment.

"Would you like some coffee?" asked Jonathan.

"Yes that would be nice," I said not opening my eyes. "Can you smell those roses? It creates an image of a cosy country cottage with heavy blooms hanging over the front door, can you picture it?"

"Would you like a place like that?" he replied.

"Of course, but I can't see me ever affording such a delight, not on my salary, but it's fun to dream," I said. "You often hear people wishing they were rich, eager to voice their ambitions should they ever be lucky enough to acquire such resources."

Jonathan was unusually quiet and as I opened my eyes, he was grinning. I got the feeling he was silently laughing at me but would never admit to it, maybe he didn't indulge in such innocent fantasising but for some this provided a kind of aspiration that managed to aid their laborious path of everyday existence. I decided to ignore his humorous interpretation of our conversation.

"My dreams for the future are very simple, to enjoy my life and work. Of course, I would like a modest home to retreat to when needed," I said. "What do you wish for Jonathan, or is it a secret?"

"I've never really thought about it," he said.

"Oh come on, you must have some desires for the future," I replied. "You wouldn't be so successful if you had no ambitions in life."

"I've been fortunate in my pursuit of a successful career. My parents wanted us all to become involved with the family business but once they realised that Andrew and I didn't share that passion they used all means at their disposal to ensure our success. Financially they supported us and at every opportunity encouraged their friends and colleagues to make use of our services," he said. "Sorry, I'm going to have a brandy, would you like one?" he asked. I nodded my head in agreement as he ordered the drinks.

"Go on," I pushed.

"Not much else to tell. Once established, things just

got better. Andrew keeps saying that he hopes to make enough money to retire at forty so he can donate more of his time to enjoyment and the various ladies he will have in tow," said Jonathan smiling.

"That doesn't surprise me at all! He's not the sort to commit himself to one lady," I replied, I suddenly felt that statement was inappropriate under the recent circumstances but it was too late to retract it now. However, from his next comment, it was clear that Jonathan had accrued a very different belief of the situation.

"That's not what I've been lead to believe, Carol. I got the impression that there was one young lady he would be faithful to," he looked at me slyly across the table.

Even though it was dark he must have seen me blush.

"Who told you that?" I enquired.

"He did," he replied. "He had had a little too much to drink one night and confessed to big brother his undying affection. I wondered if it had just been the effects of the ale that had made him spout such words but we did discuss it again, he was serious about his feelings."

"What else did he tell you?" I quizzed.

"Only that she had let him down gently. With them only knowing each other for a short time, she felt it best to wait and see how the relationship developed. He did say, however, that even on their first encounter he had a rival for her affections," he said.

"And who might that be?"

"He never said, his only remark was if that person had any sense he ought to snap her up before some other fellow came along," replied Jonathan.

He reached across the table a took hold of my hand.

"And that's exactly what I'm going to do," he said.

I was transfixed by his stare, he could hypnotise me with those eyes and he knew it. I never noticed his hand disappear into his pocket to fetch out a small velvet box. As he opened it, the light from the lamp on our table caught its contents which sparkled. It was a ring but not just any ring, a large heart shaped diamond mounted on a deep band of gold. It was, I believed, an engagement ring.

"Carol, I love you so much will you marry me?" he whispered softly. "I want to be part of your future." He removed the ring from its mounting, pushing it onto my finger, raising my hand aloft as though signalling to all onlookers that I was now dedicated to him. I didn't want that moment to pass and it was only the arrival of the waiter with our drinks that broke the magic of the moment. It also gave me chance to sit back and take stock of the situation. What the hell was happening here? I was supposed to be trying to trap this man, not committing myself to him for the rest of my life.

I looked down at the beautiful symbol of love he had bestowed upon me and began to cry, I needed to escape from his presence.

"I didn't mean to upset you," he said, concerned.

"Oh, you haven't. It was just a shock that's all," I said. "Would you still feel the same if I was a brunette?"

"What?"

"I was contemplating changing the colour of my hair." That was my cry for help. "Sorry, forget it, just a stupid idea. Excuse me, I need to powder my nose, I won't be long," I said rising from the table and grabbing the little black bag as I left.

I wanted to run but didn't. Jennifer was waiting for me in the ladies room. I furiously paced what there was of floor space. "What the hell do I do now!" I ranted.

"Calm down, Carol," Jennifer said in a strong, stern voice. "Nothing has gone wrong."

"What do you mean, nothing's gone wrong, I've just had an offer of marriage and I've all but accepted it!"

"OK, tell him yes and we'll walk away now!" her voice was raised, angry even. "But is that really what you want. Only yesterday you were so adamant in your decision."

I leaned, head bent, against the basin for a couple of minutes saying nothing. I turned, put on some lipstick, combed my hair and made for the door. "Let's finish it," I said in a cold, callous tone.

When I returned to the table Jonathan had ordered us another drink, I smiled but my eyes showed no emotion and he must have noticed.

"Are you feeling alright?" he said. "Only you seemed a little upset."

"No, infact it's the opposite, I've never felt so happy," I said looking down at my hand. "This ring is beautiful, Jonathan, but far too expensive."

"Nothing is too good for you. For one awful moment I thought you were going to turn me down," he said, "and I couldn't have taken that."

"I love you very much and I could never do anything to hurt you unless you gave me just cause," I said in a joking manner with words designed to ease my conscience.

"I hope I'll never do that!" he replied. "Would you like to dance?"

He escorted me to the small dance floor and wrapped himself around me ensuring our bodies touched as closely as good manners permitted. Our lips were never far from each others as he guided me around the floor as if treading on glass. He was a very good dancer and quite capable of compensating for my wrong footings. We danced for what seemed ages, not speaking, just taking pleasure in our nearness and I think we would have stayed there for as long as the band played but the floor was becoming crowded and I was already hot so I asked to sit down. Also, the hour was getting late and I still had a task to fulfil.

There would be a difficulty in broaching the subject let alone receiving any response and as I sat consulting my own private world for help, he spoke.

"What are you thinking of, Carol?" he asked, his words snapping me back to reality.

"Andrew," I replied.

"Oh."

"No, not like that," I said scolding him slightly. "I wish he could be as happy as us and he may have been if Angela hadn't been taken from him. I believe he did love her in his own way."

I looked across hoping for a reaction. There was a secondary moment of frost in those loving eyes before it melted again. Nearly.

"Fate does play cruel tricks," he answered.

"Yes, I know but I'm still puzzled. Jennifer told me that the police had no idea how she could have got to that area of the stream without either walking there or being carried and they could find no signs of either. Strange, don't you think?"

"I'm sure they'll find something eventually," said Jonathan.

"I've been over this point in my mind and the only explanation I can come up with is that if she didn't enter the water upstream or downstream, the only place left is the pool but I ruled out that possibility as well. The gates are always locked and it would be an impossible task to get a body over such a height. What do you think?" I must get a reaction now I thought.

He sat back in his seat looking across, his eyes showing contempt at my words. Finally he chose to answer.

"That would insinuate that Andrew killed her and if he was as fond of her as you say, he would hardly have murdered her." His voice sounded agitated. "So why not drop the subject and enjoy the rest of the evening, I'm sure the police will handle it."

"It might not have been Andrew, he wouldn't be the only suspect." I really was pushing it to the edge.

"Carol please, stop it!" he said insistently.

I had gone as far as possible for the moment, anymore and he would become angry provoking the opposite effect to what I wanted. We sat finishing our drinks and saying very little.

Suddenly he said, "Tell you what, let me pay the bill and we can go for a stroll along the river bank, it'll do us good. That is, of course, as long as you're not frightened to be alone with me in the woods." He was taunting me and although I was scared I couldn't refuse.

"That sounds like a good idea, I'll just visit the ladies and we'll go," I said cheerfully.

Jennifer was again waiting for me. She was unhappy with the way events were turning. She knew I would be vulnerable once out in such an open and unlit area, but I dismissed her idea of quitting. I had expressed my doubts and suspicions to him about where Angela had met her fate, this could be the time of truth and I doubted if there would ever be another chance to play such a dangerous game.

As I prettied myself once more, Jennifer was laying down the ground rules. They would try and follow at a safe distance. Her final comments were to just shout out if I was in danger and they would come running even though it would blow the operation. They didn't want to catch a killer at the expense of another life. I took a deep breath, gave her a hug and walked back to find Jonathan. He had just finished paying and had my jacket ready to put round my shoulders as we left the restaurant on what I felt was the final phase.

It wasn't long before we lost the security of the restaurant lights. Others must often have used this route, the grass had been trampled away creating a sort of path that ran parallel with the river's edge. Once our eyes became accustomed to the dark we could comfortably find safe footing and make out the surrounding landscape. There was a grassy area about ten feet wide that spanned between the river and the bushes that enforced the boundaries of the local farmer's land. Every now and then the river bank dropped away slightly and we could see the silted bottom of the river creating miniature beaches, suitable for children to paddle in the heat of the day.

Jonathan decided the topic of conversation, obviously it was about our future and under any other circumstances I would have been as eager as he but I knew there was no future, only now. This theme had to be changed and soon, otherwise we would be on our way back before I managed to manipulate the truth from him.

We had gone a fair way and my feet were beginning to hurt. I was not used to walking in such high heels. We stopped at the next drop in the bank which proved to be much steeper than those previous creating a natural seat, nice to sit and rest. Jonathan slipped off my jacket and began to undo the zip on my dress, I tried to stop him saying somebody might come along but if they did he said we could slide further down the bank out of sight. It was inevitable we were going to make love, and I desperately wanted to just once more. Even the thought of maybe half the police force listening couldn't deprive me this final moment of passion.

Every time he touched me it was like the first time, the excitement he stirred in me was so intense I could not resist, as he lay me back on the dense, wild grass. His lips made contact with mine before he gradually moved them down my body leaving no place untouched while his hands caressed my breasts, I was in ecstasy. Any woman who has experienced the touch of such a man will understand the pleasure I felt.

Jonathan was a tremendous lover, always giving rather than receiving and very able to read the right time for the final act and he knew that time had arrived. He was highly aroused and his thrusts were not only rapid but exceptionally strong. He found need to put his hands above my shoulders to stop me being pushed away from his fevered advance. We both lay united until nature parted us, neither wanting the moment to pass but of course it must, and much to our disappointment, it had to.

That was it, that was to be the finale of our togetherness. I didn't want to accept it but that choice had already been made by me. It was time to take the most serious chance I'd ever had to contemplate in my carefree life. Jonathan adjusted his clothing and lay back against the green matressed ground and I could see the contented smile that covered his face. I took a deep breath and once again dared raised the subject of Angela, but this time the point had to be so direct and the insinuation so accurate that the answer he gave would have to be either positive or negative and I was praying for the latter.

"Jonathan, did you kill Angela?" I asked.

"What?" he said in a stunned voice sitting bolt upright.

"Did you kill Angela?" I said once again in a cool, calm voice.

As I waited for his reply I perceived every noise and movement from my wooded surroundings, not blending in unnoticed as before but loud and disturbing. Had I pushed too far? I started to have mental apparitions of my body collapsed on the floor with Jonathan's hands clasped around my throat. What a dreadful thought for my mind to cruelly conjure up, I quickly needed to dismiss such a vision as I certainly had no intentions of it ending so. I turned and looked as he finally spoke.

"Christ, how could you think I could do such a thing!" he shouted. "You are becoming obsessed with this, I think it's a damn good idea if you stop seeing Jennifer and constantly getting involved."

"You didn't answer my question," I pushed.

"Come on then, what's lead you to such a wild conclusion?" he asked.

"Remember the night before Angela's body was discovered?"

"Yes, what about it?" his voice had calmed and he seemed less agitated.

"When I came home that night and entered the house you emerged from the pool."

"Yes, as I told you, I was checking the banks because of all the rain," he said.

"But as I remember it hadn't rained for over 24 hours and even I could see that the water entering the pool was flowing much slower than on the previous day. There was no need for you to make a check at all, was there?" I said wishing I could see the expression on his face but being too frightened to make further eye contact. Even in such dark conditions, I knew one look and I'd lose it.

"What makes you think it's me?" his voice had changed, it was cold, emotionless.

"It couldn't have been anybody else. When I returned that night the gates were locked as usual, Sabrina and Andrew were out together and you were the only person in the house," I answered.

"Go on," he said.

"It's the only explanation I can come up with and don't think I haven't searched for an alternative. A dead body can't just magic itself into a place, someone has to put it there and no matter how careful, there are always signs but in this instance there weren't any." I stopped for a moment waiting for his pleas of innocence but I heard none. This, to me, confirmed what the police had been telling me for so long but my heart and mind refused to believe.

Now for the final nail in the coffin and our relationship.

"I don't know why you killed her but I believe you did," I said. "You may have planned to dispose of her in a different way but my return disturbed you, you had to get her body out of the pool because I would have seen it, so you pushed it over the edge hoping there was sufficient flow to take her body far enough out of sight."

There was only one question left for me to ask. "Why did you do it?"

I had tried to be brave but as I sat there, tears ran down my face as condemnation of my wanton destruction of our relationship, and this was only emphasised by the self pity that enveloped my heart.

Eternity passed as I determined that it would be he who broke the ensuing silence that now gripped us both.

"She was a slut," he said vehemently, as the confession that I'd worked so hard to obtain now spat from his lips.

CHAPTER 15

I just sat listening to his mental replay of that night, about how Angela had shown up fairly early that evening, supposedly looking for Andrew but obviously knowing that he'd planned to go out that evening. In her naive stupidity, she'd mentioned that she'd met the other lads that afternoon and learnt of their intention to go bowling, Andrew and Sabrina included. Unsure of her true reason for visiting, he let her continue with her childish prank until she became bored with his mature disinterest in her.

"Yes, but how did she know you would be home?" I asked.

"Because I passed her in my car about an hour before. She was chatting to her neighbour, leaning on the fence, her ample bosom hanging out of a very low cut top, poor chap had no option but to stare and she loved it," he replied. "She looked up when I drove by, she had that self satisfied smirk on her face, the one saying, look he can't keep his eyes off me."

For whatever reason, she'd turned up on the pretence of finding Andrew at home and Jonathan unwittingly let her in, well, why shouldn't he?. He offered her a drink which she eagerly accepted and they both sat out on the patio. Angela had changed before she went to the house, she sported a mini skirt and a low cut, ribbed top that buttoned down the front. It was quite clear to Jonathan that she had no bra on and probably no panties either, but he'd chosen to ignore her clawing need to attract his attention.

He offered to drive her home but she was in no hurry to leave. Infact she made reference to being too hot and asked him whether he minded her using the pool before she left to which he had no objections, anything to fulfil her amusement. She'd made some giggling comment about not having a swimsuit with her. Jonathan told her that she could use one of Sabrina's bathing costumes but she declined and instantly removed the little clothing she was wearing. He'd been unprepared for such a blatant show and, for once, felt a little uncomfortable at her actions.

Angela had flaunted her ample carcass in front of him asking if he liked what he saw before plonking herself on his lap, face to face. He tried to tell her not to be so silly and that Andrew wouldn't approve of what she was doing, but his resistance only seemed to make her more determined. Finally he gave her what she wanted, sex.

There was no love involved just pure sex and she fed from this lust not letting him alone for one minute but after her own fulfilment, her ardour ebbed and she wanted to leave but he wasn't having any of that. He was going to teach this stupid little girl a lesson.

He struck with full force turning their final encounter

more to rape, pinning her down and taking his pleasure at will before releasing his strong grip. Although he knew she was disturbed by his brutal use of her, she put on a front as if dismissing his actions as familiar, acting as if she'd enjoyed the pain he inflicted on her delicate skin but he could see the relief when he slackened his hold on her and she retreated far enough away from his reach.

Even after such a traumatic attack, she still remained. Angela had discovered a new game, but she was young and had not yet learnt the rules by which it was being played. In theory she'd lost and paid the price, but had refused to concede defeat. He saw her staying as a second challenge, had she not understood that the stakes for losing again would be higher? Or did she consider herself experienced enough to continue?

Round two began as they both went for a swim to cool the blood in their bodies. He kept his distance not wanting to be the one to initiate further contact. He felt if they had bathed and she had left straightaway without opening that rosebud mouth of hers, she might still be alive now but she didn't.

While they swooned around in the water, she started insinuating things, taunting him with the idea of dropping a very large hint to Andrew about their little contretemps. She obviously thought it might be amusing to watch Andrew's painful and jealous reaction to her revelation.

Jonathan knew now that Angela had cleverly used Andrew, after all, he was a good looking lad and rich too, just the sort of person she wanted to be seen with, not your run of the mill type. It was apparent to him that she was a nasty, scheming bitch out to satisfy her own ambition, by whatever means. If she'd truly cared for Andrew she wouldn't have acted as she had. Jonathan could only assume one thing, if it wasn't love that was the attraction then it had to be money and there was no way he was going to let some cheap slut like her use or hurt his little brother. The more she talked, the more Jonathan despised her, becoming angry with hatred and rage filling his mind.

Her brief, devilish idea of divulging to his beloved Carol the night's little escapade sealed her fate. He couldn't have that, nobody was going to threaten his relationship with her.

Once again he slowly slipped towards her in the water. She started laughing, her simplistic brain must have presumed he wanted the use of her body again but she had presumed wrongly. This time the touch was different, he forcibly pinned her to the side of the pool from behind as his legs raised and wrapped around her body trapping her arms to her side before his hands slipped around her tender neck and squeezed.

He was surprised she put up so little resistance, being a well built girl he thought she would have been stronger. When she finally stopped moving he released his grip and she slumped back in the water, finally silent. He had planned to drag her body out of the water, throw her in the boot of his car and dump her well away from the area, but my early return hadn't been accounted for and disrupted that plan. He panicked when he heard the car pull up, above all, he knew he had to get rid of her and he only had minutes before I'd be there to witness her existence. Then it came to him, the only option open; to push Angela's body over the edge of the pool before I entered the patio.

From there on I knew the rest. I couldn't condone what he'd done. But I understood his reasons as again he had found it necessary to play the great protector.

"So you see I had no choice, I couldn't allow her to ruin Andrew's life or for that fact my own," he said, sounding regretful, as if expecting absolution for what he'd done but if he had killed the other girls as the police suspected then that gift could only be bestowed by a higher authority than mankind.

"You do understand, don't you?" he pleaded.

Yes, I had but I couldn't bring myself to say so. I also had to finish the task I had set out to achieve, any tendency toward sympathetic emotions now would allow a seed of doubt and that would surely mar my immense effort so far.

The police still had no method of tying Jonathan to the previous murders only insubstantial theories and that old gut feeling they claimed to have. The only chance was to strike again while his defences were lowered and he still felt our relationship strong and safe enough to permit me to live knowing his deadly secret.

Now was the moment of truth, he was already lured into the room of no escape, the final act was to bolt the door behind. Jonathan's response to my next question took me somewhat by surprise. I suppose I'd expected more from this man who possessed such a strong mind but he'd weakened, putting up no opposition to voice the facts of his previous atrocities.

"And the other girls, why did you kill them?" As this question poured from my lips, I could feel the strained tension of the officers that surrounded us. He didn't reply, I thought I'd pushed him too far and I'd overwhelmed the one and only chance to ever pose that question again, but no, it had worked.

"You really are very clever, Carol," he said with a little chuckle. "You're little devious brain has managed to achieve what the mighty power of our collective police force couldn't manage. What made you suspect me then?"

I had no need now to hold back, I explained each theory from which I'd amassed all the sordid details. His major mistake had been to write everything down, a sign of forgetfulness or an astute business man, his forte being the latter. My confession to searching for and reading his diary gained a reaction, it was the first time I'd seen fear in eyes, unmistakable even in this poor light. I had unwittingly struck a weak point, mentioning the only possible thing that could resemble a scrap of evidence against him.

"Have you shown it to Jennifer?" he asked, I needed to allay his fears and quickly.

"No," I replied.

"Why not, if you're so certain of your facts?"

"Not down to me and to be quite honest I didn't want to," I said hoping my reply would be enough.

"But that's not like you Carol, why the change of heart?"

"How could I help the police lock you up?" I said. "I love you, is that a good enough reason?"

He looked across and smiled, maybe my reason had sounded convincing, I was sure I'd soon find out one way or the other. I went on to tell of my other somewhat simple deductions that I'd managed to work out from snippets of information obtained from my many a long visits with Jennifer.

His preference for sleek black cars was also another area that was to be his downfall. The hire company staff, well, the young lady on the desk said they remembered him well. They had to obtain the car he'd requested from another branch as theirs was small and only kept the more standard saloon type models, possible link number two.

Then there was Sarah, a poor innocent soul whose only mistake in life was to care too much for the sick and injured beings entrusted to her care. That medical treatment for the cut to his hand lead to the meeting of a nurse, one who lovingly wrapped a protective layer around the wound of a most charming and handsome man. I bet she couldn't believe her luck when such a well turned out and affluent gent such as he took such interest in her, a humble student nurse, overwhelming her with compliments, flowers and fine dining. She'd probably never been approached for a date before but when such a perfect specimen as he asked, how could she refuse?

Then there was his liking of a fresh flower each day for the button hole of his suit. At first, it never dawned on me but just before their trip to Italy, he had been trimming back the climbing roses that hung on the outside wall, not unusual you may think but that jolted my memory. He never left the house wearing a button hole but upon his return, a flower was always pinned to the lapel of his jacket, the same colour roses as those he tenderly cared for. Obviously he plucked one from the bushes as he left each day but unable to do this while away, purchased them from a florist in his locality, thus providing the link to Jane. I thought he may attempt to deny it, after all it was a very loose link, nobody had ever actually seen them together, but he didn't, he stayed silent letting me continue.

Making a connection between him and Sammy had been more luck than anything else, pure hypothesis and again flowers played their part. In the statements of Sammy's somewhat bizarre neighbours, they'd mentioned her new man's obsession with roses, red roses at that, I remembered seeing them in a vase on her front room table. Unwittingly, Jonathan had created and left a kind of calling card. How could he have been so stupid as to provide such a blatant clue if he'd intended to rid himself of this woman? Or did he? Was it a spur of the moment decision? I had based my findings on some watery and unsubstantiated facts, if he refused to refute them then I and, more importantly the police, had no other means of proving his involvement with these girls.

I knew each clue on its own was of little merit but together they made up some convincing evidence like a jigsaw puzzle, each one fitting into place. By now he must have known that I had no real proof to hand, but I was gambling on him believing that maybe I could substantiate my beliefs or had sufficient coincidences for the police to work on. He could, of course, dismiss my theories as wild and stupid fantasies, totally unfounded, but he wouldn't have insulted my intelligence in such a manner.

Now I would play my final card; the fingerprint. I knew there wasn't sufficient evidence to be any good but he wouldn't, this gave me the advantage.

"Oh, of course, there's that incriminating fingerprint," I said laying yet more bait for him to snap at.

"But you said..." he stuttered.

"I know, at first the police hadn't found anything but after re-checking Sammy Nielson's bed, they found one under the pretty bows tied around the tail board post which had been missed, but I'm sure you remember them?" Each word I spoke was filled with confidence that I was winning the mental battle between us.

"Have the police matched it yet?" he asked.

"No, as yet they have no suspect, can't match it to someone you can't find," I replied.

"So unless you make things clear they still can't tie me to anything," he said calmly. Had he mistakenly felt some false sense of security from my words? No, his next comment put paid to that. "You're going to tell them aren't you?" he asked.

For the first time I hesitated before responding. If I said yes would I become yet another victim, or if I replied negatively would he assume I'd allow to him to escape justice, forfeiting any punishment that he would incur, implying my willingness to keep my silence on the matter? No, he knew me too well for that, if I agreed to the latter he would almost certainly know I was lying, even to the point about telling the police and that could be a much more dangerous route to travel.

"Yes," I said ," I feel I must, but first I wanted talk to you before I said anything."

"I knew your answer before you spoke, foolish really to expect anything else," he replied. "But you said before that you wouldn't, why did you lie?"

"I felt if I'd said yes straightaway that you'd clam up and not talk about it," I said.

"Probably," he replied. "You really do understand me very well, don't you?"

"Well?" I asked my heart in my mouth. "Are you going to tell me what happened?"

"Promise me you'll always love me, Carol, no matter what," he begged.

"Yes, I'll always love you, you've already made sure of that," I assured him.

"The first was a mistake you know, never meant for it to happen, it just did," he said.

CHAPTER 16

Jonathan recalled his first meeting with Jane Downing on a glorious sunny morning in August, he had been on one of his first searching missions for new company premises. At home, fresh flowers were always readily available for that infamous button hole but he had stayed overnight in a local hotel, he'd chatted with the receptionist before leaving, ascertaining the whereabouts of the local florists and apparently there were several. Most, however, were situated in the heart of town and it would have meant parking the car, which he didn't have time to do, he was already running late and was rushing to an early appointment that morning.

Although it went against his principles, he decided to do without that day but on his travels he had stumbled across a small florists where he could leave the car directly outside. The shop wasn't very special but he could remember the wondrous perfume as he walked through the door, the only thing that outshone the flowers was the pretty blond assistant behind the counter. Jonathan had found himself quite smitten by her good looks and before he had left with his purchase, he arranged for them to have dinner that night.

Their first date had been fairly uneventful. Jane being several years younger and a little less worldly than he meant that their topic of conversation was basic, she chattered on about what he described as her simple life, he just nodded on occasions. Normally he would not continue with such a liaison but found her bounce and natural beauty refreshing. She, on the other hand, was delighted to have attracted the attentions of such a gorgeous man. On the second evening they met Jane took him back to her flat, he laughed a little as he remarked about being very impressed at her choice of decor which displayed signs of a mature overtone, more than he expected.

Even though he was to discover she was still a virgin, Jane was more than eager for him to be her first encounter of love. After that evening he never stayed at a hotel, always with Jane even though it meant driving many miles out of his way. They had dated for several months but as far as Jonathan was concerned he had not regarded their affair as serious. In his eyes, the relationship was not destined to last forever. Sooner rather than later he knew he would gradually tire of her apparent lack of interest in the things he enjoyed doing. Jane liked the pictures, Jonathan preferred the theatre; she opted for pop while he mostly listened to classical; the differences between them were vast. Unfortunately she, in her naiveté, probably thought it an easy space to bridge but Jonathan was disillusioned, he'd never feel the same relish for Rambo as he did at the prospect of a visit to see Swan Lake.

One evening he'd tried to narrow the gap by taking her to watch a dramatic production at a local venue and although not up to the standards he normally witnessed, it was well acted and enjoyable. Jane, however, insisted on spending most of the evening fidgeting in her seat more interested in fluttering her eyelashes at other men within the circle of her vision. Only when they left the tiny theatre did she lose the sulky look from her baby face that had been present throughout. He'd found the delight she exuded at convincing him to buy her supper from a local burger house pathetic and he knew it would not be long before the parting of the ways.

He had continued his visitations, complacency had taken over during the colder months, discouraging the urge of change, leaving him festering in routine. However, one winter's evening he felt a difference when he arrived at Jane's place. Normally she'd watch out for his car pulling up and rush to the door to meet him but not that night, she was in a tense, nervous state and he knew something was wrong. He crushed the impulse to ask, past experience had taught him that when she was possessed of these moods swings, it was better to wait until she was ready. He'd pretended not to notice the chilled atmosphere that filled the room, making matter of fact conversation in the hope she'd tell him what was wrong.

During dinner Jane hinted more than once that it might be good for him to meet her parents but he saw no valid reason to be introduced to people he had no interest in and in the nicest possible way made that opinion quite clear to her.

Jane was upset at his refusal and became angry, shouting hysterically, accusing him of disregarding her feelings. In all the time he'd known Jane, he'd never been exposed to such an outburst, she had always shown a bubbly and happy attitude to life. No, there was something more, something he had yet to discover and as her anger turned to tears, she told him.

Jane had discovered she was pregnant with his child. The news of World War III starting couldn't have made a bigger impact. Stony faced and appetite gone, he looked across at the shaking young girl who sat before him. She was frightened by her predicament and he now knew why she was so intent that he met her parents, due to this new circumstance she was obviously hoping that their temporary relationship would become permanent.

As he comforted her, he whispered words of reassurance. He wanted things to be put right and they needed to discuss the matter calmly and quietly, but they were both tired, he especially after driving most of the day. He suggested that after a good night's sleep they would both look properly at the problem in the morning.

Jonathan hadn't expected her advances for love making that night, infact she showed more passion than normal, maybe a ploy on her part. She chose her moment carefully and when he was in the heated advance of embrace, she started rambling as to how he could move in with her and they could look for a bigger place together, the perfect little family.

Mentally he saw the net closing and wanted out. His preference was more along the lines that she be rid of the baby, a much more sensible solution in his eyes but if she insisted on keeping it, he would of course support her and the child as long as needed. However, he had no intentions of settling down and playing happy homes with a woman he didn't love. Escape from this relationship now became a priority, no way was he willing to bow down to the total commitment that she was expecting.

Panic flooded his already confused mind as the realisation at what she was suggesting sunk in. He was blind to his hands closing around her fair throat, firstly stroking the delicate skin but the pressure gradually became more severe until finally, her words were choked into silence. Strangely, the boundaries to which his mind was pushed during this experience thrilled him, he fed from it as if it were a drug, craving more, his heart beat faster but he was mentally unaware of his actions. As she became silent, he found himself panting, never had he reached such a height during any previous sexual encounter.

Finally, with the return of his senses, he was horrified to see her limp, lifeless body laying beneath him. He frantically tried to revive her but she had long departed this world. His only instinct then was to escape but although his affection for her never became more than a trickle, she didn't deserve to be found in such an uncouth state. He sat ages on the edge of the bed staring. She resembled his image of Snow White waiting for that magical touching of lips but this prince's kiss would be the finale of her life, not the beginning. That was what prompted his decision to set the surroundings for her eventual discovery.

His final touch was that of parting words he was no longer able to convey but felt should be said. He systematically removed all traces of his being there before closing the heavy door behind him. He had never been seen with Jane or met anyone she knew, also his arrival and departure was always in darkness thus making his undetected disappearance into oblivion possible.

There was only one other neighbour at home as he slid away in the darkness but he felt sure they had not seen him. The car he was driving had only been hired, due to his being in the garage for emergency repairs, and any onlooker's eyesight would have to have been exceptional to see the number plate in the murky darkness, let alone read it.

No, he was adamant he was safe from discovery as he drove away, and he knew it wouldn't be long before she was found, poor girl. He booked into a local hotel for the night and first thing the following morning collected his own car before returning home, distancing himself miles away from Jane.

Over the next couple of weeks he spent a lot of time reflecting on what he'd done and was thankful that Sabrina and Andrew were still in Italy for the Christmas break. He had not gone due to the pressure of work and although displeased, his parents accepted his decision.

He managed to isolate himself from any new romantic encounters for a long while, going out with friends as a group, frightened to be alone with a woman. That is, until he met young Sarah McDonald. He had not successfully managed to locate suitable offices and once again resumed his search. This, of course, meant travelling again but he kept to himself during his voyages.

The estate agent who'd been guiding him around the various properties had insisted he take him to the local hospital when he managed to slice open his hand on a door handle, he wanted qualified medical treatment just incase the matter went further.

He had been shown into a side cubicle where he awaited the arrival of a doctor. In the meantime, his wound was cleaned by a very attentive nurse. She was meticulous in her work, slowly but gently removing all traces of dried blood before placing a pad over the cut to absorb further bleeding. He was taken by the soft manner shown as she performed her task, only lifting her head once or twice to give a nervous smile.

He recalled her face was plain, the sort many men would pass off as unattractive but he saw more, sparkling blue eyes with long lashes fringed by perfectly formed dark brown eyebrows, a small button nose and full reddish lips ideally set against her unblemished pale skin. He felt make-up would have spoilt such a delicate face.

The doctors were extremely stretched that day and he'd waited for over an hour before being seen. During that time, his little nurse had showed him constant attention even fetching him a cup of coffee. For the first time in a long while, he felt comfortable in this girl's company, he'd managed to steer clear of females up till then but before leaving, he'd weakened and asked her out. He'd asked for her suggestion on a suitable restaurant but she admitted her ignorance in that field, not being able to afford such luxuries.

This was the date that the other girls at the nursing home had found out about. Sarah had, however, neglected to divulge where they had met, probably at his request, if she hadn't been so naive and chatty like the rest maybe she could have informed on her killer's name before the event.

He chose a local steak house for their rendezvous,

not very intimate and busy. The food was adequate, not the sort he was used to, but Sarah nevertheless enjoyed her evening out. He was able to play the perfect gentleman with her, not feeling the urge to take it further than a platonic friendship, until their final encounter.

That night in Scotland when he rang to say he had to stay out with clients I now believed to be a lie. He had arranged to meet Sarah with the purpose of ending their relationship. When I questioned his reasons the only answer he gave was, 'you'. He had picked her up at the usual time of seven o'clock, which gave her time to get ready after work but on that particular evening she had dressed differently. She had managed to borrow some clothes from one of the other girls, nothing too serious but of more modern design and a little shorter than she usually wore. He also noticed she had applied make-up which didn't suit her colouring, her whole mannerism was different, as if trying to portray something she wasn't and the more she drank, the worse she became.

He had succeeded in removing her from the restaurant without attracting attention and helped her into the front seat of his car. Sarah was totally out of context that night, even touching him under the table like a naughty school girl. It didn't stop there, as he drove her home she kept mauling his body.

Once at the nurse's home, he retrieved her from the seat making sure she stood upright before he pointed her towards the door. She invited him in but he was reluctant, it was only her threat to stand in the car park and shout at the top of her voice if he didn't concede to her demands that made him relent and enter the building.

As we already knew, her room was very near the front door and his presence went undetected. He had the intention of only staying a short while, hoping she would calm down and let him leave without too much fuss.

Unfortunately that was not how things developed, instead she put on the radio making him dance with her. As they approached the bed, she grabbed him and pulled back, inevitably he landed on top of her. Quickly he stood evading her clutches and turned towards the door mumbling that he should leave. Sarah, however, had different ideas and called to him to stay. As he turned back to voice his objections, he was faced with Sarah who had removed most of her clothing beckoning him to her.

In the end, he finally gave way to her persistence and though he knew her still to be a virgin gave no consideration to the fact. The frightened and painful expression on her face was indication that the pleasure she had hoped to experience was not evident. He was a strong man whose advances were not to be deterred and he had managed to stifle the onslaught of fists to his chest. He taking enjoyment from the pain she inflicted with each futile blow and his hands once again found themselves wrapped around a new victim's neck.

The pleasure he had experienced once before flowed through his veins with his forceful attack on a frail and lesser opponent, his victory, total defeat. He found himself with a lifeless being below him, his gaze now filled with the dead faces of Sarah and Jane. He felt sheer horror that he had yet again allowed himself to commit such a hideous act.

With the possibility of discovery ever present he had to slip away. Firstly he dressed, then he flicked through once treasured drawers searching for a suitable shroud. The best he found was a white linen night-dress that buttoned to the neck and billowed to the ground shielding any glimpse you might capture of the body it covered. Jonathan manoeuvred her into this less than suitable attire and straightened the bedding slightly before laying her back. He sought a means to tidy her hair. Upon the dressing table sat an old brush, well made but it had seen better days.

His project was temporarily interrupted, a movement in the corridor signalled him to silent stillness and though the weather was cold, his forehead began to form beads of sweat.

When quiet once again, he hurried to finish his work, he drew a hanky from his trouser pocket and methodically brushed it across each surface he may have touched. Departure now imminent, he turned for one final glance at this poor, plain girl who he had selfishly despatched from this world before time. As he looked down, his final vision was blurred by tiny smudges of make-up, this he decided needed to be removed letting the face he first saw be the picture he would carry in his mind forever. The note took only seconds to write after he'd rummaged in a drawer and found a scrap of paper and biro, cheap utensils for a person who liked to use nothing less than a gold tipped fountain pen and personalised paper. With his handkerchief he delicately wiped away each blemish until her natural pallor was restored.

With the tarnished cloth still clutched in his hand, he opened the door just enough to see down each way of the passage before sliding out and scurrying towards the entrance that offered escape and freedom. With the car started, he immediately pulled away but not too quickly, the roadway was full of gravel and to rush would create noise. He couldn't afford to be heard. Only when he exited onto the main road did he feel it safe to put on the lights.

The hour was late and the stress of the evening's events left him in need of rest and again he felt the necessity to put distance between himself and the recently deceased, speedily driving over forty miles before endeavouring to find a place to stop.

He could see the signs of a motel looming in the dark distance and pulled in, on this occasion he was lucky and within minutes was being shown to a chalet. He never bothered to undress but just lay across the ample bed falling into deep slumber almost instantly. Sleep only lasted for a few hours and he revived himself under a rather soothing hot shower. Jonathan always carried an overnight bag in the car, business had necessitated its presence and once dressed in clean clothes, he continued on his way.

He had promised to be back in Scotland to pick us up from the castle but the hunger in his gut forced an unscheduled break for breakfast before resuming his journey. Once back with us the rest was common knowledge.

There was only one more poor soul to tell of and it took very little to prompt him further.

"And Sammy?" I asked, this comment was enough, as he easily switch the topic of conversation.

"Oh Sammy, she was something completely different!" he replied.

CHAPTER 17

Apparently, this little lady had made a play for him one evening when he was out on the town with some work colleagues. He noticed her sitting alone at a table across the restaurant and every time he glanced in her direction, she stared towards him with a sultry smile upon her face and he found it amusing to follow suit.

His pals left early, they were due to attend a wedding in Dorset the following day, they had planned to travel and stay with friends that night.

Jonathan, possessing the perfect manners escorted them to the door as they left. As he returned to the table, he noticed that his admirer had vanished, he presumed that she had also decided to depart. He finished his drink and paid the bill but as he approached the door, he could see this rather brash lady was blocking his exit, she linked her arm through his, smiled and they left together. He had found her boldness in taking charge of the situation fascinating, he went willingly intrigued to find out where this strange and as yet unknown woman might lead him.

Jonathan, although young, didn't like or give much

and raising the coverage of her bosom which at the outset had been perfectly acceptable when attracting their interest.

The last stage would be his inference that they stay in more, have cosy nights together at home drinking cocoa, but if this hadn't cured her desires to have him around then the ultimate hint of cohabitation or marriage would. No matter how good he was, when things reached this unacceptable stage she'd sever the fine ties that bonded them together. Sammy made reference to only three very special chaps that had survived to the end in what, up to now, Jonathan considered her very pitiful life and these she referred to by name.

First came Roger some eight years back, he was a red-headed, burly Scotsman who swept her off her feet with his manly strength and protective ways. Any rival who came near was seen off immediately in fear of his life. This she found flattering, enjoying his dedication towards her but as time went on, she found herself unable to speak to her friends without him watching her every move, any inclination that another was vying for her affection and he was there, pushing himself between them.

Roger's proposal of marriage and his insistence that once wed they would return to his native land where his family owned a farm rearing beef cattle was the death of this partnership. The thought of isolation with a bunch of harsh and narrow minded people did not appeal. She was young and still wanted to party her way through life, not live in cold, un-modernised accommodation with the in-laws. The next thing he would suggest would be children, oh no, that wasn't what she wanted at all.

Their break-up was messy, he couldn't accept rejection, he constantly phoned her and went round to her flat accusing her of going with other men, which up until then she had not done but she thought, what the hell, go for it, and after that she had a string of affairs. Eventually she had to move, his pestering and threatening behaviour had forced the decision. Sammy put as much distance as possible between them, ending up in the small flat she now occupied.

It was over five years before the next great temptation in her life reared his desirable head. Heartthrob number two was called Martin. He was a few years her senior but didn't look it, he took great pride and care in his appearance but not to the extent of overdressing. His looks were modest which pleased Sammy, she didn't want to spend her time fighting off hoards of female admirers all competing for his attention. Martin also had money, he was not rich but very comfortable owning three or four properties providing income which was untouched and channelled straight into an ever increasing bank account. He used to joke that he was keeping that money for his retirement years when he intended to travel, seeing and doing everything that took his fancy. This notion also interested Sammy.

Martin had a good job as a chartered accountant working for a large company in the city. His job was demanding but paid well and the gifts he would bring her made up for the loss of time together, but neither of them minded and the time they were together was wonderful. She would suddenly receive a phone call, inviting her to a show or the theatre in London and afterwards they would stay at a top class hotel. He, the gentleman that he was, always insisted on separate rooms. Her wardrobe when they first met was sparse but within no time it bulged with expensive, if somewhat strange clothing all paid for by him. After all, she had to have the right clothes to wear when he took her out.

They had never gone any further than a kiss much to her disappointment but despite that, Sammy had fallen deeply in love with Martin and for the first time in her life even contemplated the idea of marriage. She had visions of a large country mansion where they'd sit out on the lawn taking breakfast whilst the children amused themselves in play but, of course, the picture was too perfect, something had to go wrong and it did.

Unwilling to wait any longer, Sammy took the liberated stance one evening when they were alone together to propose marriage. The request had left Martin speechless and Sammy waiting with anticipated excitement, she could think of no reason for him to refuse.

At first she took his silence to be shock at her brazenness in asking a question traditionally reserved for the male of the species but the awkward look upon his face and the delay to reply turned her excitement to distress, had she hurt his feelings? Was he going to ask the same question and she'd spoilt the moment he had been working towards?

His suggestion that they were unsuited met with the natural reaction, Sammy just flipped. She desperately implied the opposite, their relationship had been almost too perfect. They had never made love but surely any little problems there could be dealt with, there was no way she would believe that was the true reason.

Knowing her persistence when it came to obtaining what she wanted Jonathan knew she would not let up on Martin until he told her the truth, but even strong natured Sammy was not prepared for the words she was about to hear.

Martin was gay.

She slumped into a chair, unable to speak, he made some futile attempts to explain himself but Sammy couldn't hear them, her only response was that of asking him to leave.

Once alone she felt the first tears trickle as her cries turned to uncontrollable sobbing. It took her several days to recover and come somewhere near to acceptance of the stark facts. The reason they'd always had separate rooms was his avoidance of the inevitable and this was why he'd never made love to her even though she was willing. She had fooled herself that he was the perfect gentleman, not wishing to tarnish her chastity. What an idiot she had been.

When they met again it was as strangers, they sat opposite one another at the dinner table both uncomfortable and embarrassed at what had occurred. Sammy had nothing but coldness in her heart for him now and politely listened as he tried to heal the heartache he had caused. His comments that he had never professed to wanting their relationship to become anymore than friendship were true but the least he could have done was be honest with her, not allow her to fall into a situation he knew could never be.

The only thing now she could take consolation in was that the truth had been told, how long would it have continued, her hoping, he staying silent. There was no chance that Sammy could keep the same feelings for him, there had to be a break, clean and final. Martin wanted them to remain friends, asking her to call him but once they parted that night she never made any efforts to communicate with him again.

This breakage had seriously damaged her confidence in men, she portrayed the vision of a cold, hardhearted bitch who wasted no time on those who didn't fill her requirements. The only trouble was that the more she practised, the more she became that person until eventually there was no need to practice anymore.

Sammy was determined, no man would ever get close enough again to hurt her as much as Martin had, returning to her old ideals of non-committal dating and this lead to her involvement with many strange people. She giggled as she told of their unusual peculiarities, one chap she'd become entangled with liked to play games, she found them harmless, enjoying acting out his little fetishes. He used to ask if she minded him tying her to the bed, hence the ribbons around the bedstead.

When quizzed as to the third person in her life she looked at him and just said 'you'. He was flattered but uncomfortable knowing the feeling would never be mutual, and hence her reaction at the mention of another woman.

It was obvious that Sammy was not going to give him up without a fight, no woman was going to steal her man, not with her scheming mind. She would track her enemy down and remove her from the contest. Jonathan had to do something to rid himself of this medusa-like woman, but how?

Sammy was in good humour that night thinking she was winning him over and he went along with it. They inevitably ended up in bed. Lying back his eyes caught sight of those pretty yellow ribbons. Of course, there was the answer staring right back at him, and his suggestion to make use of those ribbons bought an alluring smile to her face. She obviously hadn't mastered the art of reading other people, otherwise she may have figured out his real reason.

This removal of life was premeditated, unlike before. He sat astride her hips caressing her body up and down. Sammy was purring with pleasure, she hadn't noticed his hand slipping closer and tighter around her neck until it was too late.

Her realisation that his hands were restricting her gasps for breath made her open her eyes. She was struggling violently against her restraints but was unable to break free. His bodily weight stopped any movement of her torso, he had rendered her helpless. Her death was inevitable, her defence becoming lesser and lesser, he wanted to make sure she was unmistakably finished keeping a tight pressure around her throat until she lay perfectly still and limp.

The body had to be moved, he didn't want her found in bed even though it was her favourite place. He had carefully chosen her final attire, something he felt appropriately defined her character, an enticing little number she'd picked up from some boutique that specialised in 60's style clothes. There was very little of it and although it wasn't transparent, it left virtually nothing to the imagination, imposing the suggestion to her discoverers that she'd been out for the evening and had met her end in the garden from person or persons unknown.

Another reason for his choice was influenced by a previous conversation with Sammy regarding her dress manner. She'd found his insistence that she curb her lust to show off as much of her body as possible quaint, even a little eccentric and wasted no time in relaying that point whenever she spoke of him.

He did as best he could to touch up the heavy make-up that covered her face before carrying her out and laying her across one of the sun loungers. Upon re-entering the house he made the bed and, as if by natural reaction, once again went through the routine wiping all the surfaces he may have touched with his dampened handkerchief. Then he washed the dishes before turning to leave, but he had forgotten something, oh yes, some appropriate parting words.

There was only one that stuck in his mind, 'temptress', something she would always have been, funny, she prompted her own epithet. He could only find some yellow coloured paper upon which to place his message and used one of the brightly coloured crayons laying in a large woven basket to write the words. He gave her one momentary glance before slipping discreetly away undetected, leaving her for eventual discovery.

I had listened to his story of events almost sympathising with his justification of his actions until I'd learnt that Sammy had been murdered because of me. He'd made this death personal, how terrible to know that I was the cause of such an irreversible violation.

"There, you know it all now," he said. "Oh God what a bloody mess!"

"What are you going to do now?" I asked.

"What do you want me to do?" he replied looking across. For the first time I saw a weariness in those once bright eyes.

"Should I confess all to the nice policemen or say nothing? After all, you're the only one that knows."

What was he hinting at? Was he about to remove me from the picture? He couldn't without casting suspicion upon himself and he daren't do that, his vulnerability once in their clutches would give them reason to look further. Then again, he was maybe expecting me to stay silent, keeping his secret safe, but I was sure he knew me better than that. No, he was well aware of the only option left open to him after such a frank confession.

"It's late, shall we go back to the car?" he suggested.

"Yes." What else could I say? It was becoming increasingly uncomfortable, I knew there were police scattered around in close proximity but I still felt total isolation.

No words were spoken as we walked back to the restaurant car park, which by now had emptied. Only a lonely van sat parked in a far corner. The restaurant itself was in darkness, only the coloured lights remained lit.

As we approached the car, I became aware of bodies appearing from the blackness, they came closer forming a tightening circle.

"Are you alright?" Jennifer asked. Jonathan looked at me with a disbelieving stare.

"Yes," I replied, nervously glancing at Jonathan.

"Have you got the bag?" she asked and I handed it over. "It worked very well."

"Good," I replied.

Two burly officers stood forward of the restraining ring and approached at a quickening pace. His arrest was imminent. I turned to Jennifer and mouthed a plea for just a couple of minutes alone before they took him away, she nodded and they all retreated to a reasonable distance to allow a brief moment of privacy.

"Of course," said Jonathan quietly. "Stupid of me, I thought you a little brave to be alone in such seclusion while I bared my soul."

For a man who was about to be taken into custody and ultimately charged with murder, he managed to remain calm, aloof even.

"Jonathan...I'm sorry, I'm so sorry," I cried.

"Why?"

"I didn't want it to be you but I had to know one way or the other."

"Well, now you do and thanks to you, so do they." At that moment he must have relented on any decision he made regarding my continued existence.

"I did it because I love you so much, I couldn't have carried on with uncertainty, do you understand?" I said hoping but not expecting him to condone what I had done.

"Yes, I think I do," he said.

"Oh God, I don't want to lose you!" I cried.

He pulled me to him and wrapped his arms around me for one last time, the brief touching of lips was a reminder of what I had had, and now thrown away.

We could see the officers who'd been hovering discreetly, edge nearer. Jonathan pulled away and smiled, brushing the hair from my face.

"I still love you, Carol," he whispered, his voice almost sounded forgiving. "Life is unpredictable but love never changes. Don't worry, part of me will always be with you," he said as his hands ran down the front of my body. What a strange thing to say.

I couldn't bear to watch as they took him away, I turned my back to them and walked across to a waiting police car where I remained until I heard the vehicle in which Jonathan sat pull away.

"OK?" asked Jennifer

"No, but there's not much I can do about that is there?" I said in an angry voice.

"I'll get the constable to take you back to my place tonight," she suggested.

"What about Sabrina and Andrew, who's going to tell them?" I asked.

"That task has been given to David," she replied.

As we drove away, I knew that David would be knocking at the door of that lovely house for the last time as an invited guest and friend. Once the knowledge of tonight's events had been told, any future visitations would be in a professional capacity. There was no way I could return, even though all of my available clothing was still hanging in the wardrobe at the house. There was no way that I'd dare go near the place again, I'd leave the task of collecting them to someone else.

I didn't envy David one little bit, I remember thinking 'poor bastard', that little meeting would put paid to another wonderful relationship. Sabrina would, of course, take it badly causing a scene, her Italian blood you know. I only hoped he was stronger than me, the battle I'd just faced had left me exhausted and feeble, disinterested in fighting on.

I was sat quietly at Jennifer's dining table staring blankly across the room at the television when David telephoned me. As I predicted, Sabrina had reacted just as I said, cursing me when she became aware of my involvement, crying, shouting and lashing out at him in her fury before expelling him from her home and her life. Andrew had been more reserved, saying very little in his brother's defence. Not only had he endured the pain at the loss of Angela but the discovery that Jonathan was to blame must have been an even bigger blow. This whole affair had turned into a nightmare for all involved.

I asked David if he'd mind calling by to pick up the set of keys that I possessed and returning them and whilst there, gathering my belongings and dropping them off to me at Jennifer's. His reluctance to my plea was expected but nevertheless a chore I'd given him no other choice but to fulfil.

Jennifer was hardly at home during waking hours over the next few intense days and I took advantage of the quiet time to make peace with my mind. There were only a couple of weeks before the start of the new term. Sabrina's decision not to return was of no surprise, I don't think either of us could seriously have coped together now, she would have been unable to control the hatred she felt for me and I would spend most of the time saying sorry. The only possible hope was that eventually, that she'd not forgive me, but at least understand why.

CHAPTER 18

The new academic year was slow in starting and the loneliness of the little flatlet didn't help matters. Jonathan had insisted he still pay the rent until I'd finished this trial period of study. I wanted to keep occupied so that my own self-pity didn't have time to manifest itself. I had been feeling a little off colour, not ill as such and at first put it down to the strain of the past few weeks but when I started having sickly bouts each morning, decided it time to visit my doctor for a check-up.

He was thorough in his examination, checking my blood pressure and heart, you know, the general type of thing. I sat back in the large comfy but worn out leather chair that had occupied the same spot for as long as I could remember. At first I was relieved at his assurances that he could find nothing wrong with me, well nothing that the early stages of a normal, healthy pregnancy couldn't account for. I was stunned, I knew I had missed a period but I 'd blamed shock for that. I questioned the validity of his findings but he was almost certain and a urine test would confirm it.

I sat on the bus home unsure whether I wanted to sing or cry. At this time it was not the news I wanted to hear, I'd only just managed to establish some normality back into my life. For the first time in my life I felt an insecure, childish urge to be with my mum, something I'd never experienced before. I'd always shown strength to cope with any problems that life threw my way but I had to do some major thinking, rearrange my life to revolve around an imminent new arrival and for once, the answers would have to come from elsewhere.

How would I manage? I needed to finish my course and hopefully, I could study right up until the child was born, and afterwards sit the final tests but what then, when I became the sole provider for a new, innocent and vulnerable life? The very idea of aborting was dismissed immediately. Even though it would be a struggle, the child was part of Jonathan and I wanted this baby, the only thing good to come of our relationship.

My mother was shocked, of course, but soon rallied offering her full support. Her sensibility towards the situation amazed me, suggesting various options as to the child's future care, but finally I opted for the most sensible even though it meant a sacrifice on my part. It was agreed that, if possible, I would stay at the flatlet until the baby was born, then while I sat the final exams mum would have the child at her house and I could join them at weekends. Dad had been given no choice other than the prospect of playing taxi driver, transporting me to and fro. After all, whilst I was not earning and relying on state handouts for a while, there would be no spare money for expensive train fares.

My father said very little, chastising me at first for being foolish and allowing myself to get into such a predicament but secretly proud that he was to become a granddad. As to the future, well that would depend on many things. Obviously I'd need to find a job in order to support us in the short term once the child was born but there would be too many changes to plan too far ahead.

Mum really wanted me to go home at weekends straight away but I'd convinced her that I could cope adequately for the time being and promised to phone her every Sunday, her decision only stemmed from concern but I knew that she would fuss.

I heard through Jennifer that Jonathan had been to court and that bail had been denied even though mummy and daddy were on hand ready to muster together any amount set, but though they engaged the very best of solicitors they had proved unable to sway the judge's mind on allowing Jonathan any freedom. Mummy had taken a turn when it was announced and had to be assisted away by officials, leaving daddy, Sabrina and Andrew huddled around the flustered solicitor in a vain attempt to coerce him into appealing Jonathan's case. However, the learned gent knew the judge of old and any attempt to question his judgement would only be met by a stubborn resistance to further discussion on the matter.

The police, for once, were delighted to hear that old 'thunder face' had been put in charge. Apparently, he was well known for handing maximum sentences, any attempt to sway his opinions normally resulted in having the opposite effect to that desired, often causing a backlash when final sentence was passed.

Jonathan's case was set to be heard in January and

as a witness, I had no choice but to attend, yet another test of strength on my part but I was determined not to let it upset me. I may have lost my man but my baby was the most important thing to me, no way would I let anything or anyone jeopardise us.

Of course, there had to be that meeting with Jonathan. After all, he was to become a father and it seemed only right that he should know. I left it for a while before contacting Jonathan's solicitor to arrange a meeting, that's if he would agreed to see me. Naturally, his family had voiced their objections but he overruled them, he wanted to see me.

Dad had kindly volunteered to drive me to the prison, saving the prospect of changing from one bus and train to another and would allow me to stay for as long as necessary. My pregnancy was about midway and my belly already sported visible signs of growth and although I'd kept myself well nourished and took gentle exercise, I was beginning to notice my energy not lasting much beyond tea time.

It had decided to rain that day making the grey walls of confinement a depressing view from the car window. Dad dropped me outside the hefty metal door that barred entry to the outside world, he'd wait under a large tree that loomed over the only convenient spot to park.

I stood unsure of how to proceed, should I knock, or would I be noticed? As I stood deliberating as to my next action, I saw a small shutter slide across. After a few brief words I heard the locks being pulled back and the iron barrier shudder open to let me inside.

As I was escorted down various corridors and into a waiting room, I was confronted with the smell of human inhabitation, no cleaning or scrubbing had managed to remove the stench of bodies huddled together in such a small place. The only thing that gave respite was the aroma of food cooking bringing back memories of our school canteen, the only problem being that no matter how good it smelt, the real thing never lived up to its advertisement.

The room was barren, just a couple of chairs at an old wooden table that had seen its fair share of war, various names and messages carved into its memory as if an omen from people who'd passed through its eternal life.

It was made clear to me that once Jonathan entered the room, I was neither to move or attempt to touch him in any way. His solicitor and warder would remain and under no circumstances was I to speak about the case or anything else relative to it, these had been the terms on which I'd been allowed to see him.

I stood to the far side of the room while Jonathan was ushered in and sat at the table. As I moved across to take my seat, I could see his stare fixed on the swelling stomach I could no longer disguise.

I sat silent for a long while considering the best way to approach the subject.

"How are you?" I asked, raising my eyes to look at him. He'd lost a little weight but in all he appeared fairly well.

"I'm alright, a little tired from constantly reading, but there's not much else to keep me occupied," he replied.

"I came to talk to you," I said not wishing to pass comment on his last remark.

"What about?" he said.

"I'm pregnant," I said trying to sound as unemotional as possible, "and I thought you should know. And before you ask whether it is yours, then the answer to that is yes," answering the question before it could be posed.

"I know it's mine, you're too proud to belittle yourself in coming here if it wasn't," he said. "But I knew long ago, remember that night in the car park?" Of course I remembered, it wasn't something that would just slip from your mind.

"How?"

"I could see it in your face, could feel it, I can't explain but I just sensed it," he replied.

"I'll quite understand if you want nothing further to do with me or the child," I said giving him the chance to opt out.

"You are joking aren't you?"

"Well..."

"I could not have asked for a better gift other than to be with you instead of being stuck in here."

His reaction to my news came as a surprise but a pleasant one. He wanted to discuss everything there and then; how I would manage alone, where I would live, what money he needed to make available. He was adamant our child would be born in a private establishment where all our needs would be catered for properly and in total comfort. I had to slow him down, this was not the time to make rash decisions and until his fate had been decided, all suggestions would need to be regarded as temporary.

He wouldn't let me go until I'd promised to visit him when I could, that was one request I was happy to agree to.

Unfortunately the tranquil contentment I felt was not to last. As I emerged from the inner sanctum of the room, I glimpsed some familiar faces seated on the far side of the bars, Sabrina and Andrew. The anger in her eyes was unmistakable as she rushed at the barrier dividing us and spat loud abuse in my direction.

Jonathan's solicitor convinced the guards to allow them access giving his assurances that it would be better than a scene in the hall and that he would calm everybody down. I would have much preferred to have slid away from this confrontation but the choice was denied as I was ushered back into the dingy room once more.

I initially fled to the far side but as they poured in, I gradually manoeuvred myself round the wall close to the only existing exit. If there was going to be a family scene, I wanted no part.

"Aren't you going to introduce us?" asked his father.

"This is Carol," replied Jonathan in a deflated voice.

"I was just about to leave..." I started saying, trying to avoid eye contact.

"What's that bitch doing here?" shouted Sabrina as she emerged from behind her father.

"That bitch, as you call her, is here because I invited her!" His voice was raised and angry, I thought it better to stay silent, I didn't want to be the cause of further eruptions.

"Before anyone else voices their opinion, let's just get one thing clear, I'm the one who's at fault, not Carol," he preached. "She only did what she thought right and probably I would have done the same if faced with the same situation." This frank admission felt like a weight being lifted from my shoulders, I just wanted to hold him and tell him how much I missed and loved him but this wasn't the moment for such a show of affection.

His outburst had also had the desired effect on his family. Sabrina, now silenced, sat herself on one of the chairs, Andrew mumbled as he rested against a far wall and his mother and father although not totally happy with my presence made a simple but courteous gesture of welcome.

"There is one other thing that you need to know," said Jonathan now in full dominant stride. Oh God no, he was going to tell them. "Carol is going to have my child."

Those few simple words made his mother turn pale. Andrew had to rush and take her arm helping her to the only remaining seat in the room, she looked quite overcome. Father only raised an eyebrow and Sabrina said nothing, staring into space, unmoved by my joyous predicament.

Talk about tell it to them gently. It came like a bomb from the sky, full impact. Suddenly they all started talking at once, mostly in Italian but I got the gist, his mother appeared to be scolding him, his father dishing out some sort of advice and the other two contradicting. Jonathan finally shut them all up, he told them we were extremely happy about this child and that only he and I would decide what needed to be done.

This was an appropriate moment to escape and I voiced my desire to the burly guard by whom I now stood. I nearly managed to disappear without detection but the old lock clunked noisily as the key was turned and although not loud, it was sufficient to alert Jonathan that the door was again opening.

My last visions were of a flustered solicitor pleading

for calm from this small but volatile group and for once, I couldn't help but laugh.

"You take good care of you both, alright?" said Jonathan "She is going to be as beautiful as her mother." How could he know it was a girl?

"Yes, we'll be fine, don't worry," I assured him.

"I hope she is born before they lock me away for good, I'd give the world to be with you when she's born, maybe hold her. I can't tell you how happy it would make me," he said with a broad smile right across his face.

Just for a brief moment, I saw the same sight that greeted me as I turned in shock on that first night, the most handsome and gentle man I'd ever had pleasure to meet. His very look had the ability to melt away any pain, as if banishing it from our presence. It would burn into my memory to be recalled whenever needed.

As I walked towards the exit, the corridors didn't seem quite so cold and daunting as previously and as I stepped into the outside world, the sun slipped from behind a shielding cloud, its heat supplying a welcomed warmth after the chill.

Dad must have been looking out for me, his car materialised from behind a row of parked vehicles and we sloped away as silently as we came.

I wasn't in a talkative mood on our journey home, dad was happy to drive and I to think. There were only a few words between us as he dropped me outside the flat, I sounded convincing that I was OK and promised to phone mum later, she was a proper worrier and would only insist on phoning me if I didn't ring her.

I spent the evening happy in my own company. I made the promised call to mum after tea, she wasn't totally in agreement with my decision to visit Jonathan, her only concern was that it might upset me too much and that if he reacted in a negative way to my news, I'd be deeply hurt. Thinking about it, she was probably right.

Jonathan was to remain part of our lives no matter how distanced he was from us. As to his remaining family, well, I'd have to tolerate some contact with them for the baby's sake, after all it was part of their line. The only thing that worried me was that they'd try to interfere, and the fear that if allowed to visit them there was the possibility that my child would never return. Apart from that, access on regular basis would be acceptable but only on the understanding that I knew when and where.

Our next meeting was to decide the future. Jonathan's was already mapped out for an unknown number of years and although he may not be with us, I felt it important that his ideas for the upbringing of our child should be aired and if amicable, complied with.

Jonathan, at first, wanted me to quit university, take a modest house staying at home with the child and he would furnish whatever funds necessary to cover, but I had already decided I wanted to continue my studies. Reluctantly, he accepted my wishes and it was decided that I would stay in my lodgings until the child was born.

My suggestions of living back home with mum and dad afterwards were met with a little despondency and though he didn't say, I assumed it would be to do with his parents. However, he understood my reasons but as soon as possible preferred me to find a suitable house to move into. There was mention of hiring a nanny but I was adamant that I wouldn't let a stranger take care of my child at least until school age, then I may consider the possibility of a child minder.

A bank account in my name was to be set up and monies transferred each month. I had partly agreed not to work for a while but that time span would be of my choice. The final hurdle would be that of family access, I had no objections to free access, only interference or meddling would change that course. If I put restrictions on his mother and father and not mine that would be unfair. All in all, things were sorted fairly rapidly and by mutual consent we would only visit once a month when possible but I promised to contact him if anything was wrong.

Most of the pregnancy was uneventful, a little morning sickness, backache and tiredness, nothing unexpected. By chance, I 'd managed to find a small two bedroomed terraced house with just enough garden, close to my parent's home and, luckily, the current tenants were to vacate about a month before baby was due. This would be most suitable, allowing me time to add my own homely touches before moving in, freedom for both me and my parents. With it being only a few minutes walk, it cleared all the obstacles with regards to mum minding the child and secretly, some relief for Jonathan.

CHAPTER 19

An unscheduled telephone call from Jonathan confirmed the worst. His trial was set for March and with his plea of guilty, would not take too long to finish.

I had seen none of his family since the rendezvous in that prison room and I had made no effort to bridge the gap, but it was inevitable that with us all now within these walls of justice, our paths would again cross. Being a witness, I was to stay outside the court room until called and could only re-enter when sentence was to be announced. Strange, here I was one of the people who loved him, most ready to assist in his internment, but I no longer felt guilty or saddened by the fact. My only hope now was the length of sentence the judge found fit to bestow on him.

His mother and father made courteous attempts to acknowledge my presence and enquire about my health but were really only interested in the baby, not me. Andrew just smiled when he thought his parents weren't looking but apart from that he stayed silent. Sabrina, however, was different since our last encounter, her eyes said we should speak but her pride was blocking her route through the barrier. By now, she must have adjusted to what had happened and given initial anger time to subside, the relationship we had would never be the same again but there was a chance we could be sociable to one another, it was a case of wait and see.

As I stood in the witness box, Jonathan watched my every move. My stomach was extremely swollen and a court official had thoughtfully provided me with a chair. My evidence took some time to tell but each hesitant moment was overcome by his warm smile. How could he be so laid back as every word I spoke made the hole into which he would fall deeper?

The case presented by the prosecution was that of evil inhuman form, branding Jonathan a scheming demon hell bent on murdering as some form of self gratification, taking pleasure from the demise of another, trying to manifest him to the jury as an uncontrollable, volatile maniac who should be forever isolated from human contact.

Jonathan's defence lawyer was good, crushing all manipulation by the prosecution to blemish his character. His determination was that any decision should be made purely on the acts Jonathan had admitted to and not influenced by pathetic attempts to slur him and sway the jurors. Judge 'thunder face' Simms was known for his harsh approach but deplored unnecessary irrelevancies from the courtroom benches, fairness ruled above all else and his judgement was based on pure fact only.

After five days of hardened benches and only two

hours deliberation, the jury returned to give verdict. There was no doubt as to the outcome, only how severe the sentence was to be. As Jonathan was being retrieved from his cell, I slipped in the back of the courtroom undetected and out of sight of staring eyes.

As we waited I scanned the room, it was filled with tired faces, their eyes fixed in an unseeing stare. Most were in their mature years which pointed to them probably being parents or relatives of the victims, who'd sat silently as if to bear witness that justice was carried out, that the bastard who'd prematurely robbed them of their babies suffered for his actions.

The verdict was fifteen years imprisonment for each count all to run concurrent, a long time but less than I'd anticipated. I watched the agony that now spread across the same faces, it was clear that however long this beast was locked away, it would never be justifiably long enough. The shock caused his mother to pass out and in the commotion to assist her, I withdrew turning in the opposite direction. Once through the doorway, the press rushed towards the source of their next story while I slipped un-noticed through one of the many side entrances. Now it was over, I wanted to divorce myself from its future repercussions. The media were present in large numbers but as yet my involvement other than that of witness had, by some miracle, remained undetected and that's how I wanted it to remain.

Jennifer had promised to keep the knowledge of our continued personal relationship secret, it had been difficult as the media can turn into wild dogs at the mere scent of scandal. Jennifer admitted that on more than one occasion she'd been followed by persons unknown during the trial and had been hounded by press men hoping for that exclusive story.

I found myself a small coffee bar where I sat and rested, taking in the consequences imposed within that last hour of life. I hadn't fooled myself, I was to be alone for a long time but I had prepared myself, my loyalties now lay with the new life I carried and my sheer determination to succeed would help me through. There was also the cheery fact that with good behaviour Jonathan might apply for parole and be released in a shorter time.

Mum and dad whisked me away for a few days to some hotel in the middle of nowhere, mainly to let things die a natural death and also to ensure I was not present for any media interest. The break was lovely and with my time close, the rest did me good. Mum was happy that at last I looked healthy again.

The first painful hint was during a morning lecture, just a niggle, nothing positive, excused as a little wind, but by mid afternoon, I knew it was more than that. I found myself systematically checking my watch and the pain increased with each spasm; contractions. Being a midwife, I knew all the technical details but until now had no personal experience.

I excused myself. My explanation of a more pressing engagement was taken a little strangely by the teacher before a few short words hurriedly whispered into his somewhat hairy ear advised that I was in labour and should leave. He instantly voiced what I'd said and his statement caused the other students who were in different levels of conscious sleep to sit and cheer as I left.

My mother had never asked outright to be with me, her hints had always skirted around the edge with, 'If you want I can come with you', that type of thing but what she was really saying was, 'I'd like to be there', and as Jonathan couldn't be with me I could think of no better person than my mum.

The birth was straightforward, no complications and I wasn't at all surprised when the midwife gleefully stated that I had a perfect little girl. As I gazed at the small pink bundle that nurse handed to me, Jonathan's prediction was complete, she was beautiful. I know most mothers think their child is beautiful even though some are not, but my little girl was. Her skin although still wrinkled felt silky, her head was topped by a mop of golden honey coloured wispy hair and her eyelashes were long and curled, she had a little button nose and her little mouth was rosy pink and full lipped.

The thrill and pride on my mother's face as I held out the first and probably only grandchild I would ever produce brought tears of joy to my eyes. Her arms extended to grasp this tiny being, pulling her close into protective arms, her whispers familiarising the child with the sound of her voice.

I received flowers and cards of congratulation but all were outshone by the huge basket of red roses that had just been delivered. I didn't need to read the card to know who sent them, it was Jonathan of course. I had not been able to telephone him yet but the grapevine was obviously working, his message simply said, 'I love you and I long to see our daughter.'

My confinement only lasted a few days and I was grateful to leave the stuffiness of the hospital behind.

My father was there as always to collect us and drive us to our new home. It would take some getting used to, planning my days around another but many women before me had managed so it couldn't be that difficult.

I had arranged a prison visit to see Jonathan and take our baby for him to see and again father played taxi driver. As I entered the prison, I heard the gates slamming behind, a cold atmosphere emitted from the building and the numerous faceless guards as I passed by. I was shown into that familiar room that contained a table and two chairs, there I was asked to wait. As Jonathan was brought into the room, two guards also entered and stood in front of the now closed door.

"I'm sorry," he said quietly, "but they have to stay."

"That's OK," I replied. "How are you?"

"Much better now that you've come," he said smiling. I could see him looking across at the white bundle in my hands, it was time for father and daughter to meet.

"Want to hold her?" I asked. No answer was necessary as his hands reached out.

As he sat down, he pushed back the blanket that closeted his view. He just stared for ages and just once, I caught sight of a small droplet of water seeping from the corner of his eye.

"She is even more beautiful than I imagined, so perfect," he whispered.

"Just as you predicated," I replied.

"Perfection," I heard him mutter.

"I waited to see you before naming her, have you thought about it?" I asked.

"Rose," he said.

"Why that name?" I asked.

"Because she is as perfect as one, a delicate bud waiting to blossom into full flower to be admired by everyone who is fortunate enough to cross her path," said Jonathan.

"Then Rose it shall be."

The time we had been allocated was all but over, a kiss and short embrace was all that was allowed before I was escorted away from a place that Rose and I would become all too familiar with over the coming years. Although the inside of prison walls was not the best sight for such young eyes, there needed to be a bonding between father and daughter which shouldn't be denied, however restricted. Life would be tough enough for them both, he devoid of freedom and she, suffering the stigma and cruelty that arise from said circumstances. I promised to have some photos done of Rose, he could keep one with him and I'd also supply some for his parents to take back to Italy with them.

Jonathan wanted his parents to see the child before they departed to which I had no objections. A swift meeting to bring together an old and new generation was well within my control.

I arranged for Rose to be christened, a choice opportunity to introduce her to her second set of grandparents. It was a strained affair with both parties avoiding each other. His parents were reserved in permitting any over indulgence of emotions towards their first granddaughter but they couldn't disguise the pride that radiated from old eyes each time they caught glimpse of her beautiful little face.

I felt sorry for the photographer, he worked hard in

getting all parties to smile in an acceptable way for the camera. He seemed most relieved as he pressed the button to create the last negative, he almost ran from the church, clutching his equipment but he had managed a promise to rush the photos to me within a couple of days.

My mum and dad had courteously invited Jonathan's parents to their house for refreshments but the reply was already known. 'Thank you but we have urgent arrangement.' Very convenient. Secretly I knew we were more than happy that they'd declined and with my duty now completed, I smiled as each bid farewell. His mother and father wished us good health while Andrew nodded nervously as he passed but as our eyes met, I saw a momentary grin flush across his face.

Sabrina was the last, she'd almost succeeded in divorcing herself from the proceedings but couldn't resist a last look at Rose as she pushed back the edges of the frilly bonnet that shrouded her from view. Sabrina may have felt some kind of affection but couldn't bring herself to show it, the expression on her face never changed and as she looked up I felt the coldness that emitted from her. I wondered how long the bitterness within would take to wilt and die.

Mum had generously prepared a buffet which the remaining family and guests tucked into and with the production of a couple of bottles of sherry, all enjoyed what remained of the day.

The photographer was as good as his word, a courier arrived and deposited a large bulky package full of colourful pictures. With the photos now in my possession I arranged to visit the house for one last time.

I caught the train this time and took a taxi the rest of the way, my father was very good about ferrying me about but I considered it unfair to take advantage. It also meant I had a selfish excuse to carry out this mission alone.

The necessity for a taxi vanished as I stepped out of the station. David was standing at the ticket booth enquiring about trains to London. He, at least, was happy to see me and it was nice to see a familiar face. Thankfully, he offered us a lift. Rose had slept the whole way the train hadn't bothered her, nor was she disturbed as David locked the carry cot in the back of the car.

"How's it going?" I enquired but really asking how are you and Sabrina.

"Getting there," he replied.

"And Sabrina?"

"I don't know," he said. "I've only seen her while in the company of others."

"Do you think you'll ever get back together?"

"Doubt it."

"What makes you think that?" I asked

"You weren't there when I told her about Jonathan, she went for me in a big way, fists flying and screaming," he said shaking his head. "The only feelings she holds for me now are hatred and contempt. I've tried phoning but when she hears my voice she just slams down the receiver."

"Oh," I said.

"I even went to the house a couple of times but she refused to see me."

"Well, maybe things will change," I replied trying to offer some reassurance.

"No, I think it's too late and the wound too deep for even love to heal it."

"Don't give up will you?" I said. "You may be surprised."

He gave a sideways glance to that last comment that said it all. Who in hell was I trying to kid, nothing short of divine intervention or complete memory loss would reunite them.

"What about Jonathan, how is he?"

"As well as can be where he is, but he dotes on Rose," I answered. "Maybe she was born with a ready made purpose."

"Maybe."

"Thinking of taking a trip?" I asked, changing the subject.

"What makes you ask that?"

"Weren't you enquiring about trains to London?" I said

"Yes Miss Nosey," he replied. "I've got an interview at Scotland Yard next week and it's easier to go by train than car."

"Really?"

"Jennifer rang about an opening in her section and wondered if I was interested," he replied. "She'd recommended me to her governor, seeing as how well I'd worked with her."

"Going up in the world," I said. "Can't blame you for that, if that's what you want."

"Well, there's very little to keep me here now and the prospects of promotion are better."

I didn't want him to take me right to the house, the station would do being only a short walk away. He didn't ask why but I'm sure he understood.

When we arrived, he helped me to get the buggy sorted out. He insisted that when ready, I was to return to the station and he would drive me back.

The gate had been left open and I parked Rose's buggy on the patio, shading her slightly from the strong spring sunshine. The door opened and I was confronted by Jonathan's father. I picked up Rose and entered, even though I was outnumbered I stayed relaxed drawing from the knowledge that it was a short lived event.

I stayed what I considered was a reasonable length of time during which I saw little of Rose except for her being nursed by either her grandmother or aunt. They needed some time together, no matter what their opinion of me, Rose was still related by blood, I didn't want to spoil any future relationship she may want with them.

Just before I left I remembered the photos, for the first time I felt a little warmth in his mother's smile as I handed them to her, and she asked me to send more as Rose began to grow. Andrew, as normal, smiled from afar as I walked towards the door, Sabrina was again last to hold Rose and as she handed her back, quietly suggested she call sometime.

At last the first signs of the frost melting and I'd do my best to encourage its thaw, if she was softening towards me there was still hope for David.

Father offered to drive me to the station but I declined telling him I had already made other arrangements. His parting words were, if ever I needed anything I was to contact him. I thanked him but it was an offer I never anticipated taking up.

The stroll back to the station was pleasant and it brought back familiar memories of last summer, amazing how unpredictable our lives are, you spend most of it planning its course but invariably fate decides the direction not the simple mortal mind.

David would be a few moments so I'd have to sit and wait. The officers took a keen interest in my tiny tot, the men being worse than the women, cooing and tickling her cheeks as she lapped up the attention that was abundantly thrown in her direction.

Leaving Rose safely in the care of her many admirers I walked to the glass wall where I could once again view the house, how different it looked now. Strange how things that happen can alter your image of material objects, a bit like the dress you'd bought to stun everybody when worn and your eagerness to show it off dashed by coming face to face with an identical vision, turning excitement to embarrassment and the wish for a large hole. I'd arrived as an inexperienced young woman, my only desire to enjoy the holiday but left transformed, having taken a ride on the express train of life.

CHAPTER 20

In just one year I had fallen in love, played a dangerous and deadly game, lost friendship and ultimately become a mother. What a hell of a trip.

What next? To sit those exams, to find that job with wondrous career prospects and bring up a child, not much really. The idea had crossed my mind to return to Saudi, not to marry the prince of course, he wouldn't want me now but maybe I could talk him into funding a clinic for anti and post natal treatment and education for women, well at least his wife or in future his wives would make use of it.

The only problem with that idea was the inability to visit Jonathan and Rose's education, but the prince was extremely rich, rich enough to pay for tutors and plane fares and who knows, when Jonathan was finally released he could with help start a new outlet in Saudi aiding the ever increasing European customers that were flooding in to fill its vast space of business opportunities. It may necessitate more study on his part but he'd have plenty of time for that, plus it was far enough away to defer constant visitations from the in-laws.

The more I thought about it the more I liked it, I would discuss it with Jonathan and then the prince. As I looked down, I was subconsciously twiddling the gold ring the prince had given to me. I had, up till then, hardly taken it out of its box but had decided what's the use of owning such a gem if never worn to be admired? Maybe it was a good omen.

My dreaming was disturbed by a voice in the distance.

"Are you ready, Carol?" it was David.

One last glance through the window before it was time to close one epoch of my life and open another. I had already decided that this new era was to be successful, both professionally and personally, I would draw on past experience to ensure it so.

"Yes," I replied turning round to smile at him.

"Let's go then, if we hurry the next train is in about 15 minutes," said David ushering me out.

"Good," I said, "I need to get home and write a letter to an absent friend."